ABOUT THE AUTHOR

Mártin Howe is a journalist who has worked for the BBC, Channel 4 and a news agency in Washington DC. Writing literary fiction is his escape from the constraints of factual news. *Dead Right* is his fourth novel.

mbhowe.com
Facebook.com/MartinHoweAuthor
X : @_MartinHowe
Instagram: @martin.howe.925

Also by Martin Howe

White Linen

The Man in the Street

Coming Down

For christie and Brian

Dead
Right

All the best

Martin Howe

Martin. Howe

Troubador Publishing Ltd
Unit E2 Airfield Business Park,
Harrison Road, Market Harborough,
Leicestershire. LE16 7UL
Tel: 0116 2792299
Email: books@troubador.co.uk
Web: www.troubador.co.uk

ISBN 9781805142638

British Library Cataloguing in Publication Data.
A catalogue record for this book is available from the British Library.

Printed and bound in Great Britain by 4edge Limited
Typeset in 11pt Minion Pro by Troubador Publishing Ltd, Leicester, UK

For Dulcie

Foreword

The inspiration for **Dead Right** came from a real event. The discovery on the 12th July 2000 of the bodies of four women in a three-bedroom semi-detached house in Leixlip, County Kildare, 15 miles west of Dublin. The women had shut themselves in their rented home and starved to death. They were all related (three sisters and their aunt) and aged between 47 and 82. They left no note explaining clearly why they had done it. **Dead Right** is a work of fiction and the characters bear no relation to the four dead women.

Prologue

Kut War Cemetery, Kut el Amara, Iraq. July 1995

Bulging and rippling, the oily liquid was alive, an army of green frogs patrolling the viscous depths. Their frenetic motion disturbed layers of decay, sending myriad bubbles of fetid gas jittering to the surface where they coalesced in a froth of dirty suds. A yellow-hued haze hung low over the steaming water and drifted across the piles of garbage scattered between sodden graves. The sun-bleached air was heavy with the reek of putrefaction, the intense heat broiling. Swarms of insects, black against the aching blue of the sky, clouded the stillness, the faint hum of their wings the only sound. Overhead a raptor circled, a dark stencil, searching.

The great inundation had been encroaching for weeks – Eden abandoned, sinking back into its natural state – the River Tigris reclaiming its ancient course. The antiquated pumps that had kept the cemetery unnaturally dry for over seventy years were now silent, the water rising higher each day. Sewage from the surrounding dwellings was backing up and brimming over. The constant seepage undermined fragile foundations, loosening mortar, dissolving clay bricks, weakening ramshackle wooden partitions and walkways. Solid earth gave way, collapsing into the quagmire, dragging down neighbouring houses, their walls cracking, their basements slumping to reveal dusty underbellies – contorted beams, dangling wires, and broken pipes. The land was bedding down, returning to the swamp it had once been. The local residents no longer had the wherewithal, the tools or spare parts, to prevent it, and powerless, lived in fear for their health, for their children and their livelihoods. They were watching and waiting, for nothing was as it had been before.

The stone memorial cross at the centre of the graveyard, leaning lopsidedly now, still towered above the flood-tide, yet its lower steps were submerged and a damp brown smear marred the corroded concrete plinth.

Gravestones – over five hundred of them marking the foreign dead of two world wars – marched resolutely in serried ranks, ten-deep, from the crumbling houses that flanked one side of the cemetery into the deluge. Those nearest the weed-choked riverbank were barely visible, their stained and chipped off-white crowns pale stepping-stones in the lapping water.

The dry sandy soil offered little resistance. Close to the reed beds fringing the main channel, gravestones had been toppled and graves flushed open, exposing their contents to the merciless sun and the rats. Bones lay scattered in the shallows, the rags of khaki uniforms drifted, tarnished brass buttons and tattered badges settled into the greasy sediment, broken skulls stared.

A bubble – an amphibian eye, matched by hundreds of others blinking – contorted the slimy green field of algae, its taut surface diffracting the intense sunshine into a vivid rainbow flare. Its brief colourful existence ending in a roiling release, adding to the stench. It was followed by another, then another, in a quickening stream, foaming the surface. River water was leaching into another grave, breaking through the walls, flooding into the interstices, soaking the friable wood of the coffin, forcing out stale air. The desiccated ground, a sponge sucking up moisture and losing its strength and form, fell away into the pressing flow. The heavy gravestone of Private Sean Fanning of the Kings Own Royal Regiment, killed in a shooting accident on 20th May 1941, lost its footing and toppled over, the forceful momentum of its slide shearing off the end of the decayed coffin and revealing the private's pale skull, lying face upwards, stripped of all flesh, bone the colour of antique ivory, a dark patchwork fuzz of desiccated hair still attached. A grotesque throw of the dice that landed with the four uppermost – vacant eye sockets, collapsed nasal cavity and the neat bullet hole in the centre of his forehead. A symmetrical diamond of death underscored by the gormless gape of slack jaws and yellowing crenated teeth. Fine fractures radiated outwards across the shattered brow, worry lines ossified into a permanent frown of consternation. A parody of Private Fanning's concern for his own luckless humanity.

Part 1

The Early Bird Catches
The Worm

"… and then was a widow until she was eighty-four. She never left
the temple but worshipped night and day, fasting and praying."
Luke 2:37

The small modern house – narrowly detached from its identical
block-faced neighbours – stood in the middle of a row of five,
mirrored on the opposite side of the street and in myriad other
places on the sprawling estate. Now a permanent remembrance of
an economic bubble, recently burst, the property presented to the
world a facade of banal utility – grey painted front door, red-tiled
step, white plastic stoop, crème double-glazed windows, one down,
two up, vacantly admonishing the infrequent passersby across a
small unkempt front garden.

Sparsely populated, anonymous and unprepossessing, Eden
Avenue was this morning incandescent. Nothing stirred, yet the
air was ethereally alive, suffused in a delicate pink sheen, with

the rising sun dappling the bland walls of brick, pebble-dash and plaster with a ruddy vitality, its rays glinting fiercely in closed-off casements. Swollen by the balmy humidity of summer this infant haze, oblivious to the depredations of builders and developers, nestled the ancient landscape in a serene natural blanket.

Dead to the world the residents slumbered, dream figures mingling with the perpetual ghostly presence of pilgrims past trudging the ancient byway that crossed this place, a staging post of the devout, seeking a salvation now balked by the hard-edged barriers thrown up by an uncaring, modern sensibility. Some were more attuned than others to the recent vandalism inflicted on the centuries-old sediment of sanctity that had settled over the site. Daphne Fanning, from number 57, was among them, a passionate believer, sensitive to the existence of spiritual value in people and spaces and scornful of others who were not or, even worse, simply didn't care. She had not lived in Eden Avenue long but had drawn solace from the vibrancy of recurrent visions, teeming with a religious cast that spoke vividly to her in old age.

But she was now dead.

The car, a silver-grey Ford Mondeo, crawled slowly along the street, side lights lit, its wheels whispering on the degraded road surface. Curls of cigarette smoke wafted out of the cracked-open side window, the mundane drama of its progress underscored by the faint twang of a slide guitar coasting over a thumping double-bass line. The driver was staring intently at the passing houses, shaking his head in time to the music and paying no attention to where he was heading. As the avenue gently curved to the right his front tyre nudged the kerb and he jerked involuntarily. Loudly swearing he swerved into the middle of the road and straightened the steering wheel, before resuming his count of the empty buildings in the street. There had been five so far … they were easy to spot – a shabby air of immobility, litter-blown doorways, closed empty windows, front lawns, always to the left of the driveway, weed stricken, gone to seed, uncut, the stillness of abandonment, of lives never lived in … and number 57, his destination, made it six.

"A moonlight flit. I bloody knew it."

Collecting rent door-to-door was challenging work and Owen Cavanagh, who had been at it for years, was finding it increasingly hard. Today, was a case in point, it was shaping up to be a major pain in the arse. He drew up outside the house, dragged heavily on his roll-up, and stared up at the blank windows. The only mark of his former tenants a curling sun-bleached picture of the Virgin Mary, propped askew behind the frosted security glass of the front door. Revving his car impatiently, he stubbed out his cigarette, before turning into the driveway.

"Over a grand they owed. I should have known!"

Muttering he switched off the ignition and peered through the smeared windscreen. He noticed that the downstairs curtains were drawn, unlike those upstairs, and that the letterbox was sealed shut with what looked like brown masking tape.

"Odd!"

He understood now that there was no hurry. Lighting another cigarette, he switched the radio on again, leant back in his seat and closed his eyes. Smoke caressed his face. It was his third early start this week and it was taking its toll. He was tired, slightly hung-over and had had no breakfast and now it looked like he'd get no rent this morning either. It was endless the cat and mouse game he played with his tenants. He won some, usually at this time in the morning and this early in the week, when they hadn't spent up all their money and were asleep at home, still too groggy to come up with a reasonable excuse. But he did lose some as well and this looked like one of them. The house had that aura about it to him, lifeless, abandoned, he could always tell. He just hoped they hadn't done too much damage, crapped in their own backyard, left it fucked over after all he had done for them … he was working himself up and he didn't want to do that. He had been in the collection game too long for a few women to upset him, but it was annoying the liberties people took. He inhaled deeply and let the cigarette smoke infuse, moving his head gently to the calming rhythm of a familiar country ballad.

He had been too easy-going with this bunch. There had been nothing from them for over four months. If it hadn't been for the Social paying half what they owed he'd have been down on them sooner. He was a soft beggar with women, he knew it, and that Anne had been a bit of a looker.

"Sod it."

It was time. Winding down the side window he flicked out the smouldering butt and watched it skitter and spark across the striated concrete surface of the neighbour's driveway. His neck and back ached and stretching his arms upwards he tenderly massaged his temples. The dints in his skull moved beneath his chilled fingers.

Standing wearily on the parched grass he stared at the house confirming what he already knew – stained curtains drawn haphazardly across dirty closed windows, weed-choked flowerbed, sweet wrappers, newspaper, a plastic carrier bag blown into a ragged heap against the wooden boundary fence and a solitary coke can, crushed, lying in the yellowing grass – that it was empty.

Shuffling across the lawn he struggled to extricate a large bunch of irregular-shaped keys from his jacket pocket. A key-bit had snagged on the lining and he felt the material ripping as he tugged. Irritated he kicked the can into the road, where it clattered to a halt against the far kerb. The sound was startlingly loud and he glanced around to see if he had disturbed anyone. The keys held fast and he was obliged to take off his jacket, rest it across his arm and carefully lift the bunch out of his pocket, inverting the grubby inlay. One of the many Chubb keys had become entangled in a loose thread protruding from a fraying seam and his efforts had already torn a large hole in the perished material.

"Fuck it."

Needing two free hands he squatted down on the concrete path that ran beneath the front window and carefully unpicked the key.

Then jangling the collection in his palm he searched through it for the keys to number 57.

"Shit."

A number of the small cardboard address labels were missing from their key rings, short loops of white string all that remained. He had been meaning to ask Tracy in the office to sort this out for him, but he hadn't and number 57 Eden Avenue was one of the missing labels.

"Bloody typical."

Getting unsteadily to his feet he separated out the first unidentified key to try and stepped up to the front door.

"Oh, fuck it."

The keyhole was blocked. There was no way he could insert a key. Looking closely the lock appeared to be stuffed with chewing gum or faded Blu-tack.

"Fuck them. What's the point of doing that?"

Shading his eyes with his hand he peered through the tinted glass of the front door, but could make out very little. A bed sheet, or something like it, had been hung across the hallway, blocking the view from the door and the adjoining side window. Its upper portion was taut and pressed against the pane by a large object leaning against it. He pulled at the masking tape that sealed the letterbox, cursing as it came away, bringing with it flakes of grey paint from the door. Lifting the metal flap he pushed in the faded newspapers that had been stuffed into the gap, intending to call out, even though he knew it was pointless, but the hot fetid air that wafted into his face, forced him back, and he let the flap slam shut.

He tried the doorbell a number of times, the muffled chimes ringing out into silence. He rapped on the glass, then pressed the bell again, calling out as he alternately hammered and rang. Frustrated he gave up and sighing rummaged in his jacket for his mobile phone and rang the office.

"You're in!"

He smiled as Tracy swore at him.

"As I thought 57 Eden Avenue have done a runner and left it in a right state by the look of it. It smells like something has died in there …"

"They haven't, have they?"

He laughed.

"No, there were four of them so not likely. Probably rotting food or something. Anyway, we'll need the cleaners ASAP. Give Ron a ring and see when he could get over. They've buggered up the locks so I'm going to have to break a window to get in. Ask if he could bring some boards with him to patch it up."

"Will do. Take care out there."

"Copy that. See you about 11."

Standing in front of the door, alone in the enveloping silence of a dead conversation, he suddenly felt overcome by boredom, unable to summon the energy to carry on. The job was nothing but unnecessarily hard work and he was weary of it. Dealing with the dregs was not what he wanted to do, day in, day out. People's dishonesty, their messed-up lives, sick behaviour and interminable problems – they were not his concern. Yet he couldn't escape them, it was his bread and butter, grubbing around in their dirt to earn a crust.

A thought occurred to him. This door was blocked from the inside so they must have left by the back door. A strange thing to do, but maybe they'd left that one unlocked. God damn it, maybe his morning was looking up?

The gap between the house and the border fence was narrow and blocked by rubbish bins and a scattering of recycling boxes. They were all overflowing with their lids balanced askew and heavy to move. Strangely many of the discarded cans inside appeared to be unopened and the bottles full or only partly used. The bins stank. Holding his breath he squeezed awkwardly past, fending off the dirty plastic rims with his hands and shifting the boxes, where he could, with his feet. Brushing himself down, he noticed, with surprise, clouds of steam billowing from a black plastic pipe in the wall above his head. Drops of condensation dripped from the corroded lip trailing an off-white stain down the bricks. They'd left the heating on. Christ what were they playing at? It made him angry and he didn't want that. Stepping out of the alleyway to check the rear of the property a flock of starlings startled him, exploding from the long grass in a flurry of cracking wings and squawks of alarm. The back garden was neglected and overgrown, a rusty barbeque lay on its side on the weed-covered patio next to a collapsed deckchair. There was a black and white chequered tea towel pegged neatly on the sagging washing line – one of its rusty tubular supporting posts bent at an angle.

He glanced up again at the rushing steam cloud and shook his head in incomprehension. If he ever met any of the women again, he would give them a piece of his mind. Age and the fact that they were women would be no barrier to him letting go.

The back door was locked, as he now knew it would be, the keyhole sealed like at the front and it looked like the fridge-freezer had been pushed up into the doorway, blocking off any view into the kitchen.

"Fucking hell. Why is nothing ever easy?"

The light wavered as dark clouds scudded across the sun, scarring a clear sky. The day dimmed and in anticipation of rain the temperature perceptibly dropped.

He hammered on the dimpled glass, the door rattling in its frame. He called out.

"If you're in there, open the bloody door. I'm not going anywhere."

It was hard to conceive but how did they manage to leave the house if both entrances were blocked from the inside? There was no way those ladies, particularly the old one, were climbing out of any windows – and why would they want to do that anyway?

"Open the sodding door and stop messing about will you."

There was no answer.

"Come on I've had enough. I'll be breaking in soon enough if you don't open up."

7

Behind him on the other side of the fence the neighbour's door cracked ajar and a woman's voice called out.

"There's no point in shouting there's been no one in the house for weeks."

"How do you know?"

"I've seen nobody. I'm stuck in here all day and would have seen or heard someone if they'd been there."

"When did you last see them?"

"Don't know exactly. It must be at least a month or so, maybe longer."

"Isn't that a bit odd? Wouldn't you have expected to see them around? There were four of them."

"Well, yes I suppose. But they always kept to themselves, you know, barely said a word to anybody round here. Certainly not to me anyway. As I said I don't get out much."

"They always had plenty to say to me the few times I saw them."

"I'm telling you they've gone. There's no lights or nothing on at night…"

"But the boiler's on."

The neighbour shrugged.

"I dunno. But they're not there, I'd swear my life on it."

"But both doors, front and back, are barricaded up on the inside. How did they get out?"

"You what?"

"Both doors are blocked on the inside. There is no way they could leave except through the windows and they are all shut. And I can't see them climbing out anyway at their age, can you?"

He laughed.

"Suppose not. But I'm telling you I've not seen them for a good while."

She closed her door. He shook his head, then pounded again on the glass. There was no response. He listened intently, but could only hear the deadened roar of the boiler. Walking round into the back garden he felt the first drops of rain and glared up at the darkening sky. There was an air of dereliction and no sign of life. The curtains were drawn both upstairs and down and a wooden chair was wedged up against the door handle of the large patio doors. The seat of the chair caused the heavy drapes to bulge outwards lifting them slightly to reveal a small gap at the bottom of the doors, which he tentatively peered into, but could see nothing against the reflected glare and the darkness of the interior. He backed away from the house staring fixedly at the upper windows, uncertain what he was expecting to see. He had a strange feeling about things and was uncertain what he should do.

"What were they planning for, a siege?"

If he broke in when they were inside it would not look good, victimizing poor women, frightening them half to death. But he couldn't let this go on; they had already been given masses of leeway. You can only take the piss for so long. He lit another cigarette and inhaled deeply letting the smoke soothe his growing irritation.

"But what are they doing in there, if they're still around? People are fucking weird."

The rain grew heavier and he scurried back to the house, avoiding the scattered garden furniture, to shelter under the back-door porch. He hammered again on the glass.

"Open up, it's Owen. Come on now, be reasonable, we can sort this out."

The last time he had spoken to one of them soon after they had moved in – it had been the old biddy – what was her name? Daphne that's right. Ancient but on the ball, mind – it had been about getting them a new fridge as the old one was on the blink. He had promised to send someone round to take a look and see what they could do. But she had not been happy and had pestered him relentlessly. After somehow getting hold of his personal mobile number she called at all hours until he gave in and bought them an old "new" one. It had pleased him at the time to get one over on her. It took only a moment for his mood to change. He shivered involuntarily and glanced down at the bottom of the glass door.

So why was this new fridge now blocking the back door and not connected to an electric socket? Through the scalloped glass he could clearly see the plug dangling on its flex.

"Fuck."

He stepped out into the downpour. The icy drops lanced the bald patch on the top of his head, stinging his eyes and cascading into mouth and ears. Wincing, he fumbled for his phone, intending to call the police, but thought better of it and slipped it back into his pocket. Drenched he came to a decision and stepped back out of the rain. He had to break in, there was nothing else for it. Weird or not it was his problem. Spooked by the actions of four women, what was his world coming to?

A screwdriver might clear the lock and he had the backdoor key somewhere on his bunch. He would end this nonsense once and for all. Hunching against the deluge he purposefully returned to his car, rummaged in the boot for a screwdriver narrow enough to fit into the lock, a glass-cutter and his sledge-hammer. Lugging his tools back along the cluttered alleyway his resolve started to waver and he wondered if he should get someone else here to witness what was going on? He'd been in this situation once before, breaking in to one of his houses only to find the bastards had gone away to the Costa del Sol for the sodding winter, without telling him or paying him. Cheaper and warmer there! They came back accusing him of burgling the place, saying stuff had gone missing – money, family heirlooms (for fuck's sake), jewellery – it had cost him all they owed in back rent and a new door to keep them quiet.

This felt different though – everything closed up and barricaded – and the neighbour seemed sound, but the boiler niggled him. You'd be mad to leave the heating on if you were doing a runner. It was no skin off his nose if you ran up a massive debt, it just got you into a load of trouble and stuffed up your credit rating. Didn't those biddies think about these things? Trouble was knowing them they probably did. So, what was going on?

Spurred on by his growing annoyance and the soaking he was getting from the rain, he forced the screwdriver into the lock and managed to twist it back and forth several times before it stuck fast. He closed his eyes for a moment and exhaled. Levering the protruding handle up and down failed to loosen it, as did further twisting, which painfully cramped his fingers and made him yet more angry. The lock was useless. Raising the sledge-hammer he tapped the end of the screwdriver tentatively a couple of times, before swinging it back and hitting the handle hard. The result was dramatic. The dull thud of metal on plastic masked the splintering of wood and the cracking of sheet glass, as the impact wedged the screwdriver deep into the lock, forcing its shaft through the obstruction and into the back of the fridge, puncturing membranes. There was the high-pressure hiss of escaping gas. The back door popped open several inches.

Success was a fleeting moment of elation – he would remember it as a distinct mark in time – there was everything he had known up to that point and then there was his understanding of all that came after.

He vomited, even before his mind registered the appalling smell, an inconsequential dribble of pallid bile splattering onto the wet concrete step and fouling his shoes and trousers, his stomach muscles straining. Doubled up, he staggered back, hand clamped over his nose and mouth. It was too late.

The stench was a noxious farmyard cocktail dressed with a sickly odour of ordure sweetness, an unassailable memory. He gagged as he clattered his way clumsily over boxes, squeezing past the bins, weaving back to his car.

Head down, hands resting on the bonnet, his stomach churned.

"Someone had died in there. Or something worse?"

He shook, craving a cigarette.

"But what could be worse? What the fuck else smells like that?"

Alert, suddenly aware he was being watched, he turned his head. The woman in the neighbouring house was peering round her front door at him, the safety chain on.

"Are you alright?" her voice tentative.

"I'm fine love, just had a bit of a turn," he croaked, "I'll be OK in a mo."

"You sure. You want something to drink?"

Head throbbing, it was a pleasant thought. The chain clattered, she stepped out onto the front step.

"You don't look so clever."

"I'd like a glass of water, ta."

He pushed himself upright and turned, then sat back on the bonnet. She tightened the belt on her pink dressing gown, gathered both lapels together and held them firmly at her throat.

"Is everything OK in there?"

She nodded towards number 57.

"I'm not sure love. It don't look quite right to me."

She grimaced and glanced at the upper windows of the house. Her body trembled.

"What you gonna do?"

"Break in, I expect."

She frowned at him.

"I'm here to collect the rent, by the way. I work for the landlord."

"Oh ... What about the peelers?"

"Maybe ... probably. But I'll take a look first."

Company was therapeutic. He felt better. The panic was subsiding. Let's be realistic it could be anything – rotten food, blocked drains, a dead pet – in that heat stuff would go off in no time. And if they had done a runner, just leaving everything, locking the doors ... it could have starved to death.

He shuddered then stretched his arms wide and flung them backwards, opening his body up to the falling rain, which for the first time he appeared to appreciate. The drops were cold and wet on his clammy face, refreshing.

"God I'm getting soaked".

"Come and stand over here out of the rain and I'll get you that water."

"Thanks, I will. By the way did they have a cat or a dog here, do you know?"

He nodded at the house. She gave it a moment's thought.

"Not that I ever saw, no. Never saw them out walking a dog, nor heard any barking either."

His disappointment was palpable.

"But as I said I didn't have much to do with them. They could have had a cat or something."

He nodded. There was a cat flap in the back door, he knew that. But they were not supposed to have pets anyway, under their rental agreement.

"Why?"

Fuck it could be anything ... and in that heat.

"Sorry love what was that?"

"Why did you ask about pets?"

"Oh, it smells a bit in there. Was wondering if it could be animals?"

She shrugged.

"I'll get you that water."

Composed and slightly embarrassed at his behaviour he stared out at the rain. It appeared to be easing off and overhead the sun was breaking through the dispersing clouds. He looked for a rainbow.

"Here you go."

He leant back against the wall and took a sip of water and the burning in his throat eased, a rapid succession of gulps followed and he felt settled, his head clearing. Straightening up he smiled wryly at the woman who had retreated into her hallway. He wiped his face with a handkerchief.

"I'll be getting on. Thanks for the water."

He raised a hand in farewell, pushed himself away from the wall and nodded towards number 57.

"I'll let you know what's happening."

She inclined her head and closed the door. Around the corner of the fence, out of her sight, he grimaced, cleared his throat and spat into the long grass.

"You idiot. You complete and utter idiot!"

Sliding his way along the passageway towards the shattered back door he sniffed the air. He couldn't be certain of anything, but drawing closer there was definitely something rank and repellant in the atmosphere. Placing his damp handkerchief over his nose and mouth he gingerly pushed at the door with his finger. It opened a short distance before hitting the fridge. At first he could smell nothing and he realized he was holding his breath. Reluctantly inhaling, the awful stink bore into him, a pungent pile-driver punching deep into his being.

Standing back, he turned away. The rain had stopped and the sun was warm on his damp skin. Wiping his face with his handkerchief he realized it was too small to tie round his head as a mask, so he would have to hold it over his face or, sod it, manage without.

"This is ridiculous, let's get things sorted."

Holding his breath he stepped up to the door and with his shoulder pushed against it as hard as he could. Nothing happened. Readjusting his position so that he could apply more pressure against the lower wooden part of the door, he tried again. The bulky obstacle suddenly moved, skewing anti-clockwise, allowing the door to judder open several inches. The squeal of the fridge feet scraping across the linoleum floor was drowned out by the frenetic buzzing of a swarm of black flies that lifted into the air as a cardigan-clad arm slumped into view from behind the barricade, the hand, desiccated and palely blue. Beyond it a slippered foot projected vertically into the air, the exposed leg bent slightly askew.

Recoiling he slipped on the wet step and ended up on his hands and knees. The flies were everywhere, they drove him to his feet and he stumbled to his car, the imprinted image forcing him to acknowledge that all the fingertips of the hand had been missing.

Blue light pulsed regularly across closed eyelids, there was a tapping on glass, a shadow loomed to his right. Rousing himself he looked up. The patrol car had pulled into the driveway behind him. Another was parked at the kerb. Two police officers were gazing at the house from the pavement. The tapping again, a hand circling. Wind down the window.

"Did you call us, sir? About a body?"

He nodded.

"Do you live here?"

He shook his head.

"Do you know who lives here?"

He nodded.

"Are you a relative?"

He shook his head again. There was a hammering sound, loud and intrusive, a constable, it could be a woman, was rapping on the front door of the house.

"Sir, can you please get out."

He opened the car door.

"Now."

Stumbling to his feet, he staggered against the vehicle. The officer stepped back.

"Have you been drinking, Sir?"

He looked up at him and shook his head.

"You'll need to tell us what is going on."

Leaning back against the bonnet, hands on knees, he garbled.

"Smell is awful. Flies everywhere."

He shook his head.

"In the kitchen, a body dead behind the fridge. It's obstructing the door. I can't believe it. I work for the landlord, collecting the rent. Thought they'd done a runner."

"They?"

"There were four of them living here, all women. Related I think."

"When did you last see them?"

"Months ago, next door said the same. Haven't paid rent or anything for a while."

He had trouble swallowing.

"That's why I'm here today. Chasing up what they owe. That's why I tried to get in."

"The back door is open?"

"Yes, but it's blocked."

"Blocked?"

"By the fridge."

"You wait here with my colleague. I'll take a look."

"You can see an arm and a leg inside. There's a gap. You can see ..."

He reached out with his hand, as if to restrain the officer, then let it drop resignedly. The constable disappeared behind the bins at the side of the house, but returned almost immediately, grimacing.

"Better get Serious Crime here and call an ambulance."

"Four bodies, Sir. Looks like they're all women, though it's difficult to tell. Advanced state of decomposition in a couple of cases. Possible they all didn't die at the same time. One is wrapped up in a blanket beside the sofa in the living room, another on the floor in the dining room covered in a duvet, the third is the one the rent collector saw in the kitchen leaning against the fridge which had been moved to barricade the back door. The last one is curled up in the hall. It's all a right state in there as you'd imagine. Also, some sort of animal has got in. Don't know if it's a rat or what. But it's had a go at ..."

"Thank you, Sergeant. That's enough for the moment."

"Yes Sir. No obvious cause of death that I can see – no smell of gas or anything like that. Boiler is working fine and it's like the tropics in there. The thermostat has been turned right up."

"What about upstairs?"

"All clear up there. But it's very odd, everything is incredibly tidy, beds made, bathroom spotlessly clean. Clothes hanging in wardrobes, no clutter on the shelves or bedside tables. It's like nobody was living there. There is no mess, not like downstairs."

"OK thank you. Anything else?"

"Yes, Sir. There is one more thing. On the ground floor there's paper everywhere, scattered throughout the rooms, on furniture and under it, behind cushions, wherever you look."

"What, newspapers?"

"No, every kind of paper – normal stationary, sheets of A4, shopping receipts, envelopes, pages torn from books, any old scraps – but it's been written on. All of it and not by the same person either. Different handwriting, scribbles, drawings, you know. There is masses of it. Hard to make head or tail of the few bits I looked at. No obvious sense to it. But it's all over the place. Might give us some clue as to what happened."

"Yes, thank you, thank you. Is the doctor here yet?"

"Yes, Sir, just arrived."

"Get him to take a look will you then get forensics in. Any idea who the victims are?"

"Yes sir. Rent collector's come up with some names. Oldest one, Daphne Fanning, was in her eighties apparently. The others are sisters and related to Daphne in some way, he's not sure how. They are Mary, Bernadette and Anne Walsh, he thinks."

"Get talking to the neighbours and see if they can confirm the names and find out when they last saw the women."

Police patrol cars now lined one side of the street, an ambulance had pulled into the driveway next door, blue light revolving. The driver leant forward on the steering wheel, resting his head on his crossed arms, his colleague stood at the open rear door, smoking. Officers idled on the front lawn, waiting, the urgency of the initial call-out dissipated. An occasional resident peered from downstairs windows, alerted by the unusual activity in an otherwise quiet street, but none ventured out. Only the woman from next door stood on her front step, holding a steaming mug and watching.

The air felt electric – charged by the sun's rays breaking through wan glowering clouds and the potency of death – burning off the imprint of summer showers. Colour again drenched the day, fringing the houses in the street, defining them, painting their exteriors with a character and substance that was normally lacking. She sipped her tea. There was a ghostly beauty in commonplace things, even in the effacement that was the ending of life, part of a deeper natural order that would outlast them all. It was a powerful feeling, one she had experienced on occasions before, while living in this street. It was temporary, a passing interruption to the flow. Her dead neighbour, Daphne had felt it too, she knew that. Wary of each other they had spoken only infrequently, but that had been enough for her to establish an understanding. She took another sip.

A faint distant reverberation, it could have been a scream, then a flurry at the shattered front door of number 57, a police officer beckoned urgently to the paramedic standing beside the ambulance. Extinguishing his cigarette, he jogged across the grass.

'What's up?'

"Bring a stretcher and get in here, one of them is still alive."

Part 2

Death By Numbers

"In weariness and painfulness, in watchings often, in hunger and thirst, in fastings often, in cold and nakedness."
2 Corinthians 11:26-28

Belfast Coroner's Court – Ten months later

The rain beat down on the glass roof of the Coroner's court, it's incessant hammering faintly audible to those below. A few bored faces staring upwards were illuminated in the dull glow of an overcast morning sun filtered through grimy panes high above. All colour washed out in the aura of insipid radiation, any animation draining away in the hushed stillness of the courtroom. The Coroner was late and the jury, lawyers, journalists and members of the public were idly biding their time. An explanation had not been given, so no one knew how long they would be waiting. The inquest, scheduled to begin today, had a macabre interest – the case itself received widespread media coverage – that had drawn in a larger than usual crowd of onlookers. There was no suggestion of foul play, the Police were not looking for anyone else in connection with the deaths and yet there were many questions unanswered about how three women, all related, came to die – a fourth had been at death's door when they were found – seemingly at their own hands, in a small house in a quiet suburb of the capital city. People had been shocked when it happened, collectively experiencing a sense of deep unease as the lurid details had been revealed in the press. To perish alone, unremarked, was a sad, familiar fact of an increasingly individualistic society, but to die in the company of others was a corruption of the belief that there was safety in numbers, in being popular, in not being lonely, in having friends, and particularly in this case, of having family around you. It was all very unnerving. A couple of the women, the twins, were in their forties and considered too young to die. The oldest, the aunt, was ailing and in her eighties. But still they had all been regular church-goers, devout God-fearing women according to their local priest and yet … it was hard to believe, difficult to take in. It was perverse, that was what it was and it was this fact that had drawn people to the courtroom in central Belfast on a wet weekday morning.

The wind buffeted the roof, smashing raindrops in pneumatic waves against the shimmering glass, agitating the air in the room, unsettling the composure of the people below. Shifting on the hard benches, leaning into whispered conversations, the solemnity of the occasion dispersing with the rustle of unfolding newspapers, overcoats being removed, a bunch of keys clattering to the floor. The clerk, censorious, looked up, then glanced at the silent clock at the back of the court, its juddering hands clearly signing the pressing extent of the problem.

"Five more minutes, then I will go and inquire. Please be patient".

Silence wrapped itself around the pattering rain and held – it was as if the courtroom had emptied – until a door swung violently open, banging hard against its stop and the Coroner swept in carrying a bulging briefcase, a dripping umbrella under his arm. The Clerk leapt up, reaching out to offer his assistance, others struggled to follow him to their feet. A whispering crescendo then a dying away. The Coroner moved uneasily around the bench, handing off coat and umbrella, pouring and drinking from a glass of water, sifting through papers, distributing them evenly before sitting down and adjusting the height and profile of his chair. The courtroom settled.

"My sincere apologies for the delay to today's proceedings," his voice wavered and he sipped again from his glass, "I have had an eventful commute in to court. An accident caused huge traffic problems, which unfortunately I got caught up in, making me inexcusably late. This rarely happens I hasten to add, but I thank you again for your forbearance. Now to the business of the morning."

He nodded to the Clerk.

"Belfast Coroner's Court number two, Mr. Stephen Mulvaney presiding, is now in session, please come to order. The purpose of today's inquest is to consider the circumstances surrounding the deaths of three women, who were related to each other: Mrs Daphne Charlotte Fanning, aged 84, Mrs Mary Elizabeth Reivers, aged 51 and her sister Anne Edna Walsh, aged 48. Mrs Reivers and Miss Walsh were the nieces of Mrs Fanning. They all resided at 57 Eden Avenue, Ballyrange, Belfast, where they were found dead on July 16th last year. The aim of these proceedings is to establish the facts surrounding their deaths and to place those facts on the public record and to make findings on the identification of the deceased, the date and place of death and most importantly the cause of death. You …", he indicated in the direction of the jury with a slight nod of his head, "… will, if all agree, return a verdict in relation to the means by which the three deaths occurred. The range of possible verdicts available to you, members of the jury, are accidental death, misadventure, suicide, an open verdict, natural causes and unlawful killing." He paused and raising his hand to cover his mouth discretely cleared his throat. "Questions of civil and criminal liability are not for your consideration and will not be investigated at this inquest. Also, no person can be exonerated from responsibility for the deaths at this hearing. Those are matters for another court to decide if so required."

The Clerk sat down. In the hushed court the rain drummed overhead. The Coroner looked up, reassured himself that the relevant papers were aligned on the desk in front of him, then declaimed in a sonorous voice.

"Call the first witness."

There was a flurry of activity as an usher pulled open the heavy door to the courtroom and called out imperiously.

"Constable Sinead Brennan."

The young woman appeared almost immediately, in uniform, and strode across the floor of the court. She placed her hat on the chair behind her, grasped the low rail of the witness stand firmly with both hands in an attempt to suppress the faint tremors that foreshadowed a growing apprehension, glanced at the jury seated to her right, then drawing herself upright looked over at the Coroner.

"Will you please tell the court your name."

"Sinead," her voice faltered, "Elizabeth Brennan."

"And how long have you been a police officer?"

"Just over fifteen months."

"Constable Brennan you were on duty on the morning of July 16th last year?"

"Yes, I was with Constable Martin Hanrahan."

"You received a call to attend at 57 Eden Avenue, Ballyrange, Belfast?"

She nodded, her anxiety building.

"That address is situated on a new housing development to the north-west of the city, is that right?"

"Yes, that's correct. I believe the estate was built four or five years ago."

"Will you tell us what happened when you arrived at the house."

Swallowing, her mouth suddenly very dry, PC Brennan experienced a moment of panic and she feared she would forget the statement that she'd rehearsed. Her appearance in court as a witness, only for the second time, wouldn't be difficult, she'd been assured, as there was no pressure on her to present critical evidence

22

that would be challenged, all she had to do was lay out what she had seen on that grisly morning. It was, she knew, ridiculous to be nervous about something so straightforward – and part of the job – but she was and it annoyed her. She hated herself for having no confidence, had lain awake the night before berating her lack of assertiveness. She worried that the pitch of her voice would veer erratically, the faltering squeaks shaming her in the eyes of everyone – the court, the jury, her colleagues.

"We received the call …" her voice quavered but did not break and she pressed on, the nodding attention of the Coroner fixing her rhythm, "… at 9.35 in the morning. We were only five minutes away. We were the first to arrive, closely followed by two colleagues in another squad car. All we knew," the Coroner's faint smile an encouragement, "was that a male caller had reported that someone was dead in the house. He turned out to be the landlord's agent, Mr Owen Cavanagh, who was sitting outside in his car waiting for us when we got there. One of the neighbours, Mrs Irene Daughty, from next door, number fifty-nine, was standing in the driveway as well."

"And then?"

"Mr Cavanagh was in a bad way, stumbling over his words, incoherent. If it hadn't been so early, I would have thought he was drunk. He was mumbling about a body in the kitchen and the awful smell. He kept asking how could they have done this? But couldn't tell us what this was. It appeared that the doors to the house were all barricaded and the locks blocked so we were going to have to break in. I knocked on the front door, but got no response. The neighbour told us that four women lived there, all related she thought, kept themselves to themselves, but even so she had not seen any of them for weeks"

"What were your first impressions, Officer?"

"There was no reason to believe they weren't telling the truth. The house had a shut up, abandoned feel, as if no one had lived there for a good while. I'd have thought it was a simple case of tenants absconding without paying the rent if it wasn't for Mr Cavanagh insisting there was a body leaning against the fridge in the kitchen, which was a strange claim to make if not true. It made me suspicious. My colleague went to check it out. There was a body… of a woman. We called in for assistance and an ambulance and prepared to break in through the front door using an enforcer."

The door cracked, bowing inwards as the lock gave way and the lower glass pane fractured at the second blow from the battering ram wielded by Constable Hanrahan, but did not open. The bolts at the top and bottom of the frame held fast and the wooden chest of drawers pushed up against it withstood the brunt of the bludgeoning force. Thwarted the police officer stepped back breathing heavily, he nodded at his partner and she kicked out the broken shards of safety glass protruding from the shattered frame, knelt down on the concrete step and pushed against the chest moving it slightly away from the door. It was heavy and its legs scraped noisily across the linoleum. A table lamp with a tasseled brown shade that had been placed on top of it, teetered, appeared to steady, then toppled over, crashing onto the floor in an explosion of shattering ceramics. Constable Brennan undid the lower bolt with difficulty – it appeared to have been glued in place – conferred with her colleague, counted to three and together barged open the upper intact half of the door with their shoulders. The glass snapped on the diagonal and the splintering door folded over the chest, skewing it across the hallway, opening up space to enter. Their momentum carried the officers into the house, driving forward against the physical obstacles, only for their progress to be reversed by a breaking wave of clammy pungency that swilled the pair out onto the front lawn, ending there with faces covered, gagging and coughing, gasping for breath. They recovered, while others looked on, as the ruptured house seemed to empty, draining miasmas, the cloying reek of death dissipating on the rising tide of fresh air. It was a release, far from a cleansing, but an end to excess, the opening up of a sealed fellowship, where the domineering actions of a few had achieved extreme ends.

"Officer Brennan we know you found three bodies inside the house on Eden Avenue as well as one survivor, Bernadette Walsh. She was the twin sister of one of the deceased, Anne Walsh, and the younger sister of another, Mary Reivers. Will you please tell us how you made these discoveries?"

"We initially didn't notice Bernadette Walsh when we went into the building. We only later discovered that she was lying in the hall near the door to the kitchen and away from the front door where we came in. Moving the chest of drawers out of the way so that we could squeeze in, meant that we couldn't see her as we entered. It's a small passageway. Both of us headed straight into the living room, which opens immediately off the hall. It was stifling, the temperature must have been in the eighties. I touched one of the radiators and it was scalding hot. It was difficult to breath."

The fug of death and the grotesqueness of the dead had blunted her sensibilities. She was observing the details in a daze. Bodies curled, shrouded beneath duvets, quilts, eiderdowns, in spite of the heat, animal damage, hair neat bundles of tight curls. The women were all downstairs – the bedrooms on the first floor were eerily empty, the beds made – that was where most people died wasn't it, particularly old people? – everything was immaculately tidy, no clutter on the dressing tables or window ledges, wardrobe doors closed, no mess in the bathroom, washbasin sparkling, bleach in the toilet, the vestigial scent of lavender infusing the tropical air. Their bodies resting among dirty clothes, torn rags, soiled towels and flannels, stained mattresses, bottles and cans, toilet rolls, dirty mugs and streaked glasses, amidst the detritus pots and pans of urine and human waste were strategically placed. Strewn everywhere were pieces of papers of all sizes, colours and types, crumpled and torn, carpeting the floors in a confetti of communication: most were covered in hand written scripts of varying ink tones and legibility, there were scribbles and sketches of cartoon like stick figures and propped on the mantelpiece were a profusion of letters in a variety of envelopes, some addressed to named individuals, others not.

The first body she had come across, was in the living room wedged beneath the sofa, a cushion gripped between her knees, arms outstretched; the second in a nest in the dining room, bedcovers and clothes piled on top of the upper part of her body, face leering out of a deep fold, exposed legs clad in two pairs of stained and laddered tights, one foot bare, the other wearing a new brown check slipper, the price label clearly visible on the sole; yet another body was in the kitchen leaning awkwardly against the fridge which had been pushed out of position, scouring deep runnels in the linoleum floor, to block the back door, her clothes were disheveled as if someone had been trying to tear them off, bedclothes were scattered around her feet and her head lolled to the side, wide eyes staring down at a saucer and coffee mug at her side, her fingers were raw, gnawed down to the first knuckle. Her stomach had turned when she had noticed this detail. There appeared to be an open diary wedged beneath the body – writing densely marching across every available space, blackening the pages – a pencil with a Mickey Mouse rubber head nestling in the spine. The urge to pick the book up and read it, searching for an explanation, was strong. The fourth body was in the hall, stretched out on her front, her limbs splayed to the sides so it looked as if she was attempting to crawl out from under the duvet, which now barely covered her ankles, and head away from the kitchen towards the front door, face buried in the carpet, keeping her head down.

It was incomprehensible. How could this have happened in this day and age to four women, one of them elderly? It was a disgrace. They looked at each other, her colleagues new and old, perplexed. There were no obvious signs of violence, man-made ones anyway, that could be seen. The victims were related as well, that's what they had told her outside. Old people occasionally died like this, she knew that … but abandoned and on their own, not in the company of others. Loneliness frightened Sinead Brennan, her innate sociability making the thought of dying alone and unloved unconscionable, yet these people apparently died … in the bosom of their family.

There was nothing more that could be done. Forensics would be arriving soon, a doctor too, although there was no hurry, it was a mere formality. She had switched off the central heating, the pipes were bumping and ticking as they cooled, and opened a window in the kitchen. A welcome breeze wafted down the hallway to the open front door. She sneezed, but with no handkerchief, she lifted her mask and wiped her nose, lips and chin with her gloved hand.

A wisp of breath – a ripple in the stagnant air, a deflation – had alerted Constable Brennan to the possibility of life in this house of death. She had already passed the woman in the hallway twice before – once on her first rapid search after rushing into the house hoping against hope there may be someone alive, the second time as she returned from checking the upstairs rooms and knew there was no hope and that things were stranger than expected – stepping carefully over the twisted arm that protruded diagonally across the faded runner and not really noticing the emaciated form cocooned loosely in ill-fitting clothes. On this occasion alert to the strangeness of the scene the constable stopped and noticed that the watch on the wrist was still going and making good time. She sneezed again, loud and percussive, the sound reverberating between narrow walls. Holding her breath, suppressing the repetitive urge, she picked up the echo, a rasping. Clearing her throat, she heard it again, this time a rustle. An independent movement in the air, free-formed. Her first thought was a rat, cornered. Stepping back in horror, scraping her shoulder along the wall, she righted herself and looked again. Was that a slight lifting of the stray grey hairs coiled across her mouth? Oily, slick and heavy the curl appeared set, immobile. But there was a shifting. Bending down, she watched intently. There was the faintest murmur. At the Police Academy she had learned about air escaping naturally from long dead bodies, first the swelling then a slow deflation, a feeble imitation of life. A deception? She had to make sure. Grasping the wrist, limp not stiff, warm not cold – a body in a post-rigor state of decay or a sign of life? Fumbling for a pulse, she waited silently, then she felt the tremor.

"I cried out, I was so surprised, shocked. Constable Hanrahan appeared. I think he had been in the living room. I shouted that this one is still alive. I had no idea then who she was. He pushed the chest of drawers away from the door and back against the wall to make room for us on the floor and let some fresh air in, then went outside and called for a paramedic. I held the woman's hand and started to talk to her, you know, the usual reassuring stuff about how she was safe now, help was on its way, that type of thing. There was no real response, possibly her breathing quickened, but I may have imagined that. I stayed beside her until they came with the stretcher. I left her then and went outside. It was a relief to get some clean air. I hadn't realized how fraught it had been inside. Then finding that Bernadette Walsh, as she turned out to be, was alive, was hugely emotional. I had to sit down. I needed a cigarette, even though I hadn't smoked in months, was trying to give up."

Several members of the jury smiled tentatively, uncertain of the seemliness of such emotion. It was a relief, a comprehensible sentiment and they grasped it. Nobody looked from side to side. In the hiatus the rain thrummed on the glass roof. The courtroom was still. A cough punctured the moment and the shuffling began.

"Thank you, Constable Brennan. You may step down. Members of the jury we will be hearing from Miss Walsh later in this inquest, but first I'd like to call the pathologist who conducted the autopsies on the three women who died at the house in Eden Avenue, Dr. William MacAleese."

A tall, gaunt, grey-haired man entered the room as Sinead Brennan left, they nodded at each other as they passed. Immaculately dressed in a black suit and waistcoat, red silk tie slightly askew he carried three identical blue files, which he placed next to each other in a row on the table beside the witness stand, before looking across at the Coroner.

"Dr MacAleese you carried out the autopsies on the three women of interest to this inquest. Will you please summarize your conclusions for us."

"I performed all three autopsies on July 19th and 20th of last year at the mortuary at Craigavon Hospital. I was assisted by my colleague Dr. Enda Logan."

He spoke in an authoritative deadpan, that held the jury's attention, the pause pregnant with anticipation. He glanced down at the files in front of him, nudging one of them gently into line, before continuing.

"All three women were heavily emaciated and had been dead for a period of several weeks to over a month before the autopsy. They had not died at the same time. In all cases decomposition had begun and as you would expect from what I've just said was more advanced in some cases than in others. The condition of the bodies, however, did not stand in the way of my general conclusion that the three women died from the consequences of starvation. There was no sign of any physical injuries to the bodies that would suggest coercion, which leads me to conclude that they starved themselves to death voluntarily. Given the time span over which this fast took place – I believe they were all last seen alive on April 10th and their bodies discovered on July 16th – then it is certain that they were drinking water throughout this period, prolonging life but having no ultimate impact on the final outcome. Medical opinion generally holds that in adults, complete starvation, that is not taking any food, but drinking water, leads to death within eight to twelve weeks. There are cases of people living up to twenty-five weeks, but these are rare and are generally younger, fitter individuals than those we are concerned with today. So, in this case death as a result of the effects of self-induced starvation occurred within 10 to 11 weeks for all three individuals. Inquiries by the police appear to support this finding of voluntary starvation. I can offer no explanation as to the motivation behind these individual acts, which appear to have been entered into collectively, that may come with the questioning of the surviving relative and the interrogation of the extensive documentary evidence left behind by the four women, but what I can say in conclusion to my general opening remarks is that the deaths of these three women and the suffering of the survivor will have been prolonged and distressing, extended over a period of many days and will have ended in a period of painful incapacity in which it was impossible to reverse the course of their actions even if they had wished to at that late stage. This demonstrates to me a collective determination to end their lives, more deeply felt than anything I have ever come across in my more than thirty years' experience in this field. Suicide is the ultimate prerogative open to all of us, cast around with all the moral and religious prohibitions we are only too aware of, and is so often an individual affair, resolved and acted upon alone. Mass voluntary suicide is rare, if this is in fact the case, and you, members of the jury, need to reflect carefully on what could induce four related adults, all but one of them apparently in reasonable health for their age, to set out on such a course of action, fraught as it was with the certainty of an extremely miserable and degrading death."

The jury stared at him as he poured a glass of water and sipped it. With his free hand he flipped open one of the files, the top sheet of paper lifted in the back draft, tethered in one corner by a green tag, it billowed upwards before settling askew.

"I will give the detailed results of the individual autopsies in the order in which I believe they died. This information on the timings has again been corroborated by the police investigation."

Dr MacAleese took another sip of water. The luminosity of the room darkened as grey clouds swept overhead obscuring the hazy sun that had begun filtering weak light into the court room, subtly shading the dull gloom of the fluorescent lights; the high wind chasing a heavy downpour which clattered across the glass roof. He looked up diverted by the striking sounds.

"The first to die on or around June 15th was Daphne Charlotte Fanning, aged 84 and the eldest of the three women. I should say something here about the timing of death. Forensic investigation based on the condition of the body and rates of decomposition is by its very nature an imprecise art providing only a window of time in which death may have occurred. In this instance we are fortunate to have both a witness and, as has been mentioned, extensive written documentation of events in the house, including a fairly comprehensive diary kept by one of the individuals, which is for most of the period we are concerned with remarkably complete. This has allowed me to be far more accurate with timings of death than would normally be the case. I can, therefore, say with confidence that they are accurate to within 36 hours.

Mrs Fanning's body, which was found lying beside the sofa in the living room, exhibited the classic signs of starvation – massive weight loss, shrinkage of her vital organs, widespread hair loss, and skin discoloration. It appears she would have suffered irritation from pressure sores brought on by immobility. There was extensive evidence of significant muscle depletion and atrophy across all areas of the body. She would not have been able to walk, lift even the smallest of household objects, nor support herself independently in an upright, seated position. Mrs Fanning had a pre-diagnosed heart condition for which she was taking a daily regimen of statins and aspirin. Toxicology indicated that she had stopped taking these medicines some time before her death, even though she had redeemed her prescription just before her fast began, the day before in fact, and had ample supplies of both statins and aspirin in the house. Opened packets of both were found alongside her body. Her blood tests were clear indicating that she was not taking any form of painkiller, nor was she drinking alcohol."

Turning a page in the file the pathologist ran a finger over the papers, diligently searching for the pertinent figures. He sipped from his glass. The break in the flow of his words opening up a space for the conjuring of disturbing images and the body of the court stirred. People shifted in their seats, stretching legs, adjusting raincoats damp on their laps, looking up at the kaleidoscopic torrent of rain water streaming in rivulets across the glass panes in the roof, backlit by a pale sun partly obscured by clouds. One person sneezed then another. No words were spoken. He waited.

"Her medical records suggest a fit body weight of 9 stone 12 pounds, fairly normal for a woman of her age and height. Her body weighed just under 6 stone – a weight loss of almost 40% – a figure almost universally recognized as being incompatible with continued life."

A sigh, clearly audible and prolonged, rose from the public benches. The Coroner turned and tracked the sound to its source. A man was slumped forward in his seat, holding his head with his right hand. A woman leaned into him, an arm draped across his shoulder. Suddenly aware of being watched. they straightened in their seats and looked around. He wiped his eyes.

"I would like to conclude by saying that in the common parlance Mrs Fanning starved herself to death, but that was not the actual cause of her demise. The aforementioned heart condition holds the key. She died from a myocardial infarction, more commonly known as a heart attack, induced by starvation conditions."

The Coroner nodded at him.

"Thank you, Dr MacAleese. I think we should take a break for lunch." He turned to face the jury. "We shall reconvene in an hour."

The woman sat erect and unmoving, watching the people stream out of the courtroom into the wide echoing hallway, where she had been waiting resolutely all morning to give evidence. Her hands rested on top of a brown leather handbag, which was planted firmly in her lap. She had barely moved in over two hours, finding it easier that way, less painful, her body settled somehow, there were none of the spasms and twitches that normally plagued her waking hours. This way no one would see her trembling hands and the facial tics that still embarrassed her when she was out in public. She had made a remarkable recovery they told her, someone as emaciated as her, so close to death, rarely came back unscathed. She knew this to be true, but her doctors were so cheerful and exuberant about her progress and the efficacy of their treatment that she, the good Christian that she was, hadn't the heart to tell them the truth. That physically she still felt hollowed out, her body fragile and empty, that the sensation of her dissolute flesh dissolving into the heady balm of her faith that had permeated her final days in the house had never left her. That this sensual spirituality absorbing her wasting body and replenishing her immortal soul had been so intoxicating, so addictive, that she never wanted to give it up. And she hadn't. She held on to her faith with a renewed passion, forging a grim determination to succeed, but there was a price to be paid. Now she constantly ached, twinges of pain flaring then dying away – shoulders, back, hands, thighs, no part of her was immune – her skin burned, erupted, flaked, itched with a trying persistence that she found redeeming. Such tribulations were a penance for her actions that she was only too happy to perform. No soothing face creams, no makeup, no more pride in superficial appearances. Wavy auburn hair now straight and completely grey, almost white in fact, brittle and thinning in patches, impossible to style as she had once liked. So in response she had been shorn like a sheep – rising from the white wispy remnants of her vanity curling in heaps at her feet, reborn. A new compact with God had been fashioned that for her engendered a spiritual transformation but not a physical one. It was their secret. She had not told the doctors that her heart thumped in its cavity, racing erratically, whenever she ate, food hurting her, its texture cloying in the mouth, teeth aching, its mass sticking in her throat, clogging her stomach. The best things from her previous life were no longer any pleasure, taunting her with their plasticity and drabness. She was often sick, her body rejecting sustenance, it was, she felt, as if her material being had an intelligence of its own, determined to divorce itself from her confounded spirit. Water, cold and pure, was what bound mind and form together, plus a little help from doctors who gave her regular vitamin injections. She agreed, wholeheartedly, with this new imprint of herself, only too delighted to sign her own name.

Bernadette looked older than her forty-nine years, her frame bent, limbs thin and bony, no longer filling out her clothes. Her face pale and pinched, red blotches flaring as angry bursts of colour, lines etched deep into her forehead and around eyes, which were once a lucent dark brown, now a wasted, watery, taupe. Her expression, often hooded, revealed nothing of her steely faith in a destiny pre-ordained. She simply offered up a level of unwavering vacancy that was disconcerting to well-wishers hoping to alleviate her suffering with their compassionate concern for her ordeal, only to have confirmed by their own eyes the extent of the damage done.

Humility, of which she was an adherent, dictated a balancing out. The Bible was clear the meek not the arrogant would inherit the keys to the Kingdom and she believed in the Book's literal truth. So, faith in her eventual triumph undiminished she was only troubled by the future that she had been unexpectedly handed – a time undetermined – and how to fill it, physically impaired as she was. Nagging at her mind was the corrosive knowledge that her bodily collapse was not meant to have happened. She was to have perished with the others, pristine in the beauty of their immolation. She had been a pilgrim, processing with the others along the path to transcendence, but she had been diverted, become separated, never reached the end. Left alone. Abandoned. For what?

Father Conlan had smiled when she had told him at her first confession after her restitution that she was in limbo, unable to find herself and return to her former life with beliefs intact, stuck in an unfamiliar place, paralysed with guilt, staring into the flames.

"Bernadette, limbo is not for you. You have been baptized after all. Purgatory maybe. But there are ways forward from there. With God in your heart, with the power of prayer and a true confession, you can be reborn and your sins cleansed."

She was in purgatory. Her sins were pardonable then. Surviving always seems a good idea to the living, but what about to the dead? To Nanny, Mary and Anne? No, not to them. They were not so forgiving. She would be forever guilty in their eyes, and they were everywhere now.

"Guilt can be instructive, Bernadette, but it can also be very destructive, you must learn from it and put it behind you."

The priest's unctuous tones were sickening. She had never felt it before her fast, only afterwards in that first awkward exchange of words at her bedside as she resurfaced into this world. Later trying to communicate her experience dislocated their relationship. He did not understand, couldn't comprehend, the journey she had been on. From where she had reached, his authority was much diminished. He was wrong about almost everything, except that guilt was constructive. She had let them down, Nanny most of all. She was guilty about that, the culpability of the survivor played on her mind – was she to blame for their deaths? Why her? Why had she lived? She had let herself down and she had failed God. Maybe? There had to be a reckoning. What did she have left? Just guilt, stoking her resolve, fuelling her indignation and making life here on earth hell. Was that it? Was that her purpose? God knew.

And she had her brother, John, who she spotted crossing the hall towards her, upset, his hair dishevelled, tie crooked. He had been in court listening to the morning's evidence and not liking it. Her younger brother, a lapsed Catholic, unlike his sibling sisters, had been distraught at their betrayal, as he saw it. It had taken him weeks to be consoled and finally cautiously reconciled. But even now, months after Bernadette had left hospital, he was still wary of her, edging delicately into conversations. The question of why was never far from the surface, John eyeing her suspiciously whenever they were together. The police, after they had finished their investigation, had handed over to him all the diaries and papers they had found in the house, a decision Bernadette was not happy about. These documents were very personal and honest, and not for him. Who knew what poured forth when people were in extremis? But he was deemed the only remaining responsible adult in the family, their mother long dead, their father lingering in an old people's home and Bernadette one of the protagonists. They would be used in evidence at the inquest, she had been informed, and she sensed John was diligently reading through them. Their relationship had subtly changed over recent weeks and he had become increasingly taciturn. This had not been the case earlier once they were back on speaking terms. He had been bursting with questions then – why, why, why?

Bernadette had never actively disliked her brother and she tried to explain things to him in as simple a way as possible. He was an agitated listener and, she came to realize, was not really paying attention to what she said. He was fixated on the idea that someone had forced them into it and couldn't accept that it had been their decision. That his sisters and aunt had acted alone. That they had chosen to end their lives. He could never accept the fact that they had not spoken to him, remaining convinced he could have talked them out of killing themselves, changed their minds. The fire had eventually gone out of his enquiries and their conversations had settled onto the practical issues of her rehabilitation, of her future, of her life. He had proved very punctilious, for which she was grudgingly grateful. There were worse places to be living than his spare bedroom – a legal requirement – a secure room in Mount Carmel Hospital being one.

"How's it going?"

John sat down beside her, his face severe, eyes reddened, he pulled at his shirt front as he spoke.

"The Coroner was late so they haven't got as far as expected. You may not even be called today. That young police woman was up first then they moved on to the pathologist ... he was talking about Nanny, how she died ..."

His body shuddered.

"How could you Bernie, how could you?"

Face vacant in his anguish, he stared at her uncomprehendingly.

He was a lost cause, she knew, but she would have her chance, if not today then tomorrow. She would give her evidence and explain the fast to everyone. Her faith would win through and convince them of the righteousness of their actions. People would finally understand why they had done it and not think, as they did now, that they were simply insane.

She was not mad.

"Anne Walsh died on June 23rd, she was aged 48. Her body was found in the dining room of the house on Eden Avenue. As with her aunt I estimate that she had lost close to 40% of her body weight due to self-starvation, but had been drinking water for most of the duration of her fast, thus prolonging the ordeal. Again, there were no external or internal signs of injury that would suggest any form of physical coercion.

Her failure to take any nourishment resulted, as you would expect, in significant changes to her external appearance. She would have experienced extreme discomfort and standing or sitting would have been impossible from a fairly early stage. There was extensive hair loss, as well as a lightening of hair colour. In areas her dark brown hair had turned almost white."

Punctuating his remarks, the pathologist straightened and turned slightly glancing at the Coroner before returning his attention to the jury.

"I would now like to turn to the cause of death. Anne Walsh appears to have been a healthy woman for her age, not significantly overweight, a non-smoker, very moderate alcohol consumption and by reports she exercised regularly. Yet my internal investigation found a pronounced shrinkage of a number of her vital organs. As a result, she would have suffered in the last stages of life from heart arrhythmia, palpitations and experienced difficulties breathing. My estimation given the damage sustained internally, which makes a precise determination of the cause of death difficult, is that she died from the failure of one or more of these organs."

The fatigue in his voice as he spelled out his findings was palpable. His demeanour, closed in and reticent, suggested unease at the implications of what he was detailing – a weary consternation at this evidence of human wastefulness. Gathering himself he emphatically moved Anne Walsh's file aside, placing it on top of that of her aunt's, then rested his open hand on it as if in benediction. The jury, attentive, stared up at him. They waited, the room silent, the heavy rain having eased. A slight drizzle was now misting the windows in the roof, softening the pasty afternoon light. Layers of the commonplace already settling over the graphic evidence.

John was horrified. Undone by what he was hearing, he felt nauseated. Distraught he had sought Bernadette out, once again seeking enlightenment, but she had just sat there in the hallway, enclosed, unforthcoming as always. Her shrunken frame and blank expression exciting thoughts of violence that he had never known as a child. He had loved the twins then, or thought he did, playing with them into his teens, well past the stage when his friends had cast aside the company of girls for street gangs and football. They had been pretty, vivacious, fun to be with, their mischievous games endlessly challenging and inventive and he had worked hard to contribute and keep up. Almost identical in looks – dark auburn curls, framing wan faces of lean charm, brown eyes flashing, animated mouths forever chattering, their slim lithe figures invariably draped in boyish clothes – they had differed markedly in character. Anne, despite having an almost indeterminable symmetrical aspect to her appearance that marked her out as the more beautiful of the two – a quality of which she was completely unaware, but her twin was most certainly not – was the follower. She constantly deferred to Bernadette's wishes and the hard edge of her sophisticated creativity. In that relationship, John knew only too well, Anne had always been a cipher.

Mary had been different from the twins, older, maternal – particularly when their mother had died – strict, censorious, lacking a sense of humour. She had shouldered her responsibilities heavily but conscientiously, plodding through life, exhibiting a manifest lack of sparkle which made her suicide the more mystifying.

The actions of his sisters were a mystery. All Bernadette maundered on about was the sanctity of the fast; the sublime healing powers of belief; the resurrection of an ailing soul through the scourge of self-negation; sacrifice by virtue of pain; their faith. Such a lack of consideration for him, for his feelings, for their mutual upbringing was galling. He had tried to be a good brother, keeping in touch as their paths diverged in adulthood, visiting them on and off over the years but ultimately the austere spinsterhood of the twins had been alienating and Mary's husband had been difficult and he had met up with them less and less often. Now he deeply regretted not having gone to see them in Eden Avenue, had been meaning to, but somehow the three of them together with their aunt were so formidable and self-contained that he couldn't face it. Yet he was their closest relation. Their father didn't count as over the years he had fallen out with all his relations. John, in his fraternal vanity, believed he might have been able to change things, talk them out of it or even at the barest minimum, understand their actions. He wished more than anything that he had acted – he was certain he had called them on the phone during their fast, but they hadn't answered – he would have discovered what they were up to and would have been the one to save them. Decisiveness would have changed everything – his sisters may even have loved him again, eventually. It was killing him. There had been no forewarning, just a yawning gap in his understanding and knowledge of them, no explanation, no goodbye. All they had left him as an inheritance was a black hole into which his history and sense of self had disappeared.

His family life had been a sham. Disaffected from his brutish father, who was languishing lucid but physically incapacitated in a care home, he had been disavowed at an early age. With his dead mother, Maureen, a distant imperfect memory, his sisters had been his only kin, a source of continuity and stability in a tricky world. No longer. Love had died or, as he often now thought, been deliberately slaughtered.

"Mary Elizabeth Reivers was the elder sister of Anne and Bernadette."

John started, straightening his body on his seat, prickling in anticipation at what was to come.

"Her body was found in a sitting position in the kitchen, leaning against the fridge freezer, which had been moved to block the back door. I estimate that she died on or around the 29th of June. The exposed position of her body, uncovered, and in the kitchen with easy access to the back garden through a cat flap, meant that some of her limbs had suffered from severe degradation by animals."

A jury member gasped. There was a cough and a shifting of alignment.

"As with the other cases, there were no further recent signs of violence on Mrs Reivers' body, suggesting that death was the result of voluntary starvation. However, there were extensive signs, both internal and external, of old injuries. Her body was heavily scarred on her back and stomach. The scar tissue was superficial but suggested that on a number of occasions she had been beaten with a belt or some similar implement and slashed or scratched with a metal object. Mrs Reivers had also at some point in her adult life broken her nose and sustained a perichondrial hematoma – members of the jury may be more familiar with the term cauliflower ear. A number of her ribs had been broken at different periods in the past, as had her collarbone. These injuries are consistent with police records detailing a number of physical assaults on Mary Reivers over a period of years, one of which resulted in hospitalization. In and of themselves these injuries were not of direct relevance to the cause of her death, but I do think they were instrumental in her generally poor state of well-being and her persistent ill health and this will have influenced the nature of her death. Mrs Reivers suffered from a number of gastro-intestinal complaints, which would have been both painful and appetite suppressants. Prior to her fast Mrs Reivers was underweight for her height. Counter-intuitively this meant that not eating had less immediate impact on her than her companions and she lived longer than would have been expected given her general state of poor health."

John stared at the figure, indistinct features, blurred yet dark in outline, intoning before him. Every word spoken adding to the litany of painful detail that was beginning to exact a physical toll. Perspiration dotted John's lined brow, a throbbing pain arced between his temples. He felt weak. On the cusp of breakdown, John teetered. The sediment of knowledge weighed heavily. Layer upon graphic layer stifling the life out of him. One more matter of fact and he would have to leave.

"Mrs Reiver's apparent long-term weight loss also had other material manifestations which were again not terminal but contributing factors to the ending of her life."

John leant forward, losing sight for the first time of the voice, his hearing though still acute.

"The extreme fast she subjected herself to meant that she faced an acute susceptibility to infection ..."

John fainted, sliding from his chair, brushing roughly against his neighbours as he collapsed. Exclamations of alarm drowned out the testimony. The Coroner got to his feet. John, lying on the floor now conscious, felt sick, despair at his loss of control yielding to wretched embarrassment.

"There will be a fifteen-minute adjournment. Back here at three forty-five please for the conclusion of Dr. MacAleese's evidence."

Clarity returned fitfully. John was aware of movement around him, of people muttering. He would have to leave, he could not stay, he would not hear Bernadette give evidence on oath. There was a surge of relief at this knowledge – enough of dissimulation, of facile religiosity, of keening self-justification – then a rush of regret. He had to know. She would not lie in court: she might to him, but not here having sworn on the Bible. Not Bernadette. The truth, the whole truth and nothing but the truth, that was what he wanted. And she would have to give it, all rivalry between siblings aside. He needed the cool forensic hand of the law to help him understand.

"Sir, this way please."

Someone gripped his shoulder.

Ashen-faced he approached his sister. Beatific she stared up at him, smiling. She raised a hand to bless him. Absolution was hers to give and she would not be ungenerous in his time of need. He sunk to his knees to receive her benediction but gazing at her it dawned on John that she had never worn a black habit and caul before to his knowledge. And where had she got that heavy wooden cross that was hanging around her neck? Maybe he was going mad? It was always a possibility.

"Miss Walsh, your brother was taken ill in court. We'll be resuming in a few minutes to hear the rest of the pathologists' evidence. But we won't be needing you to testify today. So maybe you could take each other home. See you tomorrow."

Bernadette smiled at the usher and mouthed her thanks.

"John come on now, stop messing around and get up. People are looking at you."

She reached out but couldn't bear to touch him.

"Dr. MacAleese, please could you continue giving your evidence. And thank you for your patience in indulging the court."

"As I was saying earlier, Mrs Reivers' difficulties in eating and the extreme nature of the fast she undertook with the others had led to an acute susceptibility to fungal infection which once it had taken hold led rapidly to the organ failure that caused her death."

He cleared his throat, raising the back of his left hand to cover his mouth.

"I would just like to add that I think that in the case of Mrs Reivers, despite my uncertainty about the exact mechanism of her death, I am quietly confident that it would have been relatively painless. There is strong evidence that in such cases of extreme infection the individual enters into a state of torpidity, often resembling a coma, several days before they eventually die. There is no indication that the body exhibits signs of stress in response to this condition."

Underlining the finality of his evidence he closed Mary Reiver's file and added it to the pile in front of him, before lifting them all, tapping them into alignment on the tabletop and slipping them into his briefcase.

"Thank you Dr. MacAleese. Tomorrow we will hear the testimony of Miss Bernadette Walsh."

The hollowness – spiritual and physical – was enlightening. To have gazed into heaven's vastness only to fall back to earth unencumbered was a blessing, disguised, but profound none the less. Her re-entry a mental purgative, cleansing her mind of all thoughts of self. No recriminations, no longer any survivor remorse. Her failure to follow the others was a purposeful trajectory for which she had been chosen, that she now understood. Once in the presence of death, of loved ones and oneself freely chosen, you could never be the same again. Bernadette felt physically debilitated most of the time but the aches and pains were mere tracery binding her to the earth, swaddling her wings. With a mind that was sharp and crystal clear, she had a role to play. Her twin dead she was now paired with the infinite. Angelic, self-effacing, demure she would use her broken body as a canvas on which to paint her masterpiece. A self-portrait of her image as seen in the celestial mirror – a sublime emptiness reversed.

Her brother couldn't see it, try as he might. He was blind and always had been, not like their sisters, and certainly not like Anne, her soul companion. Ingratiating himself had been the doomed aspiration of John's childhood. Bernadette had tried to like him then, but his fawning devotion, assuredly masculine, had been an irritation to subtler sisterly affections. She had lately tried to help him come to terms with their fast and the deaths but, if she was honest, she had not used the full palette available to her, sketching out only the simplest outline of the events that had engulfed them all, leaving him to puzzle over what the bigger picture may have looked like.

He was here now, despite his collapse yesterday, couldn't keep away. Looking around the courtroom she spotted his pale face staring balefully, mouth slightly open. Their eyes meeting, she stared back impassively.

How different things would have been if before the fast she had been called to appear like this in court as a witness. Nervous and tongue-tied she would have been at a loss to know what to say. A hopeless, female stereotype conforming to everyone's expectations, even her own. Now her frail body and hollowed out mind were a conduit for a higher truth that everyone deserved to hear. She finally had a story to tell.

"Miss Walsh thank you for attending this inquest today. I understand that you are not yet fully recovered physically from your ordeal so I give you permission to deliver your evidence sitting down if you would like. Also, if at any time you feel the need to take a break, please do not hesitate to let me know."

Bernadette nodded at the Coroner.

"I would remind you Miss Walsh that you are under oath."

She had prayed for the strength to get through this legal ordeal and for guidance on the words to use and what to tell them. Uncertain as to whether her prayers had been heard until the moment she swore on the Bible, she now felt suffused with an inner resolve and the certain knowledge of where to start. Her guardian angel had descended. Nanny was finally talking, the whisper in the ear, directing her from the beyond as she had done in life. It had all been down to Daphne Fanning in the end, to Nanny. She had always been their mentor, their inspiration.

Cocooned in the hairdryer's warm embrace, bathing in the glow of late spring sunshine, a heady confection of aromatic bleaches, conditioners and shampoos filling her lungs, Daphne Fanning, with feet up and coffee cup in hand, was contemplating her own death.

Humming, she thought of passing on, of it all being over. The end of her earthly suffering, ushering in an eternity without pain.

An active woman of eighty-four she'd been feeling out of sorts for years, never quite right even in the good times. Her slide into ill-health had been gradual, time crowding out memory of what it felt like to be normal as the background chatter of acceptable pain grew ever louder.

"More coffee, Mrs Fanning?"

Daphne grinned and nodded.

"You'll be done in another ten minutes or so."

She raised her thumb in acknowledgement. Her reverie too precious to breach with verbal pleasantries. The steaming refill warmed her aching hands.

"Another biscuit?"

The young girl scurried away, slopping coffee on her blue overalls, and returned with a plate of chocolate digestives. Daphne took two, smiling conspiratorially.

"I wish I had your figure, Mrs Fanning, look at you. I've been on a diet since Christmas, but I've put on nearly half a stone."

She laughed, barely disguising her annoyance at the unfairness of it all.

"I'll be back to check on you shortly."

Daphne closed her eyes and arched her stiff back, stretching luxuriously in the capacious chair. She flexed her swollen ankles, moving them one way then the other, before slipping off her shoes and wriggling her toes playfully. The right stocking badly needed darning, she noticed, a yellowing, cracked nail protruding through the frayed wool, but she didn't care anymore. Old age had its freedoms and she was not averse to enjoying them. Somewhere above her head a radio was playing a jaunty tune, and Daphne couldn't resist, picking up it's driving melody and singing along. Alone under the dryers on this special Wednesday morning session for pensioners, she felt unrestrained, able to let go. She gazed benignly through lidded eyes at the deserted salon and the glare of the street beyond.

The lightness in the air was soporific and she dozed, her coffee cup teetering dangerously in her lap. Jerking awake, head full of a daze of bright colours, she smiled, unaware of where she was, then the worn reality of the hairdresser's crowded in.

"You old silly you've got a lot to do today."

Righting the yawing cup, she straightened in her chair, feeling suddenly uncomfortably warm. The music on the radio fading into the pips at the top of the hour caught her attention. She glanced at the clock above the reception desk.

"This is taking forever."

Savouring the taste of the weak, milky coffee, she dunked her biscuit. Crumbs scattered across the front of her overall as she greedily took a bite. The rest of the digestive disintegrated in her hand, chocolate melting on her fingertips. Licking them one by one, she listened attentively to the radio.

"Here are the headlines at ten o'clock: The Real IRA has claimed responsibility for the large car bomb that was left outside the law courts in Belfast city centre earlier this week…"

Brushing herself down she set aside the cup and saucer and picked up a copy of Woman's Own. A smiling middle-aged model stared at her from the cover. Everyone looked younger than her now, everyone was younger than her after all, there were no images to relate to, little to look forward to. She flicked through the dog-eared pages, but nothing caught her interest. She began fanning herself with the magazine.

"The French president, Jacques Chirac, has confirmed to Tony Blair that France is willing to seek a compromise on disarming Saddam Hussein, but would not accept any UN resolution that set an ultimatum…"

The cool rush of air was a relief. Where had her girl gone? The salon was quiet.

"I'm cooking under here!"

Every fortnight it was the same. They always took their time, it was part of the "pensioner's special" ritual. Sinking back in resignation, Daphne drifted. At her age and state of health, morbid thoughts were ever-present. Companionable even. Death, always male she had discovered, standing at your shoulder. Embracing him was to be a choreographed affair, no missteps, no mess, nothing left to chance, no random elements, minimum fuss, everything under control. She ran through a checklist of what had to be done: collect pension, close her bank account, re-direct the mail, buy food for tonight, stock up on masking tape, meet the girls, and last but not least go to confession. Lists had been her saving grace for many years – "the road to heaven was paved with them" – masking the encroaching failings of old age. Keeping her end up mentally was very important.

The news bulletin finished and music reclaimed the airwaves. A gentle melody barely audible over the hum of the dryer, Daphne opened her eyes. Across from her a door swung open, blue-fringed figures appeared, frenetically active.

"Mrs Fanning we hadn't forgotten you."

"I think I'm done."

The words slithered from her mouth without effect.

"Sorry, what was that?"

"Very hot under here…"

Venting her overall and blouse with one hand, she fanned furiously with the other, which was still clutching the copy of Woman's Own.

"… I'm probably overdone."

"Let's set you free then. These things can get a bit much if you're under them for too long."

The girl laughed and gently lifted the clear perspex dome of the drier to reveal a head of foil crimped red curls glinting in the sunlight.

"It won't take me a minute to get these off and then we'll see…"

Roughly untwisting each plump package, she tossed the balled foil into a waste bin several feet away – missing as often as she was on target, the crushed silver spheres scattering across the black and white tiles – as each rounded curl fell out. Daphne had always been a red head and thanks to the judicious use of hair dye and curlers had managed to maintain the same look for the last half century.

"You look real fine Mrs Fanning. A picture."

Slipping on her glasses she barely had to glance in the mirror to confirm all was well. The aura of curls, a waning ruddy half-moon floating high over a flat forehead creased with wavy lines of concern, gave her a perpetual expression of amused indifference. Puffy brown eyes, overarched by narrow eyebrows, stared myopically out over crumpled fleshy pillows. Deep furrows in these cheeks, framed a flat wisp of a mouth, whose thin pencil lips revealed when she smiled the unnatural regimentation and startling whiteness of dentures. Severe in repose, she had tried when younger to leaven her appearance with foundation and bright lipsticks, but had now given up such artifice, facing the world largely unadorned – these visits to the salon her only remaining concession to the passing years.

She lightly fingered the slight dimple at the tip of her firm chin. Never a beauty, she knew, but always presentable, she took pride in that. She had her mother's pale complexion and clear skin, which was something to be thankful for.

"You are a love."

She patted the girl on the arm.

"Help me up will you my dear, my old legs aren't what they used to be."

Standing awkwardly, as feeling returned to her lower body, she rummaged in her handbag for her purse.

"I know it's in here somewhere, this thing is bottomless."

Stepping forward she felt a twinge in her back and almost stumbled.

"Are you alright?"

"Yes," she hissed between gritted teeth, "pins and needles in the old leg. Sitting for too long, always does it to me."

"Here, have a seat."

"No, I'll be fine. If I sit down again, I may never get up. I'll stand for a minute."

Grasping the counter with arthritic hands, she paused, wincing at the sharp pain in her swollen knuckles, then eased out four pound coins from her purse and piled them neatly next to the till. Then she unzipped a small pocket in her handbag and took out a tightly folded ten-pound note. With difficulty she flattened it out and handed it to the shocked hairdresser.

"Mrs Fanning this is too much."

"It's for being a good girl to me over the years."

"I can't …"

"Yes, you can…"

Daphne raised a finger to her mouth, cutting off further protest.

"… before I change my mind."

"Ta … ta very much. I'll get your coat."

She hurried to the large cupboard at the back of the salon and slid back the door, it squealed then jammed before it was half open. Cursing under her breath, she rummaged through overalls and coats, the wire hangers grating.

"Yours is the black one, right?"

Daphne nodded.

"Yes, with the fur collar."

"Got it."

Triumphantly she held the coat aloft and tugged at the door. It refused to budge and she kicked it.

"See you in a fortnight."

Silhouetted in the bright doorway, a picture framed, Daphne put on her coat, waved her hand in the air as she left, but said nothing.

The fresh air felt chill on her face, tinged with exhaust fumes from the heavy traffic in nearby Murray Street but invigorating. She breathed deeply, glancing left then right, a hand shielding her eyes from the glare. They were nowhere to be seen.

"Late as usual."

She had taken her time but couldn't hang around any longer, she would have to get on, there was so much to do. They could catch her up.

Daphne hesitated at the kerb, the ordinary appeared insubstantial in the radiant sunlight. She again looked in both directions, drawing in the details hungrily: the vivid colours of the hoardings masking the vacant lot across from her, empty since the fire three years ago had destroyed the minicab firm and the accountant's office above it – arson everyone knew but never proved. She could still smell the burnt embers whenever she stood at the bus-stop on that side of the street. Further along, the variegated heaps of vegetables piled in boxes resting precariously on crates outside the greengrocers; next door silvery fish of all sizes nestling in bloodied ice drifts, shadowed beneath a stained brown awning that hung low over the pavement, its scalloped fringe forcing passersby to duck as they shuffled past; the ordered chaos of the ironmongers' window heaped floor to ceiling with tools, plastic household goods, cleaning products and archaic electrical devices, all un-priced and apparently inaccessible. That was where she was heading, she – they, she corrected herself – needed masking tape, several rolls of it.

The buildings and the streets were familiar and she felt nostalgia for the idea of such a neighbourhood, but no strong attachment. She had lived in the city all her life, but not around here. She was an interloper, unknown to most people; circumstances had brought her here. The burglaries, one every few months at the end, had been the ruination of her business – a newsagent and sweet shop. The spur to sell up and move had been a confrontation with a masked man armed with a crowbar, that ended with her on the floor nursing a severely bruised arm and the takings gone together with a large jar of Licorice Allsorts. Escaping the persecution – it was galling that her brother could have ended it, but didn't – she had been obliged to accept his help in another way and move in with him and his daughters. She knew it was, as was always the case with him, a duplicitous offer, the extending of his hand of brotherly friendship following as it did close on the death of his wife, Maureen. The role he envisaged for her as an unpaid housekeeper had been sugared by the usual platitudes about the need for family solidarity in the face of adversity, the emotional rewards for everyone in living together and the most persuasive of all for Daphne, the lack at her age of any other obvious place to go. Unhappy at first at the loss of independence and the thwarting of personal ambition she had eventually reconciled to being with her other family by ignoring her brother and growing close to her nieces. His recent physical incapacity and admission into a care home had enabled the women's move across town to a new house on an unprepossessing estate, where Daphne finally had his three daughters to herself. The four of them were about to embark on one last great adventure.

The house on Eden Avenue was nothing special but the land on which it was built and the domain around it was an ancient holy place, sanctified by centuries of pilgrims' passing through on their quest for spiritual redemption. Daphne felt it's divine history profoundly and had been moved by the chain of events, pre-ordained she now believed, that had brought her to such an earthly plot at such a time. In her mind serendipity had consecrated her sacred mission as a believer searching for restitution for the sins of the world.

A small crowd of young girls jostled past, forcing her to step off the pavement into the road. There were people everywhere, it was always bustling, the adjoining terraced streets home to thousands of strangers. That was the way she liked it. Since she had been forced to give up being a shopkeeper she felt there was no need to be sociable. She could blend in, talk to people if in the mood, ignore them if not. Her innate charm, self-effacing and undemonstrative, meant she was liked but not often remembered. Her conservative dress sense, subdued and dully hued – the product of a strict convent upbringing – and the anonymity of old age served as the perfect camouflage. Staid in appearance but mentally kaleidoscopic, her thoughts shaped and coloured differently from everyone else, she believed in the efficacy of her thinking, conjuring out of the surrounding drabness ideas of beauty ... and acting on them. She was a doer not a procrastinator, different from and not really of this world if she was honest; as a result she was not going to be around for much longer. That decision made she was now carrying it out, maneuvering through the practicalities, following the plan. The others – her nieces – unwitting in their simplicity, their trusting natures overriding the seriousness of what was to take place, were joining her, their final journey together beginning on that very day.

Faith was a powerful thing that had to be used with circumspection. She had faith in herself and in the others to have faith in her. Overarching it all was their faith in God, in whose shadow she could work, in order to meld disparate minds into a coherent block of belief, solid and incorruptible. Blinkered for their own protection, but always pointing forward along "The Path". Following her even though she was behind them. They would never understand and that was the beauty of the prize, the various immaculate strokes that came together to create her masterpiece. The work would be perplexing and open to interpretation, but starkly glorious in its lucidity. It would survive the inevitable opprobrium to resound far and wide.

A car horn blared. Startled, Daphne skipped back onto the pavement and turned to look. The taxi driver was shaking his head as he pulled up. Unabashed she moved away, avoiding a confrontation, which in different times she might have relished. The aggression of men was always so self-centred, she thought, always about nothing but their own neutered sense of themselves, rarely was it turned outwards to benefit some greater plan, something intelligent. Daphne enjoyed toying with their threadbare egos at every opportunity, spraying them with invective in arguments, words tumbling out in showers of meaning, deliberately obtuse, easily misunderstood. She would watch their inarticulacy in response, tripping synapses in their brains and generating pulses red-raw with rage. The furrowed brow of the seriously defective intellect inches away from hers – blemished skin sallow, breath sickly, fine spittle droplets cooling – restrained only by an atavistic sensation of rectitude that prevented them from head-butting an old lady. It was glorious sport, but of a bygone era. She was finished with men, the whole lot of them, mankind. Serene Daphne Charlotte Fanning and her small band of followers would be journeying on alone, self-contained, consequentially aware. If you believed anything was possible, which was a self-evident truth to her, other people needed reminding from time to time. Belief was fluid and she was channeling that to the full, damming – that's how her actions would be seen by some – the flow, confining the energy and the passion into a volume that when breached would unleash an unstoppable torrent, sweeping all before it, flooding the world with wonder. Who would be there to see it, was the question? The Ark would not be so accommodating this time around.

Bernadette spotted Nanny standing at the roadside, head angled slightly upwards and to the right, staring into space, her lips moving, silently she hoped. Her aunt was daydreaming again as people moved around her, had forgotten all about her nieces and their plans. Her absent-mindedness was definitely getting worse. It was a relief to have found her and Bernadette quickly pointed Nanny out to her two sisters, who were following close behind. The three of them were late, it was Anne's fault as usual – they had been to the hairdressers where they had arranged to meet Nanny, but had been told she had left half an hour before. Concerned they had hurried on, devoted acolytes rushing to catch up with their errant matriarch. Or as Nanny saw the three younger women – spotting them out of the corner of her eye but not turning to face them – as little lambs helplessly lost bleating on the mountainside, then careening towards her and safety, shadowed from behind by razor-teethed wolves and from above by hook-beaked eagles. They would never be apart again in life or the hereafter. Her little flock.

With masking tape bought, mail re-directed to the address of an empty house on the street where Daphne used to live, savings withdrawn from their bank and post office accounts and the accounts closed, the four women walked in silence to the red brick church of Our Lady and the Irish Martyrs. Its dreary frontage facing onto the busy street never failed to dampen the spirits of even the most devout worshippers, their fervour only reviving somewhat in the darkened sanctity of the cavernous interior. It was where they intended to make their final confessions. The difficult decision about whether to bare all to God had only been resolved, after much convoluted and circular debate, by Nanny's proclamation that they must purify their immortal souls ahead of such a holy journey. This was necessary in order to be blameless in the eyes of the infinite, irrespective of the interpretations placed on their actions by other mere mortals. They were acting simply from a state of purity, which would be recognized by posterity if not by contemporary Philistines. Religious history was riddled with endless schism, what had they to worry about? Nanny was intellectually forceful, or so her nieces thought, and very difficult to argue with. The lovable embodiment of the robust physical fool, sometimes joking and exuberant, then in a blink of an eye, clever, astute and serious, leaving her perplexed audience trailing, weighing the correctness of her pronouncements, then accepting them, with reservations set aside. Her fragile mortality was a coda to their love for an ageing relative. Their gullibility was the source of Nanny's strength, waxing as theirs waned, every interaction leaving them enervated yet oddly happy.

They were hoping the Church would be quiet, free of prying eyes and ears, and were rewarded. An auspicious omen, they felt. Agreement had been finally reached not to dwell on the future in the confessional, indeed not to mention it at all. This act of devotion was about the past and wiping history clean. The simplicity of the first confession was their aspiration, scripted and rehearsed, delivered meekly, with hesitation in the voice, absolution releasing floods of relief, the leaving close to joyous, the penance reinforcing then forgotten. A spiritual cleansing that was only the beginning enabling everyone to move on to the next stage with a skip in their step. With that clearly understood Nanny went into the confessional first, drawing the fading red velvet curtain resolutely across behind her, obscuring the upper half of her body, as she lowered herself gingerly onto her knees. Her nieces watched from a discrete distance, sitting apart from each other, bathed in the rarefied air, chill and mustily fragrant, the submerged light opaque, tank-like, absorbed in their own thoughts.

Traffic noise from the street, a distant rushing whisper, merged in the ambient hugeness of the nave with the quiet considered tone of Father Petrie as he murmured mellifluously, weaving an aural blanket that bound them snugly together. The discordant chirping of a sparrow, high above, hidden in the rafters, spurred Bernadette to concentrate, the bird's erratic persistence a reminder of life's ability to interfere with even the most exalted spiritual endeavours.

Nanny began speaking, her rhythmic lilt, duskily compelling, her words distinct and clear. Bernadette was eavesdropping, contravening the sanctity and discretion of the confessional, but no one else was, or that was how it appeared, so she was safe. Wryly she reflected it was a transgression she had time to confess to.

"I have not kept faith with my late husband, Father."

"Sean is that, Mrs Fanning?"

"Yes Father. Sean, Declan Fanning. I have not kept him uppermost in my thoughts as I should have done. I've gone for long periods without thinking of him at all. It's unforgiveable. I hate myself for it because it's meant I have lusted after other men and I shouldn't have done that."

There was silence.

"Come now Mrs Fanning he's been dead a long while."

"He has Father."

"In the war wasn't it?"

Silence. The sparrow chirruped.

"1941. May 20th 1941."

Again silence, the missing beats of a conversation.

"At least that's what they told me."

"Mrs Fanning?"

The large enveloping space resonated – cool air wafting fragrant with trace essences of decay – in anticipation of significance elaborated, meaning teased or the truth revealed. Bernadette, who wasn't sure what she was expecting, gently bit her lower lip.

"In Iraq. A place called Kut. Far away, forsaken place it seems like. The desert, hot and dry. He died there and he's buried there. Never seen his grave, not even a picture, until recently. Never been there. I should have gone. In all the time that's passed I should have made the effort. I should have found the money."

There was a catch in her voice and she swallowed hard.

"He's buried in a proper graveyard with a headstone and all. Looked after by the War Graves Commission until this latest mess in that country buggered it up. Pardon my French, Father."

"Mrs Fanning, you know me by now."

"It's flooded now, gone to rack and ruin. There used to be people looking after it, but God knows what's happened to them. It doesn't seem right to me. You die a violent death for your so-called country, you'd expect to rest in peace for ever, wouldn't you?"

"You would Mrs Fanning, but as we know sadly the world isn't like that. It moves on, often in ways not to our liking. But Sean's soul is at rest, that is some comfort."

"Maybe Father, maybe. My problem is that I never really said goodbye to him. When he went off to the war all those years ago I, we, didn't understand what it meant. We were so very young it seemed like an adventure. I didn't know anyone who had lost someone then – it all changed later mind – you couldn't imagine it would happen to you. He was so tall and strong, so healthy and full of life, how could he be killed? It was impossible, someone that handsome."

She laughed, a dry shrill exhalation of air, bleakly sorrowful in its mockery of mirth.

"It pains me Father to think of something so beautiful shot to pieces. Shattered in an instant. I should have gone to the grave and said my farewells properly on my knees. Told him what I thought of him. I'd never really done that, being the young flibbertigibbet I was when we first married. I really loved him. I knew that then in my heart and I know it now. I kept it to myself though never said it out loud. Sixty odd years is a long time to have that smouldering inside you Father, a bloody long time."

"I understand Mrs Fanning, it's an age to have such regrets. But you must've been telling him in your prayers surely? He would have been listening to you."

"I'm not sure Father, it's not the same. My faith isn't strong enough to be certain of that. And Sean was never a believer. Always treated the Church lightly. It's the closeness I wanted, the presence …"

The priest coughed three times in rapid succession, muffled yet intrusive, punctuating Nanny's speech. She faltered then picked up, her voice raised.

"To be next to him, to be looking at him when I said it. I wanted to tell him about the other men. Confess my sins to him. Tell him they meant nothing to me. That he was the only one for me, always had been and always would be."

"You can confess to me Mrs Fanning. Finally set the record straight with Sean and with God."

"I can Father, I can. Can you give me a moment?"

The curtain to the confessional parted and Nanny beckoned at Bernadette, mouthing the word "tissue". Ripping open the cellophane wrapper of the proffered packet she removed a paper handkerchief and loudly blew her nose.

"Thank you dear."

The interruption had physical manifestations, disturbing those seated nearby lost in contemplation, unsettling, causing involuntary movement, before calm was restored and all activity ceased with the curtain swishing to a close. Torpor regained, the atmosphere re-primed.

57

"Over sixty years without a man is hard, Father."

"To be sure," Father Petrie sounded hesitant, "I understand. It is a long time to be without companionship of the er … physical kind."

"I think there were four or maybe five others over all that time."

"You can't be sure Mrs Fanning? It seems quite an important thing to be uncertain about?"

"I would have to say five then, if I was having to be precise. But it does seem to depend on exactly what one is talking about. Although I suppose it's all being disloyal to my marriage vows, isn't it?"

"I would remind you again, Mrs Fanning, that you are a widow, so technically your marriage vows have been, how shall I put it, overtaken by events. But for the sake of today let's be precise, what are we talking about here? Does the five times you mention refer to five occasions or five different men?"

Outside Bernadette, leant closer to the confessional. Her sisters appeared not to be paying any attention.

"Five different men, Father. There were many occasions with each of them, apart from one who I only did it once with."

"How many occasions all together, can you remember?"

The slight hesitation prompted the priest to offer assistance.

"Ten times, twenty, a hundred, more?"

"It's hard to remember precisely. I want to be accurate but it was over such a long period of time and so many years ago I have difficulty bringing it back. If I had to estimate I'd say more than fifty, maybe closer to a hundred. It's difficult, it depends on what you are really talking about."

"It does Mrs Fanning, it certainly does. What are you talking about?"

"Kissing and cuddling that sort of thing. I never spent the whole night with them, if you know what I mean, Father?"

"I think I do, Mrs Fanning. You are saying that you didn't have full relations with any of these five men."

"Yes Father, that's the honest truth. Although …"

"Although what?"

Silence. Who would have thought? Bernadette had no real idea about who Nanny was and what she got up too. She had fallen into the trap common across the generations, of the young thinking the elderly were sexless and uninterested in the ways or mechanisms of love. The imagination particularly faltered when it came to envisioning a relative in any sort of physical entanglement with another person. Bernadette couldn't help smiling.

"Mrs Fanning?"

"It's difficult Father. How to put it into words."

"Try Mrs Fanning. You are a very eloquent women and I feel this is important to you. Honesty is vital if you are to purge yourself of your sins and come clean before God. Try and be clear."

"Some of them, on a few occasions, would do their, you know, business over me. It didn't happen that often and it seemed to make them happy, so I didn't mind that much."

Nanny blew her nose again. The noise a racket in the rarefied stillness of the church.

"Once I did mind though."

"Go on."

"The man, I mentioned, who I only went with once. He was someone I had known for a number of years, a friend of Sean's actually. We spent the evening drinking and had a pleasant time. He was funny and well-read, not like some I could mention from round here, and I enjoyed his company. He seemed intelligent. Not least he was good-looking, very handsome in a matinee idol sort of way, or so I thought. I was proud to be seen in his company. It was a case of pride before the fall. Thinking back, I must have been quite drunk, as I didn't normally drink that much and he had been plying me with whisky all evening. It was a warm night and we went for a walk out into the country. It was still quite light so we could easily see our way. He took me into a field. He seemed to know where he was going. There were hay bales everywhere stacked up in ricks. We climbed up onto one and there was a sort of hollow on the top.

It was very cosy with a lovely view of the stars. Gabardine blue the sky was. You know the colour of old school raincoats. It's stuck with me, more than anything else, that sky. It felt like you could reach up and touch it, pull it down and wrap it around you. I was happy until then, call me naïve, but I was very trusting, thinking he was a friend – after all he had known Sean – and wouldn't do anything I didn't want to. Then he spoilt it by climbing on top of me. No preamble, no by your leave. He was rough with me, pinning me down. Funny thing is, looking back, if he had been gentle and considerate, I would have given him what he wanted."

She cleared her throat, swallowed, and pouted, her cheeks bulging, before exhaling noisily. The priest felt the cool dampness of her breath through the metal grating and drew back slightly in distaste.

"I confess to that Father, planning to make love to a man I wasn't wed to or even liked very much. But it didn't happen. He got a good feel and I stopped him going all the way, getting my skirt messed up in the process. He wasn't too happy, stomping off and leaving me alone in the hay."

Nanny laughed drily.

"It's strange. It's a long time ago now, but I can recall that feeling of lying there, abandoned, under that sky, very clearly. I made a resolution then, which I've stuck to Father, it had nothing to do with getting my own back or anything like that it was about me and how I would live my life from then on. Never again were such shenanigans going to happen to me, I was not going to turn to a man for anything ever again and so it's been…"

Her timing was comically perfect, the retort forming in the priest's mind and about to be blurted out when she said,

"…Yourself not included, Father."

"Indeed, Mrs Fanning, indeed."

He smiled.

"It was just companionship really, that was all it was and I wasn't going to be after that anymore. Men meant nothing in the long run, just beer, sweat and wandering hands, not a word of sense ever spoken. And after all I had my family, my girls."

"I see you have them with you today. They must be a great comfort to you. Will I be hearing their confessions do you think?"

"I believe so Father, I believe so."

"Good, it's been a fair while, young people today being what they are."

"Hardly young Father, though they'd thank you for saying so."

"How is their father, Pat? Still in the care home I hear."

"He is Father and he has his good days. Not talking much now, drawing into himself. But then he always was a man who carefully chose his words."

"To be sure, Mrs Fanning. I'm sorry to hear he's not doing so well. I must make time to drop in and see him."

Nanny crossed her fingers. Her brother was the least religious man she'd ever known, a heathen, not caring about the opinion of any other man, in holy orders or not.

"He'd like that Father."

"I'll see what I can do."

She uncrossed her fingers.

"That brings me to the one last thing I wanted to get off my chest today."

"Ah, go on Mrs Fanning. I had a feeling there was something else troubling you."

"It's about my brother, Father."

"I said I'd try to go and see him as soon as I can."

"No, no it's not that."

"What then?"

Father Petrie shifted his position, readjusting the cushion on the hard wooden bench beneath him. Bernadette leant forward in her pew and idly tapped the prayer book lying on the narrow shelf in front of her with her fingers. Why was her father coming up at a confession? Nanny barely spoke of her brother and rarely saw him, calling her infrequent visits to his care home, "doing her duty".

"I'm not sure how to put this Father, it's rather difficult."

"As I've told you before we don't stand on ceremony here in the confessional, just blurt it out. God is listening and will understand."

"It's like this …"

She took a deep breath.

"… I've known things about Patrick, you know Pat, and I've done nothing about it …"

Silence.

"… and I should have done. It's haunted me most of my life."

"What sort of things, Mrs Fanning?"

He could tell she was looking at him directly through the grille, could see the dull reflection of filtered daylight in her eyes, hear her breathing, imagined he could feel the air moving. He looked down.

"I don't know how much you know, Father?"

"I'm not you brother's confessor, Mrs Fanning and in any case …"

"I know Father you couldn't possibly say even if you did."

"That's right, that's absolutely right."

"It's not that I don't trust you Father. It's just that …"

"What Mrs Fanning?"

His tone was dark, compassion ebbing from his voice, laying bare a flintiness that she had not heard before.

"What?"

There was an absence that was welcome, a subtle realignment in her relationship with this man, this representative of her Church, the institution she was about to seriously challenge. She didn't want to leave on good terms, that would be wrong and she didn't need to, so she wouldn't.

"OK I'll just say it then."

"Do that."

"Patrick was in the Provos. Still is, I suppose. Do you ever leave?"

Father Petrie stared into the darkness at his feet, while he touched his forehead with his hand and rubbed it back and forth.

"Not him. No never."

She raised her hand to the grille, the tips of her fingers protruding through, and waited. She could see the glistering top of the priest's head and just make out the dusting of dandruff on his darkened shoulders.

"He was high up for many years, a powerful big man, a brigade commander. Sat on the Army Council during much of the Troubles. He made many dreadful decisions. Was party to many more no doubt. I knew this ... and I told no one. Not even you Father, not even in confession. I never went to the peelers, never told the rest of the family, nothing."

"They were difficult times, Mrs Fanning. Your sympathies were, how shall I put it, in line with his, I'm sure. And he was your brother after all. No one would expect you to er... inform on him."

"But he killed people, Father, with his own hands. Ordered the murder of many others. I know this. It happened over and over and I said nothing."

The priest felt very warm, his forehead was moist, glancing up he saw she was peering at him, like a prisoner clinging imploringly to the bars of her prison cell seeking a pardon.

"Come on Mrs Fanning. How do you know this?"

"He confided in me Father, we were close once," she said bitterly, "wanted me to be impressed, look up to him, my big brother. You see we got on when we were young, it was us two against the rest and that included our Mammy and Daddy. Seven against two, good odds he called it. He was the clever one, quick witted, sharp and funny. That's what I liked about him, he was a charmer. It all boils down to being a natural leader, I know that now."

She paused. It was hard for her to talk rationally about this man. Her disdain for him was so deeply ingrained. Youthful solidarity had metamorphosed over the years into a dislike that she had found hard to contain. She had succeeded in duping him though as Patrick had continued to confide in her long after she had lost patience with him.

"Ironic isn't it, Father, that he used his talents for the wrong reasons."

"Many would disagree with you there, Mrs Fanning. As I say people viewed it as a war after all."

"You can never say killing is right, whatever the cause. I'm a good Republican, who isn't round here, but I didn't like the violence. It became a reason in itself. He was enjoying it too much at the end, probably always had been. Then the game changed, it all became bent, protection money, the drugs. I can tell you a thing or two."

"I think I've heard enough Mrs Fanning"

"I should have said something."

"Come on Mrs Fanning, I absolve you of that sin at least. We all lived through it, what could you do? They are our flesh and blood."

Sitting back, satisfied, she waited for her priest to pronounce. He was going to sanction her in the time-honoured way. She would listen but not act. In her penultimate act of defiance she would not perform her penance.

Bernadette touched Nanny on the shoulder and smiled at her as she left the confessional. Taking her aunt's place she settled down on her knees.

"Forgive me Father for I have sinned."

"Yes, my child

Father Petrie was relieved. It had been an unsettling experience, which didn't happen to him very often luckily, but Daphne Fanning had not been herself. Moving as she had done, for some unfathomable reason, into territory that it was well understood should be left uncharted. Now for someone more straightforward, less complicated.

Bernadette's thinking at that moment was anything but linear and uncluttered. She was a regular at confession, mopping up and making amends for her daily transgressions on an almost weekly basis. What was troubling her was if this was the last time she would be addressing God indirectly, the last time before meeting him in person, should she confess everything now or be saving some or all of her sins until later? Nanny's revelations had been just that, a clearing of the decks, but even she had not owned up to the ultimate sin they were about to commit. That was probably wise as Father Petrie was a flake. She was not sure that ultimately you could trust him, despite all his utterances about the sanctity and confidentiality of the confessional. No, had been Nanny's answer and she was an astute woman. Bernadette would do the same and follow her.

There were two serious things she had done in her life which she had never confessed to and it was agonizing weighing up what to do now. Her faith cried out for her to take this last opportunity to purify her mortal soul, utter the words that would release her from all earthly ties, but it was embarrassing. This fear of being shamed had restrained her in the past and thinking of it now she could feel the tightening in her skull, the prickle at the hair roots and the twisting of her tongue into a knot that made coherent speech difficult. The paralysis forced blood to her cheeks, reddening her face and stoking her temperature – all the physical discomforts of humiliation. The priest would sense her difficulty, finely attuned as he was to the faintest human manifestations – the colours, smells, tics and tells – of guilt.

That was it – guilt. She felt guilty, always had done. And that was not the perfect state to be in when you were about to meet your maker. But her present detachment surprised her. The clarity of thinking needed for rational decision making had often escaped her during a humdrum life, thus a reputation for impetuousness and unreliability had always hung around her, but not now the decision was taken, she would come clean. Why not? She would never see Father Petrie again, not in this world anyway, and when she did in the afterlife, if she did, it would all be atoned for by then and they would be equals. She still felt guilty about what she was about to do, killing yourself was definitely a sin, but Nanny needed her, it was sacrificing oneself for a greater good, it was the ultimate gift of true devotion. God would understand when, on her knees, she laid it out for him. For Nanny was holy, a person of perfect intentions who was failing, physical enfeeblement pulling her down. Bernadette and her sisters were supporters, the bearers of her dais on the final approach to the Gates of Heaven. They would all be uplifted and cleansed by their actions. The four of them would gaze on the face of God.

The priest listened to the woman's laboured breathing, feeling her inner turmoil, and wondered what was going on. These women were well known to him, they lived routine humdrum lives, ripples on the surface of their existence were rare and never made waves. The pebble was nearly always a man in his experience and he sat back waiting for her to compose herself. There was no hurry, he probably knew the individual concerned and that was tying her tongue. Bernadette took a deliberate deep breath, exhaling noisily through her mouth. She was ready.

"Father, it has been three weeks since my last confession. What I have to tell you happened a while ago, but it's been preying on me and I want to get it off my chest."

She immediately felt better, reassured by the clichéd phrasing of the confessional.

"I was with my twin sister, Anne. We were eleven or twelve, something like that. He was a little younger I think, at least he seemed to be, but he was in the same class as us at school."

"Who was he, Bernadette?"

"You wouldn't know him Father, it wasn't around here. It was when we lived in Drumkelty. As I say, it was a long time ago."

His chubby tear-stained face floated before her, his body pale and very white, almost bleached, muddy knees prominent. A boy of soft edges, unlike her brother with his rock-hard body and angular features, he was floppy to hold, Bernadette remembered sinking inwards meeting little resistance. There was nothing she found attractive about his physique, his pug nose, slightly upturned, incited instead feelings of irrational violence, the desire inflamed by the watery focus of his large brown eyes that constantly seemed to well with nascent tears. His muted appearance was offset by the length of his thin mousy orange hair, worn long by the stubbly standards of the other boys at their school and perfect for indiscriminate tugging. Their relationship was unequal, exploitative and addictive built as it was on a foundation of juvenile sadism, cemented in place by the voyeuristic proclivities of her twin.

"His name was Barry and he lived near us in the next street over. He was always following me around. It was fun at first, but it paled after a while. Every time I turned around there he was, smiling at me. He didn't say much and soon I came to realize he was a little simple. Why was he playing with girls anyway? There were lots of boys his age in our neighbourhood, he should have gone off and played with one of them. He began to get on my nerves, Father, and he wouldn't be told. I was quite rude to him, telling him to shove off and leave me alone, but still he hung around. My sister Anne said he had a crush on me and that only made it worse. That was a horrible idea. It gave me the shivers just to think it might be true. It also gave me the idea of how to get rid of him."

Her voice faded as the memory of the day seeped into her consciousness.

"Speak up will you Bernadette, I can barely hear you. Don't worry, no one can hear you outside."

The naïveté of the priest made her smile, steadying her. The man was of no importance and she had nothing to worry about with him.

"It was obvious if that was the sort of thing Barry was interested in, then I'd give it to him. So, Anne and I took him for a walk into the nearby woods, where we often built camps in the bracken and played house. This time we would play it for real. He just followed us as always, there were no hurt feelings from the nasty things I had said the last time we'd been out with him. I remember he had chocolate smeared round his mouth, which made him look really babyish, and this annoyed me, making me even more determined to sort him out once and for all."

She paused for effect, but the priest was silent, save for the wheezy pulse of his breathing that was already beginning to vex her. She hoped her tone of voice wouldn't betray her, flecked, as it was, with irritation.

"We took him to a hollow we'd been to before, in the middle of a clearing in the woods that was overrun with ferns and brambles and such. He seemed excited as we crawled through a "secret" passageway in the bracken. We reached the den and my sister plonked herself down in front of the entrance so he couldn't escape and then just watched – egging me on with her eyes. You should have seen her expression, Father, encouraging she was."

The heat was intense, overhanging bracken fronds greenly diffusing sunbeams, yet humid. Their skin prickled and itched with perspiration and the sticky seeds and burrs adhering to their bare limbs. High overhead the rustling wind in the tall trees sent shadows shimmering, slivers of light illuminating the dim interior of their "cave". Underfoot crushed stems wept sap and dankly scented the air, intermingling with the odour of their unwashed bodies. The atonal chirping of a bird, alarmed at the intrusion, a counterpoint to their heavy expectant breathing. Senses alive in anticipation, life never having seemed so vital, Bernadette quivered. At her core her power sizing the spite that was taking her over, its grip curdling character and self-belief.

"I just looked at him. You could stand up in the den without the ferns touching your head, or at least he could. He wasn't that tall for his age thinking back. Smaller than I was, anyway. I remember one frond hung low over his head and it reminded me of pictures you see of Romans wearing laurel wreaths in their hair. He was anything but grand though, slouching with a stupid smile on his fat face. I stared at him, thinking how bad his posture was and that he should do something about it when something flipped. It wasn't that I hated him but I badly wanted to hurt him. And so I ..."

The omission expanded to fill the confessional – the priest held his breath – and then beyond, her taciturnity silencing the sparrows and the traffic in the street outside.

"What did you do, Bernadette?"

"I don't think I want to say Father."

Consumed, her vision tinged a hazy-grey, she could feel beads of sweat trickling across the arch of her back, smell the ripeness as she wrenched down his shorts and pants, trampling them to the ground. Shoved in the chest he tripped over his own feet and fell onto his back. Anne gasped with surprise, Barry was silent, wide-eyed, teary, a hand covering his mouth. She sat down on his legs. The exhilaration was powerful.

"Grab his arms."

The order was peremptory and Anne obeyed. The feel of the penis in her hand, slug-like, cool, the foreskin wrinkled and rucked, then the swelling as she squeezed and pulled, the fascination of the thickening, the stretching out, the elimination of all folds and creases, the curvature and pulse of their first erection. Her twin sat open-mouthed.

"Come now Bernadette, I think you do know what you did," the priest's actorly tone masking his piqued interest.

He had no pubic hair, not like her own darkening, scattered growth down there. Only a shrunken, shrivelled mound at the base, where his balls should have been. They appeared to be missing, she remembered thinking later, only then feeling any pity for him. Uncertain what to do she jerked the penis back and forth violently, inadvertently exposing the bulging head with its, to her surprise, large slit-eye. Barry screeched and tried to sit up but Anne held him fast and he slumped back, tears streaming down his face. She rubbed harder, spurred on by his writhing moans, observing dispassionately as the beading liquid glossed over the blushing head of his penis. Then she stopped, bored, her wrist aching. A nagging sense of self-preservation told her his cries were too strident to be safely smothered by their leafy hiding place in the depths of the woods. She knew emotionally there should be more, but didn't care. Secrecy was paramount.

"Bernadette?"

"Sorry Father, I'm reflecting on it all, that's the truth."

"Well share it with me then. There's no good to be had keeping it to yourself is there?"

Bernadette was far from certain that was the case. He was a straightforward, muddled thinking old fool, this priest. No subtlety, all psychic corners, no empathy. She was inclined to tell him next to nothing and hang the consequences.

She let go of Barry's penis and it slapped against his pudgy belly, erection fading.

"You must tell no one about this you cry-baby."

She pinched him and he yelped, fixing her with a grimy liquid stare.

"Say it!"

Her nails dug into the soft flesh of his calf. There was a mute intake of snuffling breath as aberrant tears spilled over his dirty sweat-streaked cheeks. Her disdain inflamed by the sight of viscous froth bubbling at his nostrils she lashed out at his limp docility, raking nails across both bare thighs. The only other boy she knew well, her brother John, would have been fighting back, but there was nothing.

"Now. Say it."

His soggy inarticulacy enraged her further.

"Help me Anne, sit on his face until he swears not to tell."

Her sister appeared uncertain, bemused at Bernadette's audacity, her daring to touch a boy like that.

"He'll suffocate."

"That's the idea, you silly cow. He mustn't tell. Here give me his arms."

Abashed Anne shuffled forward on her knees, lifting her skirt before lowering herself onto Barry's face, then letting it drop back enveloping his head. There was a pause, an adjustment in his perception of the threat, then the rhythmic bucking began, waves rippling the length of his body. Anne let out a cry and squeezed tighter with her thighs.

"Hold on. He's got it coming."

The squealing, muted by the stifling bulk of Anne's body, was an incitement, his thrashing a spur to the two excited girls. They bounced and writhed, giggled and shouted, all caution abandoned, oblivious to his suffering. It was only his exhaustion and inability to move – his spasms fading away beneath them – that finally penetrated their frenzy.

"Get off stupid, you're suffocating him."

Bernadette pushed Anne and she fell backwards into the bracken with a yell.

"It wasn't me. It was you."

Sucking in air Barry gasped, chest heaving. Leaning in towards each other the girls watched transfixed by the rigours of his frantic breathing. His plump belly now concave, ribs clearly etched in pale skin, projected a tautness in his frame that only relaxed as his wheezing faded and air filled his lungs – an inflation that brought a momentary calm to their leafy chamber. Anne, relieved, was queasy and close to tears, Bernadette was glad they had got away with it. Eyelashes flickering tears Barry focused on his upside-down tormentors before groaning, curling up and hiding his face.

"We hit him Father and made him cry, then ran home leaving him alone in the woods."

Father Petrie was vaguely disappointed, he had been hoping for more – the juicier outcome the build-up had suggested – but then that was so often the case with these women, his intellect outpacing their imagination.

"That was not a very nice thing to do Bernadette. Was he alright? Did he get back home?"

"I think so Father. I mean yes he was at school the next day and he never said anything."

"Ah good and you never did anything like that again?"

"No, Father."

"Then that's not too bad then."

"Yes Father."

Bernadette nudged Barry with her foot, pushing up his mud-smeared shirt exposing his back and shoulder blades. Body gently shaking, he ignored her and she did it again.

"Barry you've got to swear not to tell."

Hands covering his face he stifled sobs.

"Barry, do you hear me? If you don't, we'll do it again. And next time it'll be worse, I promise you."

She reached over and shook him, her fury building with each docile manifestation of his incapacity. Venom was strident in her voice.

"We'll tell your Mammy and Daddy you forced us to show you our fannies and you touched them and put a finger in."

Submission was an inadequate defence against Bernadette's anger who, goaded by Barry's immobility, lashed out. Slaps resounded in the heavy air, ruddy contusions mottling his back, their pattern creeping across his body.

"Get him up Anne. He's got to swear. We can't let him go without swearing."

Reluctantly Anne grasped his shoulders, the skin slick and unpleasant to touch. She felt shamed by the excitement, the thrill of physical contact, and the enjoyable emotions sparked by inflicting pain. Her emotional maturity, intimately linked to the example set by her twin, was inadequate to express these feelings as anything other than a child-like horror at what they had done and a desire to be somewhere safer and more secure, where the events of the day could be kissed away and her actions excused. She longed for a room of her own – not one shared with Bernadette – and the company of her dolls. Wary of the cruel streak in her sister, now better understood, she knew she would always be in her thrall, a follower.

The lightness of Anne's touch opened up the young boy, his body unfurled and he turned over on to his hands and knees. Cupping him under the chin Bernadette fixed him with a narrow, impassive stare and smiled. His eyes closed.

"Barry, listen to me. You must swear to never say anything to anyone about this or we will tell on you. Look at me."

She raised his head forcing him to pay attention.

"And who do you think they will believe?"

"Bernadette do you have anything else you want to confess to today?"

"In a minute, Father. Sorry."

She fished out a tissue from her handbag and blew her nose.

"Barry, so you swear?"

He nodded.

"And hope to die?"

He nodded a second time.

"Good. Get dressed and we'll take you home. You can show us where you live."

Mute, he obeyed. The twins observed, eagerly feeding off the boy's anxiety. They found it comical that he struggled to pull on his muddied clothes in the confined space. Shamefaced, his back turned, Barry hurried, desperate to avoid their withering gazes. Cowering, unable to straighten up, he snarled both feet in one of the twisted legs of his baggy shorts. Forced to sit down to disentangle himself he revealed his nakedness again to their greedy gaze. Embarrassed, he rushed on, dry-eyed, his resolve cracking only when he discovered buttons missing from his shirt.

"My ma will kill me," he slavered.

They were the only words he uttered that afternoon. Bernadette remembered them clearly, but without sympathy.

"Come on, you little cry baby. Your ma won't be the only one if you don't stop snivelling."

Bernadette wiped her nose with the tissue. Crumpled it and dropped it into her bag.

"There is one more thing, Father."

She leant in close to the grille, anxious to ensure her sisters outside couldn't hear anything she was saying.

"You may not know this Father but me and my twin sister, Anne, used to be very close when we were younger, even had our own language that only we could understand … not so much the case now though."

"That's not that unusual amongst siblings, Bernadette, believe me the things I hear in here. You shouldn't be troubling yourself too much over that."

The priest felt the need to move things along. He sensed there was nothing interesting about these women and he was, to be honest, feeling a little jaded. There were two more to go and all he wanted was to get back to his study and relax with a cup of tea and The Times crossword.

"I know, Father, everybody has their fallings out, but I was very cruel to her. She suspects, but has never been able to summon up the courage to challenge me about it. There was no proof you see. It was for her own good."

"Really, Bernadette?"

"And if I'm honest now for mine as well. It brought the two of us closer together. We had been drifting apart."

"When are we talking about here? Recently?"

"No, no Father, more than twenty years ago, when we were in America. The three of us – Mary, Anne and myself – were over there working as counsellors at a Catholic summer camp in South

Carolina. It was a beautiful place, deep in the woods and surrounded by hills. The jobs were arranged for us by Father Dermot. Do you remember him? He had lived over there and knew the Director of the Ministry. Thought it was a deeply spiritual Christian place that would be good for our religious selves and build up our confidence. As it turned out he was right about some things and wrong about others."

"I do remember Dermot, as it happens, a fine fellow. He's been dead a good few years, if I'm correct. So why have you waited this long to bring it up?"

"Yes, it's strange but it's been preying on my mind lately. As I just said I've always thought it was for the best, but now I'm not so sure. You see Anne's never had a boyfriend since that time. Rick, who was a local boy who worked at the camp as a driver, was her first and her last and I took him away from her."

"And she never suspected? How did that happen?"

"She was going to stay there with him in the States, not come home, make a life there. I couldn't allow that. Mary was not keen on the idea either. We both needed her to be with us, me in particular as her twin, so we cooked up a plan and I made him an offer he chose not to refuse."

She paused.

"And Anne was heartbroken because she really loved him and confused as well about what happened. She just couldn't understand his change of heart and his going away like that without saying a word."

"What did you do Bernadette?"

"You understand what men are like, Father. I'm sure I barely need to be telling you. We were good girls, us Walsh sisters, saving ourselves for the right man. Anne was particularly prudish, not like me, I was curious, you could even say reckless. She would never have dreamed of, you know, giving herself to anyone outside of being married. You could see Rick wasn't happy with this, he made that very plain, but Anne wouldn't give way and he hung about because she was pretty and funny to be with. After all he was quite handsome in that clean-cut, rugged way Americans have about them. She loved him, I could see that, and was hoping he'd ask her to marry him. Whisk her away from the life she had over here with us to live the dream in the States. It was pure pie in the sky, we could see that, but Anne couldn't or wouldn't. Mary, in particular, knew Rick was a player not a stayer, he'd already tried it on with her and was always looking at other girls. There was no way he would have kept on with Anne once she had given herself to him. So, it was simple really. We decided to make him an offer that he was unlikely to refuse. I would give him what he wanted in return for him leaving Anne alone. Saving her was how we saw it. Why me? Well Mary didn't fancy him and I look quite a bit like Anne. I was twenty-two and wanted to know what it was like."

"That's a very cynical and sinful approach to a relationship, Bernadette. I'm disappointed to hear it from you. The plan obviously worked though?"

"Yes, Father. Like a dream."

Memories, hazy now, still haunted her, their tangible expressions steering her away from male intimacy and projecting her into a world of grudge bearing, unspecified yearning and inadequate, misplaced communications that had brought her to this point in life – unmarried, friendless, focused on herself and family, and about to end it all. Always impulsive Bernadette recalled the actual seduction as a dream that she had been glad to wake up from. Rick was a malleable beast, easy to stir – a hand placed on the crotch of his trousers was all it took – but less easy to control. Once exposed as an ingénue she had been helpless, lost to his physical strength and determined tastes. Not content with taking the proffered gift of her virginity and unwrapping it with delicacy and gentle concern, he had exploited her innocence, roughly making love to her, while crying out for her sister. Anne's name was the spur, whetting his appetite for more and she had gone along with him. The pain and humiliation she had felt from his ultimate rejection induced a steely indifference to other men that presented to the world as a shield of impenetrable disdain, only occasionally lowered to reveal a woman riven by contempt and a liking for violence.

She got up, her legs aching, the priest's admonishments buzzing in her ears. It was an age ago, but the event still seemed pertinent. Life's happenings were not sequential, one thing leading to another, there were those that linked to everything, a concurrence of events, and their potency strengthened over time. Bernadette by confessing had sundered two of those connections, dissimulating on earth, honest in the eyes of God, and felt ecstatic. Her load would be lighter now. She parted the faded curtain and stepped out into the cool air of the nave. Anne looked at her sister quizzically, from her artless expression Bernadette suspected she had heard everything.

Rage instantly consumed the equanimity of the confessional. Bernadette had misguidedly assumed her sister would respect the sanctity of confession more than she had done. They were cut from the same cloth Anne and her, it was just that her twin didn't know how to act; a sponge, soaking everything up and letting it steep. A barely perceptible flicker of the eyes, and she saw Anne registered her annoyance. The dynamic of their seesaw relationship was well-worn and predictable. As her anger abated Bernadette felt the twinge of regret that always followed close on the heels of any falling out. They would be leaving this life estranged, bickering to the end. A fitting conclusion to a bond that was easily the most important to her, at least as measured by the time she had invested in it. There were many weeks to go until the end and knowing Anne as she did that left plenty of opportunities to straighten things out. Bernadette was persuasive, had an explanation for everything, and Anne was, after all, very gullible.

Her sister was hesitating, pondering the need to respond – the curtain Bernadette was holding aside was heavy – then acting on her indecision she dipped her head and stepped into the confessional, her rosary beads clattering against the wooden panelling. Tugging the fading drape free from Bernadette's grasp she drew it across like a shroud. Sitting in a pew as close as possible to the stall, leaning forward as in prayer, straining to hear, Bernadette made out only the hiss of whispered secrets, her perfidy repaid.

"Keep the change, will you."

"That's too much love, you've given me a £20 note."

"Go on, it's your lucky day."

"And Christmas rolled into one."

Bernadette keen to emphasise Nanny's generosity as the taxi-driver lumbered out of his seat to open the door for them.

"You're too good, all of yous. Have a fine day."

He reached inside and grabbed their shopping bags, lifting them on to lawn.

"There you go now."

"Thanks. We'll be dandy from here."

The driver's mobile rang as he got back into his cab, which was parked on their driveway. He smiled and waved, then answered the phone.

"At least we made him happy."

"We're all happy here, aren't we? Give me a hand with these."

As she bent down to pick up the shopping – their last meal – Bernadette realized that that overweight, talkative man – he had barely stopped since he picked them up outside Our Lady and the Irish Martyrs – was the final stranger, the last male, she would ever speak to. From now on it was as if they were alone on the planet, the last human beings alive. There was a satisfaction to be had ending your days on Eden Avenue, it was certainly not paradise and number fifty-seven was hardly reminiscent of the garden it was named after, but they had chosen this course and their actions would sanctify the small patch of earth on which it stood. "It will have to do", as her late mother had always said about any outcome that was far from perfect, and for Bernadette "It would do," was divine. Nanny felt the same, waxing lyrically on the sublimity of the commonplace as a symbol of devotion and a rebuff to the decadence of the established church. To die at home in the presence of God and your family was the ultimate statement of your faith. There was not a more noble act that a person could perform. It was the supreme sacrifice. The base observations of the masses could be ignored, those people would do well to remember the humble origins of our Lord before casting aspersions. Bernadette believed she understood, felt she knew what they were doing, was convinced by Nanny's seductive narrative. They all were.

Earthly chattels cast aside, friendships abandoned, commitments squandered left the women with only time on their hands, a commodity to use as they saw fit. It was of their own making – how it should be crafted, how it should be used. Always frugal, Bernadette would not find apportioning this finite resource difficult, in fact it would be a joy. Standing here on the front lawn taking one last look at the world they were leaving behind was for her time well spent. The expansive sky, so clear and rarefied this far from the centre of the city (it was one of the things she most liked about living here), cloud-spotted, the burn of the peeping sun on skin soothed by the wafting breeze, air fresh, organically sweet yet for the moment fuddled by diesel fumes from the idling taxi, it's monotone throb gloriously marrying the high-pitched calls of stalling swifts, plunging and swerving above. She would miss the natural earth – it had always treated her benignly – but not the human inhabitants swarming over its surface. They were another level of malignity altogether.

"Come on Bernie. We need to get the food on."

The colours were vivid, bulking out the impermanent, accentuating angles, chasing shadows, conjuring up an alluring landscape out of the mundane. She was seeing her home clearly for the first time, understanding herself, discovering a more persuasive vocabulary. A falling away of inhibition that would be hard to shake off in the future, however much of that she had left, and a difficult discipline to re-impose even if Bernadette had wanted to. Lifting her face to the sky she closed her eyes, absorbing the ambience of the place, her breathing calm and regular, contentment settling upon her. She felt the vibration in the soles of her feet, of nature cowed but unrepentant. Never in her life had Bernadette been so overcome by the far-reaching spirituality of existence, touched by the sublime, finally blessed.

Nanny was calling. Her amiable voice summoning, her words seductive. Destiny lay that way, the transition beckoned, she would follow. Turning from the street, the sunlight bright in her eyes, bags weightless in her hands, she was euphoric. Floating, the connection secure, Nanny brushed Bernadette on the shoulder as she entered the house, a gentle irresistible pressure, a centripetal force. She heard the door closing behind her, the key turning in the lock, bolts being thrown.

"Miss Walsh, I think we should halt proceedings there for today. It seems like a good place for you to pick up from when we resume after the weekend. You can then tell us what happened inside the house on Eden Avenue. This inquest is adjourned until Monday. Thank you."

Her pale-faced brother was waiting outside the door of the courtroom.

"Bernadette."

"John, I didn't see you inside."

He held out his arms, his abjection was repulsive. She took both his hands in hers and squeezed them, but did not move in close for the anticipated embrace. They stood in the hallway, a picture of sibling incompatibility and disdain, until Bernadette exhausted, released them.

"B you should go and see Daddy. He was asking for you. He doesn't understand, just like the rest of …"

His voice faltered and tailed off. A base saccharine emotion underlaid his every word and it sickened her.

"In that home he's been hearing lots of strange things about us from the other residents, not to mention the staff. They all seem to like a good gossip. It's rumour and tittle-tattle mostly, but you should go and put him straight. He's not as sharp as he used to be."

She shrugged, having long since ceased to care about their father and what he thought. There had been a time when she had, when the competition with her twin sister to be his favourite had been intense and had galvanized Bernadette into extremes of duplicitous and ingratiating behaviour. She had lied and cheated her way into his affections and that had amused her father appealing as it did to his predatory sense of influence through strength. Such onslaughts invariably ended with Bernadette sitting on his knee watching television while Anne eyed the pair jealously from across the room.

"It's only right B."

"There's no right or wrong about it, John. You of all people should know that. He never thought about us when we were young, not once. It was only Mammy who did for us and she could do nothing with him. So why should I go and see him John, tell me that?"

His expression hardened, rough cheeks reddened. He spluttered words so heartfelt Bernadette was briefly moved to accord them some merit.

"For her B, for Mammy, for us, for me, for God's sake, B."

Any weakness on her part was fleeting and insincere.

"Maybe John. I'll think about it."

He looked relieved and smiling patted her on the shoulder in a forlorn parody of an imagined brotherly regard long since lost. She had loved the men in her family once, like all good sisters and daughters, loved them for longer than she ought to have done for her own well-being. But she would not fall for that again. Now she understood it was more complicated. Competing males in a household of adoring women were always going to be difficult to live with, but in their family the game was so ill-matched it was cruel, the outcome brutal and destructive of all values she ever thought worth having. The conflict was a humourless clash between the charismas of opposites. Her brother was weak, immature and feeble in his convictions, their father strong, passionate about his beliefs, committed and mercilessly violent. The inevitable outcome permanently cast the role of their mother, Bernadette and her sisters as that of handmaidens ministering to the egos of a damaged, broken boy and a monster.

Bernadette and Anne giggled, suppressing any sound, nudging each other excitedly as they crept closer to the lone car parked in the farthest corner of the deserted station car park. They noticed with innocent delight that it was rocking gently. A single street light at the entrance dimly cast its glow over the damp ground, barely illuminating the swallowing shadows surrounding the vehicle. The Ford Cortina was located exactly where they expected it would be after overhearing Mary's boastful claims to her friends about Ian, her boyfriend, and what they got up to. This information had been too much for her younger siblings arousing curiosity, jealousy and a strong desire to establish the detail. They could not resist the urge to see for themselves and gain concrete intelligence they could use to embarrass their overbearing sister.

The car windows were steamed up, but as the twins approached, they could see their sister's dark curls jerkily smearing the condensation on a side pane, droplets coalescing and trailing erratically downwards. They circled around the bonnet to get a clearer view. Crouching down below the nearside back door, they hugged, then slowly straightened up and stared through hazy glass into the darkened interior. They could just make out the yellow of Mary's dress pushed up around her waist, her pale legs spread wide, nylons bunched at each ankle, Ian's dark body settled on top of her and hear for the first time the faint groans of their love making. Enthralled, they pressed their faces to the cool glass and watched.

The sound of an approaching vehicle slowing down on the distant street alarmed them and they ducked. Headlights turning into the car park sent them scurrying into the fringing bushes. Hidden, they stopped, standing close in the shadows to await their sister's inevitable discovery and humiliation.

The van circled slowly, its engine throbbing in the dank air, the full beam of its headlights probing the dark recesses of the car park – illuminating sodden litter piles wind-blown against broken fencing, shredded polythene tangled in its mesh, broken bottles glinting, an abandoned shopping trolley upended, the blinking flare of a cat's eyes – before briefly spotlighting the now stationary Ford and being extinguished. In the darkness the twins shifted their position then shrank back as the engine rumbled and died. A nub of apprehension pressed Bernadette closer to Anne and they waited. Nobody moved.

The cloying air smelled of coal smoke, enveloping and chill. Shades of black shifted back and forth, conjuring wispy flexing shapes, blocks of dense shadow, cocooned in the shimmering orange opacity of the distant street lamp. The gloom pulsed.

The rear doors of the van swung open and two men – indistinct and bulky – stepped out, flitting into position either side of the Cortina's back door where moments before the twins had been watching intently. Leaning over they peered inside, their quarry identified they hesitated, watching, until one nudged the other and dragged open the door. Reaching inside they grabbed Mary's lover by the legs and tried to haul him out – there was a scream – and Ian clutched the doorjamb, thrashing around violently forcing his assailants to let go.

"Leave me the fuck alone, you bastards."

The cry was woeful. Scrambling to get back into the car and climb over into the driver's seat – Mary's wails engulfed by sobs as she flailed at her dress, pressing it down in a desperate effort to cover herself – Ian was seized for a second time. Kicking out he caught one of his attackers in the face, who reeled back cursing loudly, the other piled in behind him, pulled hard and tugged off Ian's jeans which were gathered around his ankles, taking his trainers with them. Momentarily free Ian again sprawled forward over the back of the front seat and stretched out for the glove compartment, his fingers scrabbling at the catch.

"Fucking watch it, he's going for his gun."

The voice stentorian and hard, a dark masked mass silhouetted in the dim interior light of the kidnapper's van, had half emerged from the driver's side of the vehicle.

Galvanized, his face bloodied, one of the assailants barged past the other and opened the front passenger door of the Cortina, punching Ian hard on the side of the head. There was a cry of indignant pain.

"Grab him and get him out of there, the fuck."

Hitting out repeatedly, smashing at Ian's grasping hands, they finally managed to drag him struggling from the vehicle before the three of them collapsed in a heap.

"For fuck's sake, enough of this."

The dark figure moved slowly towards the grappling men, the metallic two-tone retort of a pistol being cocked, distinct and terrible to the unseen witnesses. The sound abruptly halted the fighting and the protagonists separated, groaning. There was a finality to the man's actions. Bernadette could make out the outstretched arm pointing down and her stomach churned. Anne whimpered as she staggered against her. Mary cringing on the back seat of the Cortina moaned in terror, curling inwards, eyes firmly closed, her tearful face hidden behind contorted fingers.

A car passed by, the pulsing sound of dub reggae faint on the air, heads turning they all froze and watched as it was swallowed by the murk. Held fast Ian vomited, his desperation spilling across the tarmac, distressing the twins cowering in their hiding place.

"That's disgusting, it's all over my shoes."

"Shut the fuck up and get him in the van."

Dragged forward Ian tried to find his footing and break free.

"Steady now you little gobshite," the barrel of the pistol pressed against his temple, "don't you go trying anything now, will you?"

Attempting to turn and pull away he was struck on the forehead with the gun butt. Stunned, he was hauled to the van and manhandled into the dark interior. The gunman got in beside him.

The two others returned to Ian's car, one picked up the jeans, wiped his shoes with them, removed the wallet from the back pocket, before throwing them onto the front seat along with the trainers, the other opened the glove compartment, rummaged through the papers and took out a pistol.

"Mary Walsh, you need to make yourself respectable and head on home. Don't be hanging around now."

Mary started, stunned that they knew her name. She said nothing and did not move. The shadows disappeared. Doors slammed. The van moved off, engine loud, headlights stabbing the dark as it reached the street, exhaust swirling.

Bernadette understood the dynamics of violence, the overwhelming force, the weapons used, the masking anonymity, the cloaking darkness, but its weakness, her strength, was knowledge and she knew. She knew the truth that the dark powerful presence with the gun was her father, knew the silent one who lingered way too long watching his sister with her legs spread was her brother, knew that Ian wasn't who he seemed and knew that Mary wasn't going to live happily ever after.

Such information was an invaluable asset for an intelligent teenager like her, it meant they, her family, couldn't terrorize her anymore. She smiled grimly as her sisters, in their ignorance, sobbed. Her body was shaking. Bernadette knew exactly what was going to happen next.

The cattle shed smelled rank, the air pungent with the odours of the tightly packed animals that had just been driven placidly lowing into the pen outside, their hooves clacking and sliding on the uneven concrete floor, slick with liquid manure. An exposed light bulb, askew in its socket, feebly doused in an oily glow a solitary hay bale dragged centre stage, condemning the peripheries of the outbuilding to shadow. Holding back, preserving their anonymity, the four masked men waited as the taciturn farmer drew across the rickety barn doors and disappeared into the night. Silently they led the man, bruised, naked from the waist down, with his hands tied behind his back, to the bale and forced him to sit down, then removed his hood. As the fug from his beating cleared, he focused on a thin figure standing in front of him dressed in jeans, muddy brown Doc Martens boots and a green parka, hood raised over a black balaclava.

Captain Clive Stephens, or Ian Peters as he was known to his captors, attached to the 2 Field Survey Troop, Royal Engineers, one of three sub-units of a British Army Special Duties unit called the 8 Intelligence company, was coming to the end of his second tour of duty in Northern Ireland. He had trained for this very situation, had often thought about being captured and interrogated under duress but had never believed it would happen to him. An innate optimism, a resolute belief in his own abilities and the unthinking irresponsibility of youth, a combination that bordered on arrogant overconfidence in the eyes of his superior officer, sustained him and had led him to take risks. He had been posted to County Antrim on surveillance duties. His accent, local knowledge, he had grown up in Belfast, and incontrovertible nerve made him an invaluable asset. The information he gleaned was a serious liability for the Provisional Irish Republican Army – whose Internal Security Unit, the Nutting Squad, had begun to tease a pattern out of the security lapses he was responsible for reporting back on. Getting to know Mary Walsh had been one of the more dangerous, but as it had turned out, challenging and exhilarating of Captain Stephens' assignments. She was eighteen years old, pretty, golden brown curls ringing a lean angular face, soft-complexioned with brown flecked green eyes, a thin-lipped laughing mouth, and a slim, muscular body which was a perfect match for his and galvanized their love making. She was the daughter of Patrick Walsh a confirmed member of the IRA Executive and a suspected member of their Army Council. He was the intelligence target behind the wooing of Mary. It had not been easy, her upbringing made her circumspect, careful, and suspicious of over attentive strangers, while her Catholic beliefs, devoutly held and deeply ingrained, made her intrinsically cautious with men. But only initially, once a relationship had been established, all barriers fell away and she was, in the back seat of his car in secluded rural lay-bys, a passionate lover.

They had met in O'Leary's bar. She was there with two friends, already tipsy when he arrived. They had been discussing arrangements for one of their weddings, in great detail and for over an hour (Captain Stephens' partner had been listening intently nearby – while getting noisily heated with others about the Celtic v Rangers derby they were watching on the overhead TV – and had passed the information on in the watch vehicle parked down the street, before lurching off).

"Who's the lucky lady?"

The women turned together amiably curious, open to the interruption.

"I couldn't help overhearing."

"It's Mairin here. I'm the Maid of Honour."

Mary beamed at him, swaying slightly in her seat, her eyes partially closing, then opening wide. Her friends giggled. He had studied photographs, but none had captured the lopsided tilt of her head and the gleam in her eyes. The attraction was mutual. Affable, handsome, dark tanned skin, thick black hair curling over his ears and collar, he loomed physically large.

"Can I buy you three a drink? To celebrate."

They looked blearily at each other and then focused on him.

"Go on then, where's the harm?" Mary had said.

He had got in way too deep for his handlers liking and they had been attempting to reign him in, afraid of his exposure. He had been obfuscating, disappearing for days, even a week recently, not checking in, driving them spare, but he was getting somewhere. Mary was opening up, starting to trust him, believing they had a future. Details were spilling out about her father, useful information that pieced together could bring him down. Mary and her siblings didn't like him, their ambivalent feelings of solidarity and antipathy often intermingled with resentment, and that was Patrick Walsh's Achilles' heel and Ian knew it. Time was needed, that was all, and the big man would fall. He was a bully, cruel and self-evidently ruthless. A family man only in name. Subjugating his wife and daughters to a relentless regime of domestic repression, unenlightened and conservative in outlook, underscored by a religious chauvinism that brooked no challenge, yet his Republicanism was unsentimentally socialist in attitude, underpinning a concern for the Irish working man that was genuine and heartfelt. It was in this activist nexus that he embraced his son, or attempted to. Bringing John into the paramilitary organization, exposing him to his actions and beliefs. A closeness engendered by guilty association. But as far as anyone could tell his hopes for his heir never seemed quite to be met and he continued to push, assiduously undermining the character he was attempting to build. His son hated him, terrified of every action he took, fearful of where it would lead. John lacked commitment to the cause and the courage to act in its pursuit, loathing the implicit violence of his father's universe. He desperately wanted to escape, but had nowhere to go. Ian had sensed another opportunity and had already suggested they go out for drink together the three of them, or why not maybe make it a foursome? Mary had been aghast at the suggestion seeing her brother as a weaker, simple-minded version of their father. As she said, an insecure bully lacking confidence in anything but his fists was a greater thing to fear than an assured brute sitting on top of the pile. She had however thought it "sweet" that Ian was taking an interest in her family and said she would see.

He walked her home every evening they went out together, leaning close and holding hands, through quiet backstreets of compact terraces. Many of the buildings were abandoned and derelict, with shattered and boarded-up windows, splintered doors and graffiti-sprayed walls. Grass tufted through skewed paving stones, glass-strewn, young boys shouting crudely from the safety of a gang, jeering. Mary knew many of them, laughing she gesticulated furiously and told them to "fuck off".

The Walsh family lived at the end of a late Victorian terrace in a neighbourhood of narrow criss-crossing roads slightly more prosperous than the surrounding areas, yet still touched by the blight of sectarian cleansing and threatened re-development. As they approached the target residence Ian ensured they dawdled on the pavement, scanning the windows, blankly-drawn, before slipping together through a broken door, hanging by its lower hinge and wedged open, in one of the dilapidated shops opposite Mary's home. Kissing in the feverish airless shadows – mouldering damp clinging to their skin and clothing, expunging the coal smeared evening air from their lungs – he eyed the looming house across the street – light-fringed curtains, the blue glimmer of a television, smoke curling languidly from a soot-stained chimney – but always nothing. Nobody moved outside, there were no comings or goings. His support team could never approach. There was no cover, any attempt at closer surveillance would stand out and it was inevitable they would be seen. He was the intelligence services only hope of getting inside. Last week had seen a breakthrough.

"My parents want to meet you."

"Oh shit."

"Come on it won't be too bad, they've heard so much about you."

"They have?"

"Of course they have. At least my Mammy has."

"What about your Dad?"

"Oh, he never takes any interest in me. He probably won't be there."

But her father had been. Shaking hands, his palm was cool, a lingering pressure prefacing his unquestioning identification "Ian is it", before release. Privileged knowledge of Patrick Walsh's clandestine activities inflated his physical presence into an overbearing bulk, inducing a nervousness that Ian found hard to hide. He had asked what Ian did and he had given his cover story – "I work at a Travel Agents in town, organizing people's holidays and the like". There had been a lame follow up question – What's that like? – a laugh and he had turned away. No great interest, no overt signs of suspicion, but then no display of friendliness either. Over his shoulder, as he was leaving the room, he called out that Ian should treat his daughter kindly. There was no threat in his voice, only in his eyes. Mary noticing laughed uneasily. It had been chilling and he looked away, catching the malevolent glares of Mary's younger twin sisters, squirming on the sofa, nudging each other and conversing in an unintelligible language of their own. The belligerence emanating from the pair, particularly the physically larger of the two – Bernadette – was disconcerting. It seemed wilfully spiteful, aimed as much at Mary as him maybe – the sibling jealously she had often talked about – but in his current state of paranoia it had felt like a coordinated ambush by father and daughters. It couldn't be of course, but unusually for him he worried about the slipping of his façade, this lapse. Intelligence didn't take sides and while confident of his own, he felt confused by the encounter, a meeting with someone, or something, wilier than him. For once he was unsure how he had fared. Astute maybe or was it just the concerns of a father meeting his daughter's new boyfriend for the first time?

He knew he hadn't got long before he was ordered off the case, extricated and sent back to the mainland. Tactically he agreed with his handlers, understood that he was very exposed, the variable unknowns growing increasingly out of his control. But his weakness, one that his superior officers didn't know about, was that he believed he might have fallen in love with Mary and he didn't want to give that up. It was an intensely physical relationship, yet their association was polite and considerate. He had found himself behaving in an adoring, domineering male fashion, copied directly from his parent's marriage, she responding amorously to his gentlemanly respect and assertiveness. They had opened up to each other with a degree of honesty he was personally unused to, and within the limits of his cover story he had felt enhanced, not just professionally. The relationship had offered an insight into his feelings for women and their ability to stir him emotionally. Who knew in different circumstances, he had mused, they might have something, it wasn't beyond the realms of possibility, if this little caper played out, that they had a future – but then he suspected it wasn't going to.

Captain Stephens understood the deadly game they were playing with the paramilitaries. He was aware of the danger he was in. The fear he was used to in his line of work was now transmuting into terror. His mental capacity hollowed out, a sickening drawdown of strength causing the loss of physical control and facility, engendered by the violence of his kidnapping, the unspeakable tension and a strong premonition of the hopelessness of his predicament. Filthy cow sheds, he knew only too well, were the perfect execution sites, forensically speaking. The isolated farmyard ideal for the disposal of a body – he had smelled the powerful odour of pigs as they dragged him in, heard their agitated snuffling, the banging of heavy animals, disturbed, shifting in confining metal pens.

For a moment he thought the figure standing in front of him was a woman, slight in appearance, softly spoken words chiming with the ringing in his ears making it difficult to understand what was being said, but this patina of comfort was swiftly abraded. A man stepped into the circle of illumination, calloused, scarred working hands, reaching across, shaking him by the shoulders.

"Can you no hear what I'm saying to you?"

The voice deeper, a reaffirmed authority, demanded attention. Raising his head, he groggily focused, sticky eyes prickling, a taste of rust in his throat.

"We want to ask you a few questions about what you've been getting up to."

These were words that were simple to understood, translating into a line of inquiry that he could respond to. Relief at the simplicity of the task ahead barrelled him into a maelstrom of false expectations and imprecise hopes. Optimism and delusion were the twin poles of his existence now, clutching at comprehensible sounds, teasing out meaning, knowing it would be easy to lose your grip and fall, the spur, self-preservation.

"We need a few answers from you."

Thoughts connected to words. It was all so reasonable. Co-operation with his captors was the right thing to do.

"Listen to me."

Commands were to be acted upon and as a good soldier he would try his best to obey, but focus was the key. Consecutive actions were what he could manage, one thing at a time, with no confusion of tasks. He had a choice to make for every remaining second of his existence – the relief of pain or the succour of words? The shaking resumed. His swollen aching head rolled to the left then to the right. "Tell the truth" was the best policy. It had been drummed into him. He knew it should be straightforward, but there was a question that required a response. Veracity was a fluid concept, it could flood any discussion, overflowing channels of communication, sweep away meaning, even flow uphill.

"For God's sake, slap him around a bit, wake him up."

The voice was behind him, distant, sounding familiar. He attempted to turn.

"Keep looking this way you."

He was grabbed by the shirt collar. For a moment he couldn't swallow.

He loved Mary, didn't he? She was worth it. How could he ever have thought otherwise? He was a fool not to have seen it sooner. It was not every day…

The stinging clarity of a slap across the face, bursting apart his self-regard. Cheek aflame.

"Fuck."

The protocol of future pain management imagined, trained for, yet never before experienced. Boys' games played out in a time of dry-eyed earnestness. Calculated hate a trigger for clinical thinking was the tactic he had been taught. It would work or it wouldn't. The lamentable gap in this defence was the knowledge that it didn't matter, would make no difference. A short life remaining portioned into slivers of emnity was not necessarily helpful.

"What did you just say?"

The awful reality – almost pain-free now, an adrenaline-induced clarity deadening existence – was that he couldn't think concretely. His mind was everywhere, linear thinking sacrificed. Out of time he was facing a reckoning without the necessary summation of his life.

"Fuck. I said fuck."

"You bastard. You think …"

"Stop this, it's getting us nowhere."

The muffled voice again, an echo from a recent past, of no consequence to him now. How much thinking was too much? A surfeit of insight reaching a critical mass of understanding that you can never make use of? An excess of inquiry devoid of any possible utility? There is no conjuring an answer as the edge approaches, slippery, then the nauseous drop, bubbling bile in the throat, the stretching behind the eyes.

"Hold his head up. Don't let him look down."

The figure behind his chair, shadowy in his imagination, appears to move closer. Although he is not sure how he knows this, he suspects long dormant base senses stirring in a crisis. A creeping along the reverse slope of his shoulders, a flight on the spine, teasing the small of his back. He stiffened, balefully upright. Smelling the squelching reek of the soaked straw at his feet and the stale breath fugging the air. Hearing the frenetic patter of rain on corrugated iron.

Out of that downpour high above him, the voice emerged, no longer muffled, friendly and recognizable.

"Hello Ian, or whoever you are, grand to see you again."

A familiar presence, an acquaintance of recent months, Ian was unabashed to be meeting him now. It had been a forlorn hope born of a simple desire to survive, but now he knew he was dead – a functioning corpse, full of blood and guts, piss and shit, dread and fear. Soulless.

"Mr Walsh … Patrick."

As yet unseen, but looming, his words were threatening in their blandness, drilling deep.

"Always a polite fella. I had such hopes for you and I know Mary did."

Never strongly devout he maintained a belief in something other, was mindful of the intellect's power to access a deeper reality, seeing wasn't necessarily believing for him, he had faith. Yet he couldn't close his eyes and embrace it, couldn't stop looking.

"What she knows, my Mary, or what she thinks she knows is an interesting question, which I hope you can help me with. She plainly knows you're in deep trouble after our little intervention in the car park. But does she know who with and why? Ian, can you enlighten me?"

He feels his fears, sees them in plain view, the terrors of which his army instructors talked – identify, address, suppress – but his anguish has outstripped all rote techniques.

Could they know who he is? His body oozes, he sinks. They know.

"No? Well we're going to have a little chat and you are going to tell us everything."

How could they know? He floats. They can't know. He had been careful, managed the risks. They'd made a mistake? Picked up the wrong man. It had happened before. But it didn't matter, he founders, because the Nutting Squad never erred and if they did, they never owned up. So, a mistake on their part, or not, he was done for.

They are circling – he can see the main man now, a towering figure in front, hooded and dark, eyes gleaming through ragged slits seeking out weakness, sensitive spots where the scourge of pain can be finessed into a breakdown of your quarry – probing. There was no way forward without suffering, there was no delineation other than hurt to mark his remaining time. Units of torment to be paid for in full in a currency uniquely his own. His account was in danger of slipping into a bloody deficit

"You hear me?"

Thoughts snared on the inevitability of his own end, his resolve faltered. He couldn't think, speak, or exist for much longer.

"Did you hear what I said Ian. About our little chat?"

Identity hollowed out there was no response that he could make.

"Ian? Come on now don't do this. Help yourself."

A nod and two men stepped from the shadows and grasped Captain Stephen's arms, a third moved around Patrick Walsh and hit the prisoner hard in the face, then in the stomach. Taking a hammer from his parka pocket he took aim and smashed his right knee. The scream reverberated round the ironclad barn, unsettling the cows sheltering in its lee, sending them careening round the sodden yard, lowing plagently.

"Ian listen now. This can carry on or you can talk to me. It's your choice."

Again, the nod. The hammer shattered the other knee. The agonized wail, echoing, drove the cattle – tongues lolling, eyes wide – hard against the rattling metal bars, buffeting, mounting.

"Ian?"

The cold flush of water scoured open a channel, light and sound flooding through, sweeping aside barriers.

"I love her."

There was laughter. Incongruous and threatening.

"Very droll Ian, very droll. Now shut the fuck up you lot and let's get this finished."

More drenching water, shocking. Spittle dribbled from his mouth.

"Ian. You are looking at me, I can see you are, now concentrate. We can hurt you some more or you can start by telling us who you are."

His head shook back and forth, water droplets slicking from his sodden hair.

"Right you little shit. Hold his arms."

Both wrists were broken by hammer blows, his hands misshapen, fingers contorted at unnatural angles. He passed out.

The slide back to consciousness was stomach-churning, he was violently sick, the vomit cascading over bruised, ruined knees and dripping onto deadened toes.

"Fuck."

"Back with us, are you? Good, I can see you're a ballsy fella and need encouragement to help us with what we want."

The recoil of the flinching body, almost toppling him from the hay bale. The punctured intake of breath, staccato, as he regained his equilibrium, out of balance and slumped.

"Steady now, I have something to tell you. Get him back up."

Manhandling the deadweight of a crippled body, shattered joints flexing unnaturally, the pain shutting him down again, crying.

"For fuck's sake hold him up and refill that bucket."

"He's bloody heavy, the bastard. And he stinks, fuck."

Groaning in a deluge of cold dirty water their prisoner revived. Racing droplets – shimmering off-white pearls – dripping from plastered twists of hair, curled lashes, encrusted nose, dousing cracked lips and stubbly chin. Body shaking, he lifted his bloodied head, gasping for air, swollen eyes searching for a focus.

"Over here."

Disorientating the sharp clapping retort echoed off the unforgiving corrugated iron panels of the cowshed.

"Over here, fuckwit."

Voiding convulsions wracked his body, the empty retching overburdening straining muscles and he was engulfed by a paroxysm of coughing.

"Ian, for Christ's sake. Are you listening? I have a tale to tell you. One you'll find interesting, I'm sure. Bring over another of those bales, will you."

The shadowy figure sat down, off to his left. To turn and face him was impossible, yet he felt the need to pay attention. His hacking eased and he listened attentively, but was unable to understand what was being said. An incessant buzzing, crackling hum in his head got in the way.

"He's no listening. We need to bring him round. Get some water."

The liquid cooled the burn in his throat and calmed the tremors in his stomach. A fleeting serenity bore him up – the rain drubbing on the roof was a welcoming cocoon – but there was to be no miraculous transformation as the terrors again took hold and dragged him down. The real world was lost.

Unrecognized voices summoned out of the darkness, sneered at his helplessness.

"Ian, pay attention will you."

Ochre and ruby flares scarred the obscene pink of the overbearing sky, filling the gaping mouth of Cromarty Street with a lurid fire. Candy coating the tired bricks, tiles and paving stones, sugaring the surrounds of open windows, their glass mirroring the fleeting sparkle of the celestial circus. Anne stared at the clownish sheen of her hands, the washed-out rouge of her white t-shirt and sulked. The humid heat of the evening, barely easing as the light faltered, adhered sodden cotton stickily to her skin, a cloying dampness seeping through the hair at the nape of her neck. Up ahead in dark silhouette her best friend, Mona, in a short mini-skirt and tight halter-top giggled deliciously, her syrupy words dripping from her lips, leaning into and Anne could clearly see, was touching Ivan. His hand was gently resting in the small of her back. She was sickened. It had not been a good evening from the very beginning. Temperature soaring, she had been unable to get into the summer dress Mary had passed down to her. It wouldn't zip up. Comparisons with her lissom twin were infuriating. Bernie could wear anything. Defaulting to a loose-fitting t-shirt and cut-off shorts she offered no obstacle to the juggernaut of Mona's stylish beauty, Ivan sliding beneath her wheels the instant they had rolled in procession into the park. Barely a word had been spoken with the boy she had always fancied in class, his devotion now pure and focused on Mona. They were going to a party he had heard about, a friend of a friend, Anne trailing despondently, the wan trajectory of her life bearing heavily on the teenager.

"I hate. I hate. I hate."

A dragging refrain beaten out to the rhythm of ill-fitting sandals. Slapping intent.

"I hate, I hate."

Luminous colours shimmered through damp eyes and smeared her focus, hazily obscuring familiar sights.

Through the smokiness she spied an anomaly, unexpected, requiring in this fractured city an explanation. Odd behaviour where there should have been conformity. A surprise when there should not have been one. Anne's inner sense overriding self-indulgence, she halted mid-lament, wiped her eyes and looked again. Sure, then uncertain, she almost cried out but hesitated, the incongruity alarming. As the man stepped into the cerise glare bathing the corner of the public house at the end of the street, she knew it was him. A revealing sideways glance exposed his distinct profile, the cut of his hair, his loping gait. Hesitating to light a cigarette, smoke clouding, swirling pink as he disappeared from view.

"Jesus."

It was Ian, Mary's boyfriend.

"My God!"

The place he had been drinking in was Hamilton's Bar, a Protestant pub, it was well known, even to Anne, an Ulster Volunteer Force local. No Catholic would go in there. Silhouetted in the open doorway he had nodded over his shoulder to someone inside and waved. Anne recalled laughter, an air of normality, no hasty retreat, mistake realized. There had been about him a degree of furtiveness, possibly something she had later imagined, but definitely a lack of concern.

"Hurry up Anne."

Mona called from the end of the street, Ivan's arm around her shoulder, engrossed in each other they had noticed nothing.

"If you don't want to come to the party, just say so."

"I'm coming."

Suspicion was seeded – Ian was Catholic, born in Belfast, he would understand the rules of demarcation for such knowledge was imprinted in the DNA of everyone she knew – and it germinated over the following days before sprouting into vigorous life, colourful conspiracies blooming in her imagination. The heady scent of betrayal pre-occupied her, disturbing sleep and spiking the interest of her observant twin in the bed across the room.

"What is it Anne you're muttering in your sleep?"

"I'm so not."

"You are. You're keeping me awake. Something's bothering you."

"It is not."

"It is so. I know you."

Bernadette switched on the bedside lamp, plumped her pillow and sat up.

"Tell."

"No, there's nothing, leave me alone."

"Tell me or I'll come over there and make you."

"Be quiet you'll wake Mammy and Daddy."

"Give it to me, now."

The bulwark of silence – a vestigial loyalty to Mary, weak at the best of times – was easily breached by the exhilarating prospect of being able to confide in Bernadette. Anne rarely had secrets to disclose and relished the prospect of knowing something that her twin didn't. Leaning back against the padded headboard of her bed she pulled the covers up to her chin. Her sister's glinting eyes fixed her from the shadows.

"Are you sitting comfortably …"

"Get on with it."

A small stuffed bear arced through the air, spinning as it flew, hitting Anne squarely on the top of the head.

"Yes."

"Ouch. You …"

"Tell me."

"That hurt."

"It didn't. Don't be soft."

The constant rivalry between the two siblings played itself out in a familiar ritual, Anne's face wrinkling in mock anguish, huffily seeking protection beneath the duvet, Bernadette, her glacial smile frozen, reaching for her toy panda.

"You deserved it, now tell me."

"I won't. Never."

The panda bounced off the headboard, careering into the clutter on the bedside table, sending a half full glass of water crashing to the floor. Next door the bed creaked, light rimming their bedroom door.

"Shut it you two," their father's voice gruff, anger veined, "get back to sleep."

Someone shuffled past. Bernadette switched off her light, immobile and silent. Water flushed, the cistern churned, there was coughing – prolonged and racking – followed by a hushed curse, footsteps stilled momentarily outside their room, then groaning springs, followed by darkness. Anne counted silently to herself.

"… eight, nine."

"Tell me."

The whispered words were spoken inches from Anne's ear. Bernadette settled onto the bed, her weight stretching the duvet tightly across her sister's body, trapping her.

"Come on, you little rat. Spit it out."

Underpinning the threatening tone was a plea and Anne was exultant. Victories were rare in her enduring campaign to outwit Bernadette. She could afford to be magnanimous.

"OK, I'll tell you, but let me up first."

They awkwardly shifted positions until they were seated side by side. Anne was still, hands resting together on top of the bedspread.

"So, what is it?"

"You're right something has been bothering me for a while."

"So? It had better be good."

"It is."

"I know you Annie you can be a real pain sometimes. You better not be having me on."

Another pause, a deep breath.

"I saw Ian."

"Big deal, that's not difficult."

"Mary's Ian."

"Oh God Anne, obviously."

"He was coming out of Hamilton's Bar the other night."

Bernadette said nothing.

"You know on Cromarty Street."

"Yes, yes …"

The information was incendiary.

"… when I was out with Mona. He had been drinking and seemed to know people in there."

Dry connections crackled and sparked, igniting niggling doubts into a bonfire of certainties.

" … we was just going by when he came out. He didn't see me."

The heat generated created a burning necessity to know more.

"Why were you there?"

Bernadette's tone, cool and interrogatory, surprised Anne, the routine balance of their lives reasserting itself. She felt her advantage slipping away.

"We were only going through that way to a party, me, Mona and Ivan. Taking a short cut. Ivan said it would be OK."

"You never go to a party."

"Ivan was …"

"Ivan from school?"

"Yes."

"The one you fancy?"

"No Bernie, don't."

"Don't what?"

"He was with Mona."

"Oh, what a surprise."

Anne felt weary, she wished she hadn't started this. Bernadette always seemed to get the better of her.

"Are you sure it was him?"

"Positive. I saw his face. It was still light and he has that funny walk, you know?"

"When was this?"

"Saturday, in the evening. The sun was setting."

"And you haven't told anyone?"

"No just you. Why, do you think it's bad?"

"I don't know Annie. It's very odd though, definitely."

The sisters sat in silence. Steely Bernadette was unsure whether to divulge what she was thinking to her twin. Confused, Anne was unsettled by the course her revelation had taken, but aware she had lost ownership of it. The decision was made in an instant, Bernadette was suddenly certain.

"I'll tell Daddy and John. They need to know."

"Bernie you can't."

"I can and I will in the morning."

Shuffling cattle pressed against the corrugated sides of the shed, sheltering from the storm, which seemed to have eased during the fable telling. Ian could hear the heavy drops from leaking gutters splashing on the puddled ground, absent the incessant fury of the lashing rain. Mute shuddering cows, shaking themselves dry, the building quaking. In the human silence a distant rustling in the corner darkness. It was always the small inconsequential things that were your undoing – the inscrutable twins, strange teenagers, ever watchful, malign – the big thing maybe was the missing kind flattering word. His agony was growing. He had minutes, maybe less. His only option was to speak, a gush of words, but he couldn't. He was trying his best, wanted to live for as long as he could – not that it ultimately made any difference.

"And she did tell us."

The voice from way out on his left a surprise. The tricks played by space. It had all been over a moment ago, now it wasn't.

"At breakfast over the Weetabix. A good girl is my Bernadette. I suspect you didn't realize that did you? Despite being a clever fella."

Ian's head was shaking, small jerking movements, directionless and uncontrollable. Opening his eyes he searched for sight but there was nothing but smears of colour. Saliva dripped from his mouth. It was all he could do to delay the shutting down.

"John and I were very interested, as you'd imagine, in what she had to say. Turns out it was Anne who was the observant one, but had held back from telling us. Why I'll never understand. Families …"

Coughing he got to his feet and circled behind Ian.

"As I've told you Bernadette is the clever one. Sees the bigger picture, or thinks she does. If she was a boy she'd be a right chip off the old block. Wants to help her Da out, whenever she can, always has done. Was always running to tell me things when she was a kid. Got on my nerves at times, but what can you do? Paid off this time though, didn't it Ian? Had to thank both girls of course – can't show any favouritism can you – but didn't pile it on, it's not good for them to overdo it. Don't want praise going to their heads, do you?"

He glanced over at a figure standing in the shadows and held his gaze. It was the briefest of moments but Ian sensed it, one last connection. He emitted a sound, unformed.

"Is that you agreeing with me Ian? Good fella. You'll also agree I'm sure that it's never a good policy to give too much away. See the girls don't really know who their Da and brother are. Don't fully understand what we are about, what we get up to. Although I suspect Bernadette has worked out a devil of a lot more than she lets on, much more so than her twin sister. As to Mary …"

Silver yellow flares scorching tissue, the fluid of his eyes. He can feel their heat on his face. Mindless, love was, unthinking. All senses singed by her name.

"… how much does she know?"

Struggling to rise up, panic induced anaesthesia, he lurched forward landing heavily on his shattered knees then rolling sideways into the slush.

"Ah a sore point."

He lay still. The pain briefly diminished.

"Get him back up."

Contact made, he was flying then gone. One last thing to be done, but he didn't know what it was and couldn't foresee any way of finding out. A hard landing.

"Mary now, what did she know about you, the real you?"

Radiant Mary knew nothing. She wasn't very inquisitive, had no intellectual curiosity, was gullible, needy, perfect for the requirements of his job and he had grown to want her, desire, even love her. Clarity at such a craven time was a surprise.

"Ian did she know?"

Sagging head swayed. He mustn't move.

"Well that's one for later. Sit him up. I want him to look me in the eyes."

Groaning, he was hauled upright, squinting through raw-rimmed sockets he dimly made out the silhouette of his oppressor.

"Hamilton's Bar is not a place where good Catholic boys should be seen. Everybody from round here knows that. And you are supposed to be from round here. So, it seemed a little odd that you, a local Catholic fella, a friend of my daughter, a Republican, should have been having a wee drink in there. Don't bother denying it, being the suspicious man that I am, I had you followed. Turned up some interesting stuff, it surely did. Not least that you were tupping my daughter on a far more regular basis than I would have believed. A fact that really pisses me off, you bastard."

He punched Ian on the side of his head, as he slumped over, he hit him again restoring him to an upright position, dazed, barely comprehending.

"But more to the point it seems you were quite the regular at Hamilton's. Once maybe twice a week, always early in the evening, never stayed long, sometimes barely time for a pint. Now what could you be doing in there I wonder, if it wasn't for the company or the booze? To be fair to you it was a good choice if you had something to hide as none of our boys could be going into that bar to have a look around and see what you were up to. So will you be telling us or do I have to guess?"

Drooling and dread-ridden with senses overloaded, existing in a garish world, vivid colours clashing and bleeding one into another, he could do nothing.

"That'll be the educated guess then?"

Dry hollow laughter, resonated in his mind, grey as tarnished silver.

"I think you're a tout, Ian, grafting for the Brits. I think you are in the bloody army working as an undercover agent for one of the intelligence units. How am I doing so far?"

He looked at his watch.

"It's getting late Ian and we know you're a spy, so let's get this done with. Presumably your brief was to get close to me and fair play to you again you did a bloody good job. Plus having a wee bit of fun on the side eh!"

He hit Ian in the face, rocking him backwards.

"A bonus was it? Getting your end away right under my nose, you little prick. Had a good laugh with the fellas back at the barracks, did you? Gave them all the juicy details?"

The blow had broken Ian's nose, blood spurting over Patrick's hand and sleeve.

"You dirty little bastard. Look what you've done messing up my jacket. I'm getting tired of this."

Pushed hard in the chest Ian toppled backwards off the bale, cracking the back of his head on the concrete floor.

"Get him up. Ian there is just one thing I want from you right. Just one little thing and then this can all be over. I know you can hear me and I know you're not Ian, so just tell us who you really are and we can call it a day. Ian?"

Leaning in close he grimaced at the prisoner's pungent breath, but grasped him by the shoulder and squeezed companionably.

"Tell me Ian that you're a tout, come on. It'll be for the good."

The other IRA men moved closer, drawing in, aware the contest was approaching its end and anxious to hear whether they were to be the victors. They were not disappointed as Ian, dazed and in agony, conceded, croaking forth the essential truth they were seeking.

"I'm Captain Clive Stephens of the 2 Field Survey Troop, Royal Engineers, part of 8 Intelligence Company…"

"At fucking last. Thank you."

" … in the British Army…"

Slurring through his pain, the rest of the sentence – his assurance that Mary was innocent – withered into incoherence. His audience was lost. They stood arrayed behind the slumped figure, any elation felt at their success curtailed by what was to come. Patrick Walsh to the front, stepped back, removing a pistol from his belt. He motioned at his son, who horrified shook his head.

Clive Stephens, tormented and barely functioning, knew he was about to be murdered, that his existence could be counted in seconds.

"John, I want you to finish this."

Tempered by loathing the relationship between father and son was fractious and violent – harsh words and heavy blows were traded liberally and apologies never made. Their sparring was mediated by the women in the family – a mother determined her only son would not be driven from home by an overbearing man who terrorized those around him and by three sisters who on and off out of solidarity joined forces with those battling against their father's domineering energy and brute charisma. Conflicted by this support John couldn't escape the feeling that he was failing in his mother and sisters' eyes when compared with their father and he resented it. This anxiety gave rise to a zealous Republican fervour that was spurred on to even greater extremes by the desire to prove his worth. But almost inevitably his best efforts in pursuit of the cause only served to further strain the bond between the two men, their actions in its name, mutually witnessed introducing the weapon of blackmail into their individual arsenals. The son lived in mortal fear of his father, knowing him to be a killer, ruthless in the pursuit and execution of his victims. This knowledge confirmed that he was incapable of emulating him in the deadly game they were engaged in, that he was competing in a foolish contest which could only end in his mental, if not physical, destruction. He was a terrified young man, mortified at his self-inflicted entrapment. The father was disdainful of his son's abilities. He perceived him as inadequate in all he did, disliked his lack of clinical grit and ruthlessness and questioned his commitment. Their antipathy was at its height and at this critical juncture where personal affront merged with political necessity, family honour as well as the integrity of the cause were at stake, he could not resist testing his son.

Anguished, pale, afraid, John spurned the challenge.

"I can't Dad, no."

"Come now, don't let me down son."

He held out the gun. John's hesitation brought about a temporary fragility to the scene. Nobody moved. There could be no intervention from outside. The witnesses to the struggle held their own counsel weighing the damage done to the Walsh name. A waning of prestige dangerous to the powerful in an organization, necessarily paranoid, programmed to seek out and destroy signs of weakness.

"Think what this bastard's done, the damage he's caused to your sister, your family, banging away, laughing at her, laughing at us. And he's a fucking tout. God knows what he's given up?"

The pistol trembled in his hand as he pointed it directly at his son. His expression set in a furious grimace, eyes glaring from a face of crumpled tissue paper, soiled and bloody.

"You do it. Shoot the fucker!"

The words, jangling with the perils of defiance, reverberated inside John's head. He could hear his father's voice echoing back through time, never a kind phrase, an expression of encouragement, a demonstration of paternal love, just debilitating neglect, persecution and avoidance. Childhood panic stalked him into adulthood inducing paralysis at every turn. Seizing him now in a paroxysm of ineffectiveness he was unable to function. Scared to a point of brute disobedience.

"No daddy no."

Staring intently at his son Patrick Walsh lowered the pistol. Licking his lips, he clutched his chin and worked his jaw deliberately from side to side. Breaking eye contact, the binding spell sundered, he acted with the ruthless efficiency of the executioner. Stepping into the shadows, he returned with an empty hessian feed sack, folding it as he swept forward, his momentum forcing his accomplices to move aside. Placing the pad at the back of the sagging head of Clive Stephens, he raised the pistol forcing the barrel into the wadding. A loud crack, a bloody froth spattered the gleaming muck, and the body slouched. A tremor passed, the herd of cows outside shuffled as one, a solitary calf lowing plaintively.

Bernadette doesn't have to think about it, she won't be going to visit her father. It is that simple. He is powerless now, confined in that home, impotent. Drained by his infirmity and looming death his old world had shattered, and his connections had withered. It was a tragedy for him, she could appreciate that, but not one she cared to do anything about. Her father had been a cunning man of action who ruthlessly battled his way to the heights of authority in a clandestine organisation, wielded ultimate power for over a decade, fending off many assaults, some of deadly intent, on his crown. Ultimately, he was undone by his family – shame corroding his defences from within – blindsided by relationships he barely cultivated or cared about.

She sensed she had been his favourite out of all his children, but that had not been enough. A childhood of occasional off-kilter tenderness was unsustaining. Her father who couldn't abide his son yet never absolutely gave up on him, could never give his untrammelled affection or respect to a woman. A proponent of the rights of the underdog, a fighter for justice, yet he was a traditional chauvinist, unchanging, an unthinking dinosaur, of the deadliest sort. How galling for him, close to extinction, to be so uncomprehending, to have no idea what was going on and to have all his attempts at understanding fail. She had confided in her father once and he had corrupted her trusting words into a sentence of death, one that had destroyed not only Captain Clive Stephens, but also his own family – Mary, John and the twins. Bernadette had brooded on this guilty secret all her adult life and had nothing more to say to her father.

Smiling she waved goodbye to her brother, disappearing into the weekend murmuring to herself.

"Evil has no favourites among the weak."

Now who had told her that?

Part 3

Dead Centre

But as for me, when they were sick, my clothing was sackcloth: I humbled my soul with fasting; and my prayer returned into mine own bosom.

Psalm 35:12-14

Belfast Coroner's Court – Monday morning

The emptiness at the centre, the aching loneliness, the draw of the yawning pit beneath your feet, terrifying yet seductive, Bernadette had always yearned to succumb and step over the edge. Plummet onto the rocks far below, dashing her body into pieces, embracing oblivion. It was a recurring daydream, soothing in its austere bleakness, channelling her inner malevolence into an act of self-destruction. It was satisfying to muse on such violent outcomes in idle moments but when her mind reasserted control over her vivid imagination, it was fair to say she had never been convinced about the rocks, such a shattering conclusion seemed too final to her, an end with an end didn't add up, she didn't believe in it. Maybe the drop went on forever? Maybe that was where redemption lay, in flying not falling? Soaring across the face of God in the company of angels.

The court rose as the Clerk called order and the Coroner entered the room. Bernadette felt calm, at peace with herself, she knew what she had to do before she could release the shackles, unfurl her wings and fly. She had to tell the truth.

Her family was all but gone, destroyed by its own volition, only her father, brother and herself remained, each weighed down by shifting perceptions of the veracity of facts, the reality of events and the truthfulness of people. Meaning was an elusive entity that escaped John, he did not believe like she did and as a result was burdened by a guilt so enormous that he was unable to carry it. He sat at the back of the court now, pale and despondent, shivering in a heavy overcoat and woollen scarf hoping for redemptive words from her that would lighten his load and allow him to move forward with ease. Something she knew was impossible. She was certain her truth wouldn't help him and that lifted her, an audience was a blessing but a personal connection was divine providence. She would be addressing the court, but speaking only to him. He could pass on his own garbled version to their father if he wanted to.

"Miss Walsh we would like you to continue giving your evidence today. Please remember that you are still under oath. Do you have any questions relating to your testimony last week or to that forthcoming?"

"No, nothing."

"Very good. As happened last week I will allow you to give your evidence sitting down. Miss Walsh will you please tell us what happened on the day that you and your other family members, aforementioned here in this courtroom, shut yourself away in your house on Eden Avenue. Also, can you give us some indication of your motivation for taking such an action."

"Paradise was what we were seeking, Nanny more than any of us and she was certain we would reach it through the great sacrifice we were about to make. She had always made a great play of coming to live on Eden Avenue, the place not the street, drawing great comfort from the fact that her end time would be in a place of deep spirituality, pre-dating Christ she claimed, where the beliefs of our forebears were offered up and revered before they in turn became part of our Church. A powerful devotional site, Nanny believed, rare on God's earth. We were blessed.

Mary had never been as spiritually certain as the others. I understood or thought I did, but then I had always been close to Nanny, we both knew our minds on things and were together on this. Anne, my twin, never far from my shadow, was an eager follower. What Mary believed in was family and faith and saw no reason to doubt either. Both of them were leading her readily along this path away from her life of suffering and pain –a brute of a husband, who violently beat her, and no childrenof her own, which she found particularly hard – towards something better, God-willing. It wasn't as if she didn't appreciate what she had, she did,but it was time she made a sacrifice for a higher cause. Give her lifesome meaning. She had made up her mind. What else could she do? Nanny needed her and she owed that woman everything. Since our Mammy died Nanny had been there, protecting us against a hard world and our father. Mary reserved a special place in her heart for that cruel man, next to the hole left by the disappearance of her first and only love, Ian. He had been in the British Army and was probably a spy, she knew all this to be true and couldn't deny it. The press coverage after he was kidnapped and his suspected murder had gone into all that in detail. He had even been awarded a medal by the British. Mary wished she had known the truth about him at the time, sometimes wondered if deep down she had suspected. Our Daddy had been harsh with her and had questioned her denials of any knowledge, prying and going on and on about it, never letting it drop until she had broken down and told him the story he wanted to hear. She had hated him from then on for making her lie – but knew in her heart of hearts that she hadn't known anything. She had been entranced, blind to any faults, quirks or deceptions, prepared to believe everything Ian had told her. People said Ian was a traitor, but that was purely in the eye of the speaker and not as she saw it, although she had never admitted this to anyone. She had loved him and he had loved her in return, of that she was certain. More certain than about anything else in her life, even her faith. She had never loved another in the same way since. Her marriage was always second best, her husband knew that, and it had quickly gone bad and he had turned violent towards her.

We rescued Mary, protecting her from his brutal behaviour and helping clear her emotional slate. In recent years she thought about Ian often, wondering about what could have been, the stolen future and chewing over the remaining mysteries. How had they uncovered what he was up to and where they had killed and buried him? Mary was none the wiser on the answers to any of these questions. She had her suspicions of course and that had been a hard way to have lived over the decades. At the centre of her world of distrust was our father – a family man, but harsh, a stern husband, a local activist, a pillar of the community, a good Republican, a freedom fighter to some, a terrorist leader to others. There were even those who accused him of being a killer. She believed everything and nothing – he could be disarming at times – and that's why she had kept him close over the years, unlike the rest of us, visiting him in the care home on occasions, pressing gently in her own way for information. She learned very little, but she carried on, never gave up. If they had found Ian's body she may have let it go, having a place on earth to pinpoint her love would have made her life easier and it is possible she could have been happy. But they hadn't found him and she was now prepared to end it all – that wasn't happiness but it probably made her feel content."

It was a fine God-given evening, sunlight filtered through mackerel clouds, softening the hard edges of the houses opposite, burnishing the pallid hues of the parched yellow lawns, the wilting greens of the ornamental shrubs lining the driveways, teasing fragrances, sweet and organic from the desiccated soil, melding with the balmy air in a heady concoction Bernadette made a conscious effort to remember and treasure. An association she was sure the others would have made as they left the world for the last time and closed and bolted the door. Life had always been simply organized for Mary, she had seen everything in pale colours, unlike the twins who tended to be more animated and freewheeling, and she was trying at the end to be a little more observant and spontaneous. A late transformation in character Mary had hoped would carry over into the next life.

Their taxi reversed rapidly out of the drive into the street, a horn blared as a car braked sharply, its driver gesticulating as it swerved past. Mary pouted and let the net curtains fall back into place. She shivered, it was cold in the house, despite the glare of sunshine outside.

"Mr Burdin almost hit our taxi."

She was speaking to no one in particular.

"They were both going too fast. It's only a narrow street after all."

Mary was often ignored, living with others, never alone but frequently solitary. The twins existed in their own world, minds synchronized, communicating in a language that was their own, exclusive and often over the years intentionally deployed against her, she was certain of that. Nanny, her faculties failing, the terrors of dementia fluttering around her like a flock of startled birds, was often resting, her waking hours framed by irritability. The solitude didn't unnerve Mary, grateful for the safe haven she now had away from Brian, her inadequate husband, who when drunk, which was frequently, was violent, hitting her repeatedly in the stomach, because as he laughingly pointed out, "your fat belly won't show no bruises, girl." Damage had been done she sensed, a tearing and rearrangement of the pith, his gift to her. It hurt, the perpetual ache at her core, a constant reminder of her personal misfortune. No one else knew, it was her cross to bear.

Nanny looked up, but said nothing, she was laying the table in the back room for what she had taken to calling their "Last Supper". At the supermarket that afternoon they had reverentially selected what they would eat as their final meal – tinned steak and kidney pudding, new potatoes and cabbage, followed by apple pie and custard and, to mark the occasion, a bottle of red wine. Their fast, by agreement, would begin at midnight,

Ritual direction was the key to tending a flock and Nanny's nieces were very much her wayward sheep. She had introduced them gradually to the wolves circling the fold – the malign malady consuming their beloved aunt, the hostile world that would be waiting for them without her, a heartless ailing father, a distant uncaring brother, the lack of any support, particularly from children of their own. She had then subtly offered up ways to out run the pack and escape – passing over with Nanny, accompanying her on the great journey, performing one last good deed, making the ultimate sacrifice that would give meaning to their lives.

Charting the ancient drover's way on this metaphysical journey was now her mission, to keep the flock driving forward, to permit no stragglers. Laying down the laws, divinely inspired, that would take them to the edge before plunging over into the ethereal void where their final destination lay. Through the ages an expansively documented pilgrimage, but one less well-trodden by devotees.

Simplicity was her rationale, keeping everything black and white, allowing them no opportunity to enter into any foggy grey areas where they could lose themselves, no time for introspection, no space for second thoughts.

This life was not fair and Daphne had no regrets about leaving it and her nieces should have none either, she had told them that many times. She leavened the bitter message with humour, detailing the exact time, for her, when disillusion set in. Years before she had been a keen baker, in truth she fancied herself as something of a master practitioner, and had entered a Victoria sponge into a baking competition – Best Whole Cake (undecorated) – at a local fete.

She had come second and was very pleased with that achievement. It was only later that one of the judges told her she had been the only entrant in the category. It appeared that her offering had been marked down because of indentations from the cake rack on its underside. Trivial as it seemed, life had never appeared so bizarrely futile as it did at that point. The sense of injustice remained a sore point with her, rubbed raw every time her nieces laughed at the tale. Then she got serious with them, bluntly laying out the dismal trajectory their lives had taken. The death of their mother at such a young age from influenza, the robberies that had destroyed Nanny's business, the perfidy of individual family members were tragedies, upsetting and devastating in their impact yet all had a silver lining – they had brought the four of them together and moved them to this point. These dramas had created a need in every one of them to be together, it was pre-ordained and that is how they would remain forever. There could be no excuses.

Mary and Anne were little lambs, Bernadette a yearling, something more grown up and complicated, yet over time even she had been shorn of any affectations towards independence and their devoted Nanny had finally shepherded them all this far. They would soon be existing in her world of conceits cut off from all malign influences, she only had to say the word. Today they would eat together, pray together and then together they would prepare the house for their fast: clear out the remaining food they had in the larder, the fridge-freezer and on the shelves in the kitchen – there wasn't much left as they'd been running their stocks down for weeks, but they didn't want any future temptations to divert them from their path – dump it in the bins outside; double lock the front door; jam the keyhole with putty; tape up the doorframe, downstairs windows and the letterbox; draw all nets and curtains; block the passageways and doors by pushing furniture into and against them; barricade the glass back door by moving the fridge-freezer into position; then finally switching on the central heating and turning it up, it would get very cold.

Their tomb was sealed.

There would be no strays among her congregation, there would be no waverers in Eden. Their actions would consecrate the house and sanctify the garden. They would be scourging themselves on holy ground, purging their transgressions for the collective good. Seeking divine salvation together.

"Miss Walsh, I think it would be useful for the jury at this stage if you could explain the relationship between yourself, your sisters and Daphne Fanning or Nanny as you knew her, before proceeding with your statement about what happened inside the house."

"We called Aunty Daphne, 'Nanny', because that was what she was to us, the grandmother we never had. Our real grandparents died when we were very young so we didn't know them well. She took their place. She was quite a bit older than her brother, our daddy, so it seemed very natural. She was also on her own – a widow – lived across town from us in Craigmartin, where she ran a newsagent's. We saw quite a bit of her before our Mammy died…"

Bernadette halted, conjuring up her late mother's memory was difficult after so many years, her spectre warm, rose-drenched, tender, but elusive, there was nothing distinct, barely a chalked outline to observe.

"… you know weekends, when she'd stay over and the odd evening during the week – but even more after. Our daddy was very busy with his business – he was a builder – and local politics, which was very important to him and we came to rely on her more and more to look after us … and him, if truth be told. Meals, keeping the house tidy, the laundry, all that sort of thing, which he was useless at and had no interest in. Although he didn't seem to appreciate her efforts and if he did, he didn't show it. She had her shop you see so her hands were tied as to the amount she could do. Then there were the robberies, a number of them one after the other, which frightened her. It wasn't so much what was taken, but the assault on her, which she took personally, feeling as she did that she was something of a pillar of the local community, a character if you know what I mean. She said she knew who was doing them, but no one was ever caught. Daddy even got involved ..."

The sentence remaining unfinished, a question raised but left unanswered.

"... In the end she gave up, sold the business for a loss, something she never stopped going on about, and came to live with us. To be honest, it was the best thing that could have happened. It changed our lives for the better, no doubt about it. She looked after us, became our second mother, grandma and favourite aunt rolled into one and we loved her. She didn't just do the easy parenting bits either but was tough on us, kept everyone in line. Backed us to the hilt when it mattered, even against our father."

A novel concept, Nanny dead, and Bernadette was relishing it. There was an adjustment to be made, an emotional reckoning, that could not be rushed. The newness of the break was still numbing, even after all the months of grieving. The relationship had been long-standing, a lifetime really, emotional and infused with love, yet there was now, she discovered, a release. A generational severing that was both normal and empowering. The realization that the natural order had been restored slowly grew as she struggled amongst the emotional and physical wreckage of her recovery. At the beginning it seemed shocking in its heartlessness, but to Bernadette, once she had reflected on it, not that unexpected. The idea that she was free, now well developed and fully formed, was bearable, but its articulation was not to be countenanced in public, in any company.

"Things changed when she arrived. She was a stronger, feistier character than our mother, faced up to her brother more directly than Mammy ever did. Kind of kept him in check. They had a long history together, which was difficult for him to escape from. Nanny knew things about our daddy that our mammy never did, she had leverage and used it very effectively. It was more a battle of equals, one that had been raging back and forth all their lives, with wounds aplenty, but no clear winner. It's hard to explain, but after her arrival he left us alone, became less of a presence. Us girls, we all felt it, we were able to do far more, speak up, behave naturally. I suppose you'd call it a liberation of sorts. Power to the sisters. But it wasn't just us I know our brother John ..."

Through hooded eyes she watched her sibling jerk upright in his seat at the back of the courtroom, his anxious face raised, a pained gaze sweeping up towards hers searching, fixing, their eyes locking, then the shaking hand scrabbling through errant hair, a childhood habit revived.

"... benefitted too. Daddy always had him in his grasp. Ruled him with a rod of iron. Goading, pushing, expecting more than can ever be delivered, as I suppose is the case in most father-son relationships, but theirs had a particular intensity as John grew up. They spent a lot of time together ..."

Her brother raised himself in his seat, wide-eyed, fear of exposure seeding a panic that disfigured his appearance. Bernadette could sense his impotence.

" ... but that all eased when Nanny was around. It was as if she had thrown a protective cloak around him and cast a spell over our Daddy enabling him to forget he had a son. John was free to be himself, come out of his shell and notice his family for the first time. Less the headcase then, more the sweetheart. It was magical how he changed, or so I thought. Life was looking up ..."

Briefly basking in the glow of remembrances past, the comfortable warmth of recollected affection for those close to her acting as a balm for an increasingly intemperate mood, Bernadette struggled to hold her place in the story. She ached with a troubling urgency to speak the truth, to plumb the depths of her family's dysfunction and smear the accumulated dregs across the unforgiving face of a legal system that she was sure was manoeuvering her into the role of deranged female pantomime villain. It was always the women who paid the penalty, when it was almost invariably the men who were guilty. The quaking fool of a brother in front of her and the mute malignity lurking across town were cases in point, why weren't they up here in the dock explaining themselves, confessing to the part they had played, and taking their punishment? Her soul – for Bernadette a presence billowing beneath her breasts, cloaking a wildly beating heart, fanning the glowing embers of her intellect – was etched with venomous desire. Aaaaargh, but she had loved them so she would continue.

"Miss Walsh, are you alright?"

"I am your honour, I was just thinking back and my mind ran away with me."

"I know this is difficult for you but do try and concentrate on the matter in hand, Miss Walsh. It is what is wanted, now in court, some clarity."

"Yes, I'll try to do that."

"Good, please carry on then."

"… and we all fell under her spell. We all loved it. We felt she was a magician, a witch …"

How strange, thought the Coroner, that after such an interruption the witness could pick up exactly where she left off, word perfect. Her agility of mind was obviously belied by her dowdy appearance and apparent frailty. She looked older than she was, he mustn't forget that. Thinning grey hair, sporadically curly, crowned a face coarsened by the rigours of the fast, her nose and chin prominent in a countenance stripped of any bulk, only her brown eyes behind wire-framed glasses signaled any sign of vigour when she spoke – beacons of ingenuity and resolution. Bernadette Walsh was not a failing woman of doubtful intellect and rigid doctrinal beliefs, much as her beguiling performance in court may be suggesting, but something – a created entity – subtler and more refined. He returned to her testimony with a keener interest and a more sceptical ear.

"… a white one of course. But Nanny would have none of it. Even though we all knew it to be true."

She looked to her brother for confirmation, but none was forthcoming. He was slumped back in his chair, unruly head of hair nodding a-rhythmically, his eyes resolutely closed.

"That was all superstition for her. The only magic in this world she acknowledged was the Church. She was very devout, a regular at mass and confession, and slowly over time she began to instill a sense of the religious in us, and she succeeded, with the girls anyway. Our mammy had tried but she was a cowed woman and as children we couldn't differentiate between her meekness and her subjugation so couldn't see the merit of it. But with Nanny being such a powerful personality you could easily appreciate the value of her beliefs and make sense of them. The long and short of it was she was a major influence on us and under her guidance we grew in her likeness. We became one with her over time, a soul, divided four ways. It sounds daft but it is true. The three of us started out as her novices then became her disciples before the merging of the fast, the Trinity into the One. We would have done anything for her, as if it were doing it for ourselves ... and we did."

She sipped from a glass of water and glanced over at the jury. They stared at her impassively, apparently unconcerned at the blasphemous sheen that clung to her words, only one of their number was gazing at her with more serious intent. An older woman, wrapped in a thick grey cardigan peering edgily through thick lenses, and biting her lower lip.

"She was a Saint our Nanny. I mean that."

She paused for effect, the claim so religiously preposterous she was certain it could not be ignored. The authority for sanctification did not lie with her, as most of the jury knew only too well, yet she was usurping that power, directing and creating an image of divine rectitude in a human court. Cementing the impression that she, in the company of a holy one, was a woman who had glimpsed the light at the end of death's tunnel and returned with its lustre brilliant in her eyes. The female juror's mouth was open but immobile. A true believer, she could be losing her now along with the other strict churchgoer sitting there in judgment on her, unless her coded rhetoric worked its usual magic and converted them to her cause. The others, the majority she estimated from observing them for the last few days: the young, the feckless, the unemployed, the semi-insane, would think she was mad, "a religious nutter" and that suited her just fine as well. There would be enough uncertainty in their minds to either send them down the path of disengagement, letting themselves be led by the more forceful jurors or give her the benefit of any doubt on the grounds that at least she believed in something, which could not be said of themselves. Bernadette decided to double down.

"She worked miracles, small everyday ones mind you, but she did. Week in, week out she performed her good deeds. Ailing herself she looked after us and even nursed our daddy as he became frailer and frailer..."

Bernadette gasped, her voice breaking away. Fumbling with her sleeve she withdrew a small handkerchief, unfolded it and dabbed her eyes.

"Take your time Miss Walsh."

She looked up gratefully at the Coroner, a wistful smile creasing her reddened face. Another sip of water cleared her throat. "Thank you," she murmured and contoinued.

"He was bed-bound at the end. We could barely lift him even with two of us helping. It was very difficult for women to cope, you know, particularly with his mood swings and violent temper. He shouted at us a lot, much of it out of frustration I know, but still it wasn't pleasant. Our brother didn't live with us and only came round occasionally. He had his own family to care for and had his personal issues with our father so it wasn't surprising we didn't see him often. Nanny kept us going. And the big blow came when our daddy became so infirm we couldn't cope anymore and we had to put him into the nursing home – St Saviour's on Brackenridge Road. He wasn't happy about it, but ..."

She looked round seeking affirmation. A number of the jurors nodded their heads.

"We had to sell his house to pay for him to go in there, it isn't cheap as many of you possibly know..."

She wiped her eyes again.

"...and so, we all moved to Eden Avenue early last year. Into a rented house a fairly new one, nice and modern. It took though a bit of getting used to, to be honest. The move unsettled Nanny, I think. It's one of the most stressful things you ever have to do, moving house and she found it particularly hard. Things got worse quite quickly, she really went downhill fast."

Bernadette choked back tears, the timbre of her voice cloying and emotionally strained. Her body trembled. She knew she could collapse back into her chair now to good effect, but exercised visible restraint, holding out. Suffused with an inner heat that had never cooled throughout her convalescence her stomach ached, mirroring the hunger pangs she had suffered in the past – a phantom muscle memory – even though she had eaten well at lunch, attacking her food greedily to the evident distaste of her brother, who had sat opposite her toying with the sandwich on his plate. She had even offered to help him out with his food, the need in her eyes sickening him further.

"If you would like to pause for a moment Miss Walsh, please do."

Bernadette glanced up at the Coroner, catching his eye and shook her head imperceptibly.

"Would you like some more water?"

The repetition of her gesture was misunderstood, eliciting sympathy from the Coroner who motioned to the clerk of court to bring more water.

"Take a moment please, and when you feel able could you tell the court in what way things deteriorated rapidly?"

The fresh water flooded her body, its chill boring deep. She felt doused, the fire of her dissembling cooled, if not quite extinguished. A mental reordering was required, temper the melodrama, use the horror to arouse sympathy for her situation – the survivor suborned by personalities, not unknown, to follow a deathly course against which she was only just able to prevail. Her manner had to be more demure, matter of fact, aghast at the events that had stripped her of those dearest to her and almost overwhelmed her in the process. She would be a wounded phoenix rising from the smoking ruins, none of them of her making. There was to be no triumphalism, just sad reflections on the tenuous grip we have on life. And how easily it can be prized from our grasp. Bernadette had suffered a near-death experience – seen the bright flickering lights in the darkness, felt the blast of warm pungent air – and returned to bear witness. Everyone wanted to hear about that, didn't they? Just one more sip of delicious water, then she placed the glass carefully on the shelf of the lectern, smiled wanly at the Coroner and turned to face the jury.

"It was shocking how fast she went downhill physically. From the very beginning it was so unfortunate as Nanny was the sociable one of us and she couldn't get out much. Didn't really have a chance to get to know the neighbours, something she would've naturally done in her prime – mind you there weren't many of them as half the houses on our estate were empty. Still are."

A number of the jurors smiled, re-engaged by her conversational and unaffected tone.

"Making friends may have kept her going longer, who knows, but in the end, we were all she had."

Tears welled and she paused, allowing them to run down her face before catching them with a finger drawn rapidly across cheeks. She appeared disturbed.

"And she was all we had."

Shaking her head.

"It's still hard to believe that she's gone."

John was barely able to contain his frustration, shifting uneasily in his seat and brushing against his neighbours, who noticing his state of agitation, commented under their breath. The Clerk of the court lifted his head and glanced over.

His sister Bernadette was an unknown quantity to John, his childhood had passed in her presence, but she had impinged only as an assertive voice raised against their other siblings, while he had been ignored. A satisfactory state of affairs he had believed at the time being seen simply as another physical adjunct to the paltry furnishings of their family home. The female household, of which he was a disinterested observer, revolved around Bernadette, who sat at the centre playing her sisters. From an early age the central dynamic was established of Anne's jealousy of the close relationship between Bernadette and their elder sister, Mary, and her working hard to inveigle her way back into favour with her twin. It formed the starting point for the shifting alliances that made up the story of their childhood, adolescence and adult lives. Nanny had infiltrated this tight circle and changed its shape, but John was largely ignorant of how it had then evolved having married and moved out by the time his aunt appeared on the scene and had rarely ever visited them afterwards. This escape from the clutches of his family had been positive in his eyes until the recent deaths, now he strained to distance himself from the fearful thoughts that he could have made a difference had he not been so selfish. The awful truth for John was that he had loved Mary and Anne in the distant way he conducted all his relationships, even that with his wife. Nanny had been friendly every time he had met her and he held nothing against her. The only person he had not been able to get on with was Bernadette and the painful rub for John was that she was the one to survive.

Bernadette was subtly intellectually dominant and wielded a soft power that indomitably flattened all around her. She was doing it again now, here in the courtroom. It was unbearably obvious to John, but no one else appeared to be noticing. She had them enthralled. The jurors were swallowing it all, empathizing with her, feeling her anguish. The Coroner, the cadaverous old fool, was watching her covetously, seeking to woo her with his authoritarian charm. They were probably the same age – a starvation diet had changed her looks, shedding the bulk that had rendered her appearance benign, sharpening her edges – and both were seeking the other's sympathy. She was playing them, acting out a role, manipulating their minds, telling a story authored by her, all of it far from the truth he was sure. She was lying, but to what end, for what purpose? John, in essence, had no idea what his sister was doing but he knew she was not being honest and it was tearing him apart. This failure to understand fomented a rage that had no effective outlet as he struggled to control his agitated mind, keep swirling thoughts at bay and his mouth firmly shut. He was beyond words anyway – closing his eyes he could see a seething Tom staring at the mouse-hole Jerry had just disappeared into, steam hissing from his ears. He had to keep a grip though as he was determined not to be ejected from the courtroom and miss the end of Bernadette's parable.

"That first day when we tidied up our affairs and locked ourselves in the house, shutting ourselves off from the world, Nanny had been re-invigorated. Helping seal the doors and windows, moving furniture – yes well more supervising that."

The courtroom smiled, John uttered a low-level groan, looking down, hand over mouth as heads turned.

"Nanny helped us prepare our "Last Supper", as we jokingly called it. We had steak and kidney pudding, new potatoes and cabbage and a glass of red wine each – not what I would have chosen but it was Nanny's favourite meal. She said grace. During dinner she chatted a lot about things in the past, funny memories she had of us as children, her young life in the country with all her brothers and sisters. She was one of seven. It was a happy time, that evening, something I recalled later and held on to during our ordeal. I saw it as a spiritual rock anchoring the after-lifeline we were all tied to. Later we washed up and Nanny dried and put things away. She was always very neat, very organized. I slept well that night, we all did I think, still in our own beds. Everybody was buoyant in the morning, with a sombre appreciation of what we were embarking on, but tinged with a lightness of feeling then that was soon to disappear. It was, when I look back, the last decent night's sleep I was ever to get. Even now I don't sleep that well. My body never seems to relax like it used to. I'm afflicted by something I've come to call 'non-pain,' it doesn't exactly hurt but it's a persistent sense that things are not quite right and that real pain might flare up at any moment and make me suffer. It never leaves me, it's there every hour of the day and night."

A middle-aged woman juror nodded her head vigorously. The Coroner glanced at her, momentarily distracted, before turning his attention back to Bernadette, who was looking directly at him.

"I don't want you to think I'm looking for sympathy I'm not. I believed in what we were doing, we all did, I am where I am now and they are where they are by the grace of God."

She ostentatiously crossed herself. The pressure behind John's eyes eased when he closed them, he leant back in his seat, rolling his head from side to side stretching the muscles in his neck and throat. It was difficult to swallow. The words "fucking hell" rattled crudely around in his mind.

"I just want to tell you the truth about what happened and what it feels like, felt like, for me."

"Very good Miss Walsh, that is why you are here. I would expect nothing else from you. Please continue and tell us what happened to Mrs. Fanning, Nanny, as your fast progressed."

"As I think I've said she deteriorated very rapidly. Much faster than we had expected. We knew she was ill. She had a heart condition – angina, which pained her quite a bit – and worst of all she was showing the first signs of senile dementia."

Bernadette swallowed hard.

"Otherwise physically she was quite fit – we slept upstairs and used the bathroom for the first few weeks or so and she found that no problem – but mentally she was losing it almost from the beginning. Nanny knew this would happen of course, the Doctor had made it very clear to her, spelling out the stages, letting her know that she would need increasing help to do the most basic things. She was very accepting of it all, being the religious woman she was, believing it was God's will and that she had led a good life, but she was terrified of ending up on her own, in a hospital alone, not knowing anyone or anything. She used to say it wouldn't matter as she would have no idea what was going on, but we knew deep down she was joking. We all understood that ending up abandoned was her greatest fear and that was why we were there in the house to help her through it. Why she had wanted us with her and persuaded us it was the right thing to do. Not that we needed any convincing of course. She had always been the most important person in our lives. She meant more to me and my sisters than we did to each other, than we did to ourselves."

John's head was dully throbbing, the ache behind his temples unresponsive to massaging fingers, his tender scalp sensitive to their touch. He felt ill at ease.

"Once she was unable to climb the stairs on her own and we were getting too weak to carry her we made everything neat and tidy, closed up the bedrooms, sealing the windows as best we could and shut the doors, and all moved downstairs. We did this out of solidarity, to keep her company. It was much more comfortable in our own beds and the bath was up there, but we knew we had to do it. It would come to us all in the end. Nanny started to have blank periods, bless her, not remembering where she was and what she was doing. We knew it wouldn't be long before she wouldn't recognize us and none of us wanted to miss a second of being with the old Nanny.

We made a bed for her on the sofa in the living room and we slept on mattresses on the floor around her. We were all starting to have serious stomach cramps at this stage and to feel very tired so we spent a lot of time lying down, resting. We washed as best we could in the sink in the kitchen and gave Nanny blanket baths, using buckets for you know what. For a while we managed but as we got weaker and our bodies started to really hurt, we were less able to move about, fetch and carry, get water for washing and drinking, empty buckets in the cloakroom, stuff like that. Things as our mother used to say started to slip. Nanny became increasingly quiet, burrowing down in her bedclothes, complaining occasionally about the cold. It wasn't though, as we had the heating on high. The four of us talked less and less. Writing seemed to take over. They were always at it, while they could, the three of them. Notes, letters that sort of thing, passing them around. Mary had her diary. It became very furtive. Keeping their little secrets. I didn't bother, didn't see the point. I paid them no mind. We watched the TV and listened to the radio sometimes, we used to love it, but even that began to get on your nerves, the incessant sound was like a cheese grater being dragged along the side of your head."

Her words faded out with the exhalation of a breath and she stood in the silent courtroom, breathing heavily.

The murky living room light pulsed, barely filling the space. Scorched vortexes of air spiralled upwards from the ticking radiator, searing hot, motes of dust soaring upwards, wafting the curtains, conjuring shapes of shifting off-colour. Bernadette's arid eyes prickled the limited juddering horizon, back and forth, attempting to form a complete image. Lately she had seen little clearly that she could focus on, talk to, extract from it some scrap of the human universe that was slipping away. Sight, she had come to discover, was the deceiver, errant and willful, revealing only the partial. Noises, crystal clear, recognizable and familiar became mismatched with images of confusing truthfulness. Floating, fungiform cloud parades of dreamy, unexciting shades fading to an empty blackness whenever she closed her eyes. Bernadette understood it was boring, believed she had expected it to be more interesting, but it was hard to exactly remember. She had lain in this room forever. Time was stretching and reforming around them – the progression of lives remembered, speeding up and slowing down, running in parallel – ensuring that getting from now to then was an effort of immense difficulty, uncertainty and disorientation. The present always immovable then instantly the future, the past forming a history of all that had gone ahead. It had taken the passing of one second, she believed, and it was there laid out before her.

The sounds dancing in the air coalesced around a voice, a woman's, heavily accented, words verging on the nonsensical, a rudimentary familiarity with syntax implied. A prelude to a lucid intermission, in which logic had not completely abandoned her, brightly shining between meandering streams of mental fug. It could only be her twin sister Anne or her elder sister Mary, Nanny having already slipped into a comatose state at death's door.

It was Anne she decided, Mary was mute most of the time, in life and in extremis, and it sounded more like her twin now, the words were clearer, rising from a bundle on Bernadette's right, where she knew she had last seen Anne.

"Don't you remember Bernie?"

"What?"

The word exploded in her head, echoing, shocking and loud. She had not spoken in an age.

"Our secret language? We used it all the time when we were little?"

Conversation was unexpected and possibly unwelcome, it was hard for her to tell, it definitely required effort to have any meaning. The rewards were unclear, the approach of death was a solitary affair, company was, Bernadette had discovered, not a prerequisite for the transition, yet indeterminate time stood in her path and filling it was a mystery her sister could help solve. Anne's question was unexpected but not unreasonable and she had to admit to herself that she did remember. The exclusivity of their relationship had alienated others, set them apart at home and school, ostracized and ridiculed, made friendless and deemed in need of special educational measures, but they remained steadfast. Interventions and separations through the years only strengthened their commitment to be different from everyone else, be themselves. The collapse of parental authority had freed them and they had spun apart, the act of separation tearing at the soft tissues of their unique connection and stifling communication, reducing conversation to mere noise made up of words that were comprehensible to everyone. It was a price Anne had been willing to pay at the time to escape Bernadette's developing recitation that death was the only way to free themselves from linguistic tyranny. The death of one of them or both. Anne had suspected her twin's brain was wired differently from hers and it scared her, while they confided intimately in each other and conversed honestly about the world and the foibles of the people they knew, the logic of her arguments was always slightly awry. Passion and death were conflated in Bernadette's lexicon and she was passionate about many things.

Their adult life had been spent revolving around their family in distinct elliptical orbits, alone, their trajectories rarely crossing. The death of their mother eclipsed them both, darkening their worlds causing them to spin further apart. Nanny had been the rejuvenating light that had restored their well-being, drawing them closer to each other, and to the rest of their relatives, than they had been since they were children.

Now in this time of approaching rapture the linguistic bond between the twins, fragile, untested in years, was about to be reconstituted. Their minds were once again uniting, filling the space between them. Words that only they knew, sentences only they understood once again shone, freshly burnished, the grammar complex and ingenious. Surprisingly Bernadette could visualize it all, florid lettering swirling in the air, merging, forming words, personal, building understanding, which she knew Anne could see and comprehend too.

"Yes, I do. It's all coming back to me. Beautiful isn't it?"

"It is. I don't know why I'm thinking about it now. I had forgotten most of the words."

Anne's voice was vibrant, her earlier wavering frailty had vanished. The memory was restorative, opening out the mind in sequences of vivid light. The words forming rainbow sentences of random meaning and construction. To impose order on this spectral extravaganza communication was needed between the two of them. The rules – grammar and syntax – had to be reinstated and revitalized. They still had the time and the chance to connect.

"It was such a long time ago."

"It was. Another age."

"Things seemed simpler then. Everything seemed possible."

"They did in some ways I guess."

"I feel like a different person now. I don't know whether I recognize my earlier self."

Anne had raised herself up and was sitting leaning against the side of a faded magenta wingback armchair. Her drawn face was pale, her dirty dark hair, smeared to the side of her head, dank grease-heavy curls partially obscuring her lined forehead, yet she was smiling, an ashen toothy grimace. There was a joy in her voice and Bernadette instinctively responded to its novelty, rising against her nature, to the challenge of resurrecting a long-lost childhood language and breathing life into a moribund relationship. She struggled to get up, plumping the grimy pillow behind her, pushing down the piled sheets and covers that enveloped her, wincing as her cramped arthritic hands struggled to grip.

"We've all changed Anne", she hissed, "for the better mostly. Look at us now."

"Now?"

"Yes, selfless, that's what we are."

They were staring at each other across a narrow space in the gloomy half-light. Whether they recognized each other was a question neither could be certain of answering honestly. Fasting had turned them in on themselves, honing their own sense of identity, an introversion that was both disconcerting and consuming. Their current existence was a mix of corroded memories, sequentially incoherent, some recognizable as their own, others the result of the dramatic acts of strangers. Physical appearances had changed, divesting them of distinctiveness and obscuring their characters behind sculptured masks.

"Never used to be. Selfish not selfless that was Bernadette Walsh."

"You're too hard on yourself, Bernie. It's me that's selfish. I don't

132

really understand what's going on. I'm not selfless at all. I don't want to be here."

"Yes, you do Annie. You really do. Where else would you be?"

Anne shrugged, she felt too diminished to argue with her domineering sister. Her fear was now endemic and debilitating. Any semblance of truth was marbled with insecurity, but she clung on to a single belief that there was, and always had been, a safe haven in America with Rick – her only true love, her solitary serious meaningful relationship. The vivid memories of that time sustained her. Confronted now by an alert attentive Bernadette she sought solace, where she always had, in a fantasy land south of the Mason-Dixon line, where deserted highways lined by gnarled oaks festooned with Spanish moss, dipped and curved through endless bright verdant marshes teeming with birds, stretching out to blue-sky horizons.

"South Carolina maybe."

"Carolina? Why South Carolina?"

Bernadette knew the answer and was wary, acutely conscious of the devastating emotional impact on her sister of Rick's rejection. Anne had talked often, over the years, about her first boyfriend, pining over the lost opportunity but ignorant of the circumstances surrounding his disappearance. That was until recently Bernadette thought, but then, who knew, maybe she hadn't overheard her confession after all or had forgotten it under duress. The loss remained with her, Anne insisted, weighing heavily on her mind. Throughout her twin managed to evade any engagement, brushing aside inquiries, but recalling everything with guilty pleasure. Bernadette had had some experience of sex – six men in total, none of whom could be described as serious or long-term – but only one brief serious affair and it was those furtive couplings, rough and emotionally brutal, that she remembered with erotically charged clarity and not the pedestrian love-making of her more prosaic relationships. It was to the consequences of those few memorable nights in South Carolina that her sister was in her naïvety tangentially referring to.

"I used our secret language when speaking to Rick," Anne spoke softly, "he had no idea what I was talking about. Couldn't understand a word."

"Did you? I never knew."

Bernadette anxiously spat out the words, she needed to think clearly, but couldn't, the pain in her stomach was, at that moment, intense. A faint memory signalled alarm. Betrayal was a dangerous territory into which she knew she should not stray, but she was trapped lying immobile only feet from her twin who appeared to be inescapably leading her there. Did Anne know? She was never meant to, her sisters had seen to that, but Bernadette's recent indiscretion during their last afternoon in a mote-clouded church had breached their defenses. It was unsettling not knowing what was known and what was not, particularly as Bernadette had spent her life avoiding such uncertainty. Yet now it seemed a conversation about Rick was inevitable.

"It was so funny he used to get very annoyed at first, but then he played along."

"That was our language, Anne, just for us. Why did you use it with him? You knew he wouldn't understand?"

"It didn't matter. It was fun."

"How could it be when he had no idea what you were going on about. That's weird."

"No, it's not. We had a great time when we were alone, if you know what I mean. He enjoyed it."

Bridling at the superior, condescending tone of her sister and shrouded, as she was, in a mantle of mortality Bernadette felt the conventional constraints on her behaviour falling away. She could do or say what she wanted, when she wanted, there was nobody to stop her.

"I'm sure he did."

"Stop it Bernie. You were always jealous about me and Rick."

Coming clean, confessing, before a higher authority than this one had set Bernadette free. The knowledge of her encounter with Rick was no longer confined by the personal but was out there in the sacred realm. Open to all interested parties and Anne was surely one of those. Why shackle her soul-development now when they were facing eternity? Telling lies had never seemed so pointless.

"I had no need to be."

"What do you mean?"

The quizzical surprise in Anne's reply was a spur.

"It's obvious what I mean I had no reason to be jealous of you and Rick."

"I know you were, I could tell."

"You're wrong Anne. So completely wrong."

"No, I'm not."

Bernadette fell silent. Dappled shade from the Palmetto grove burnished her tanned skin. She could feel the warm sea breeze on the back of her neck as she lifted her damp hair, sense the soft white sand sticking to her sleek, sweat drenched body, smell the salty fish-tang decay of the nearby creek, see through narrowed-eyes the pelicans bobbing between the moored shrimp boats out in Saint Helena Bay. The boy lay beside her, his hot body pressing against hers, eyes closed and mouth open, his ruddy face beaded with perspiration, his chest rose and fell, his hairless nakedness a fascination. It was vibrant, real and she was living it – a vivid figment of her increasingly infertile imagination.

Anne capitulated first, breaking the silence with an emphatic appeal.

"If I'm wrong why is that then?"

Bernadette didn't hesitate.

"Because I had it off with Rick myself, I had no reason to be jealous of you."

"You didn't. You're lying."

"I thought you knew."

"No."

"I thought you overheard my confession? At the church."

"I didn't. Why would I do that, it's a sin to listen. How could you think I'd do that?"

Anne's immobile, desiccated face barely registered her horror, but it was enough for Bernadette, so familiar with every emotion of her sister's, to read and comprehend.

"Oh my God!"

"You're lying. You didn't sleep with Rick, you're just doing this to upset me, like you've always done."

"I did several times. I'm sorry."

The physical contact had always been rough and energetic. They had been slick, breathless, their hearts pounding at the climax. In her innocence Bernadette had felt degraded and used at the time, seduced and outplayed by experience and guile, yet for years afterwards her body had thrilled at the imprinted sensations. Even now they were cherished memories.

"No, you're not. How could you? You always do this. Why do you hate me so much?"

The emotional edge in her voice betraying the burgeoning fear that her spiteful, troubled twin might have been capable of such an act and was telling the truth. Anguished feelings choked off by doubt and uncertainty made her stumble over her thoughts. Words were difficult. As an afterthought she posed the obvious question.

"When?"

"The first time was on the beach on St Helena Island, you know where we used to go swimming. We were hidden in the palms, shaded and out of sight. It was beautiful."

"That's impossible. We were always together. If I wasn't with Rick, I was with you. So where was I? You're lying, I know it. You're teasing me again."

Bernadette's snigger was cold and calculated. The pleasure she derived from baiting her younger twin had never lessened. Adulthood had not mitigated her desire to inflict pain, just wrapped it in a cloak of respectability that tempered the opportunities available to make her sister cry. Together and dying, with time playing tricks, the cloak had been cast aside, their love had only ever been skin-deep, never much of a defence. Anne understood, how could she not, they were almost identical, Bernadette having only an eight-minute advantage over her. Yet for their whole life this small difference had been sweeping in its influence. She felt sick.

"You were with Mary. We'd had an argument about something or nothing I can't remember and you'd stormed off. Mary said she'd take you shopping to cheer you up. You bought those cowboy boots you were so proud of …"

Anne remembered the day clearly. Strolling with her older sister along the shady boardwalk and discovering the dingy shop at the top of Main Street – PHM Western Wear. She had been exultant finding the boots – they were upstairs now in the bottom of her wardrobe – and had rejoiced at having bought something that would make Bernadette jealous. The delicious sweetness of the celebratory chocolate milkshake at Dexy's Soda Fountain afterwards still lingered. Sitting up at the counter she and Mary had talked nineteen to the dozen – that had happened rarely – Bernadette was so often the centre of everything.

" … and never stopped reminding me of. While you were doing that Rick and I went to the beach."

There was an emptiness in the air between them, the sultry truth leaching its heat into the vacant space. Anne was finding it difficult to breath.

"The second, third and fourth times we did it was in his room in the house he shared in Beaufort. You know where he had that large Crosby, Stills, Nash and Young poster from their 1974 tour up on his wall."

Anne began to sob.

"He was a passionate man, very physical, but he didn't have much to say. Not a keeper if you ask me. Not someone to settle down with."

Anne wailed gulping air. Her words when they finally came were mired in remorse.

"It's not for you to say, I loved him."

"He wasn't a good man, Anne. He wouldn't have stayed with you long after he got what he wanted. I know that for certain."

"How do you know? He loved me."

"No, he didn't. He just wanted to get his end away, like all of them. You were just one pretty girl out of many, just like I was. But you were saving yourself. You wouldn't sleep with him, would you?"

"And you would."

"Yes."

"You gave him what he wanted and he didn't stay."

"My point exactly."

"What did you do to him? Where did he go?"

"I don't know and didn't care, that was part of the deal."

"What do you mean deal? Oh my god Bernie how could you? How could you do that to me?"

Mary stirred beneath the window, where she had stretched out beside the radiator. She craved the heat, the arid radiation suppressing fear – anticipation of the chill finality of the grave was a constant companion – and easing her suffering. Her chapped-red face glistened as it emerged from the cocoon of blankets, her thinning grey hair damp. She had been woken by the incomprehensible mutterings and high-pitched yells and was irritated, as she always had been when younger, by the unintelligible sounds.

"Oh mother of God, you two have started that nonsense up again. I thought you were done with all that. You never seemed to realize how left out I always felt. How dare you, talking in tongues like that."

"We were reminiscing about Rick."

Surprised, Mary hauled herself up and glared at the twins who were sitting scowling at each other. Anne's face was wet with tears. She was sniffling. Bernadette sat meekly vacant, hunched, round-shouldered but resolutely defiant.

"I told her about me and Rick."

138

"You didn't!"

Mary was shocked. There had always been a reckless streak running through Bernadette, which was dangerous to be associated with, but until now Mary had largely managed to avoid being dragged into her games, unlike Anne and John.

"You promised you never would."

"What's the point of secrets now. The state we're in?"

Anne looked aghast at her older sister.

"You knew, Mary? You knew about Bernadette and Rick?"

The truth was that Mary was secretive by nature, she enjoyed the closeness that came with confidences exchanged, appreciated the strength of character that keeping secrets demonstrated, understood that such knowledge made her a more exciting person, if only in her own eyes, simply liked possessing information other people didn't have and resented giving up such an advantage with no obvious gain to be had. In the case of this devastating secret, hidden for so long for good reason, there were distinct disadvantages to it being revealed. Eternity was a long time to live with the enmity of a younger sister, who had looked up to and admired you her whole earthly life. Mary was not a cruel woman, always acting in what she saw as the best interests of everyone, and didn't want events to unfold in this way, but the sisters were being swept into the maelstrom stirred up by their baser sibling. As so often in the past, Mary's response was indistinct, the sounds draining from her mouth.

"Ummm."

"Know! It was her idea."

"Bernadette no, don't. You can't say that."

But she was unstoppable, agitating with glee. Determination coarsening her voice as she spat out words.

"Neither of us liked Rick, did we Mary? He was an insincere, shallow swine, handsome I admit, but not good enough for you Anne and interested in only one thing. And we proved it. It was dead easy. Just one hint I was interested and he wouldn't leave me alone. He was very engaged and boisterous in a boyish sort of way. It was exciting."

"You slapper, how could you?"

"Don't call me that. It was for your own good."

"Oh Jesus, how can you say that? How did you have the nerve to think you knew what I wanted?"

Anne's hysteria was uneven, out of control. With effort she had crawled out of her nest of bedclothes and was crouched on top of them as if about to pounce. Her sunken face contorted and pale, yellow eyes bloodshot and teary.

"Calm down darling, please. This is not doing you any good. Rick wasn't who he seemed, we could see it but you couldn't."

Mary shuffled forward, hand outstretched, dragging bedding behind her. She nudged a brimming chamber-pot, its contents slopping over the rim, staining the pale carpet. Her face crumpled in disgust.

"Don't darling me. You're as bad as each other and I never thought I'd say that of you Mary. Never. Oh God…"

Anne slumped forward burying her head in rumpled sheets, gripping the stained linen with clenched fists, her muffled sobs disturbing the sanctitude of the darkening room.

Bernadette smiled benignly, her fixed, off-centre grin irritating Mary, who glared at her.

"How could you have brought this up now? For Jesus' sake, Bernie."

"We should keep it down or we'll wake Nanny."

"Oh God, you're impossible."

"Just being considerate."

Nanny lay motionless on the sofa, her low rasping breaths a reassurance of her undisturbed presence.

"We need to be honest with each other."

"Why for pity's sake?"

"Because we have so little time."

"Christ!"

Breathless and exhausted Mary lay down, twisting awkwardly to stare up at Bernadette, who appeared to be malevolently looming over her stricken family. A gaunt harpy, Mary thought as she fainted.

"To do otherwise would be irresponsible. The godliness of our soul is what matters …"

She gazed contemptuously at Mary.

"… to me anyway."

"What was the deal?"

"Ah, the youngster returns to us."

"What was the deal? You said it was part of the deal."

Anne's tone was surprisingly firm.

"You were paying attention then despite all your shenanigans."

Bernadette couldn't help but smile at the absurdity of the melodrama playing out in front of her on the sitting room floor, the actors lying down barely able to move, one comatose the other manically alert, her eyes staring intently.

"Tell me."

Bernadette, relishing her starring role, paused, moistening chapped lips, before answering.

"You knew in your heart of hearts that Rick was not right for you …"

"That's not true."

Dismissively she raised a hand and pressed on.

"… not the one. You knew he was shallow and only interested in getting you into bed, but you wilfully chose to ignore the fact. Focusing only on the superficial – his good looks and fit body – and not on the important things: his character, his heart and soul. He wanted your body and nothing else."

"No!"

The cry was eerily mournful in the muggy twilight air. Mary stirred.

"Yes Anne, double, triple yes. That's what he was. Mary and I could see the truth, but you were blind to it. We tried to talk to you but you wouldn't listen, you were caught up in the passion of a boy. He was your first, I know, and that is always special but he was not the one to be your last."

"But he was, wasn't he?"

"Oh, Anne no …"

Bernadette was momentarily at a loss for words.

"He was my last."

Anne was crying, her face crumpled, her skin crimped around the eyes, but the tears had stopped.

"I'm alone because of you."

Breathing was difficult, her words congested.

"I have nobody because of …"

"No Anne you have us."

"No, I don't. I really don't. You're the reason I've never been with anyone. I'm still a virgin because of you."

Angrily she struggled to rise up on all-fours and lunge at Bernadette, her distraught wail piercing. Mary opened her eyes, Nanny above them on the sofa lifted her head. Too weak to be effective, Anne's assault came to nothing and she fell back, Bernadette kicking out at her.

"The deal with Rick was if I slept with him he would go away and leave you alone. And he did just that. I've no idea where he went if that's going to be your next question. He wasn't for you Anne, he really wasn't."

"How many times?"

"What?"

"How many times did you go with him?"

"Several."

Anne moaned and clutched her head.

"Four or five, that's all, I swear to God."

Mary groaned. Sobs forced the air from Anne's heaving chest, leaving her breathless and unable to speak. Nanny slumped back, her head sinking into the heaped blankets. The sofa shook, a pale wrinkled vein-rippled leg, suddenly protruded, a thick dark-blue woollen sock gathered at the ankle, her arms reached out palms spread, there was a knocking as the wooden frame hit the wall, then everything stilled. In the silence they heard Nanny's final gasp of surprise followed by a ragged exhalation.

Around them there was a hazing of the light, a swirling hint of splintering form, then an absence in the room, a vacating of the spirit, as Bernadette was to recall later, Nanny had died with her soul rapidly exiting. The sisters sensed it together – the communion profound – quieting panic and soothing bruised feelings. Anguish curdled in their throats, the taste of grief distasteful. There was no ceremony, no transition, no before and after, no lingering farewells, no last words. She was gone.

Those left behind were integral to the story too. A chapter had closed, not with an unexpected plot twist, but with a foretold ending. It was a fitting conclusion to Part One. As the leading characters they were eager to read on, anxious to learn if the final scene of the whole saga was as expected. Their problem was to disentangle what was fact and what was fiction, what was an astute observation of the real or the upwelling of an emaciated sensibility, a hunger induced hallucination or a genuine revelation. The Scriptures were their preferred literary template, they all desired to emulate the divine, but they were difficult texts to follow with fading eyes and weak constitutions.

Bernadette possessed a practical streak, she discovered, layered deep within, that was throttling her grief. She momentarily reflected on her lack of feeling, her heartlessness, but it didn't resonate and she cast such thoughts aside. Action was always an antidote to mawkishness and introspection. She got unsteadily to her feet, the effort was immense, every fist-like breath pummelling her chest, until the violence of the attack forced her to stop, gasping, head giddy. The room swirled and dipped and she feared she would fall. Flashes of burnt gold seared Bernadette's eyes, blistering her sight, bleeding smoky visions into corners, crackling static interfering. She fell against the sofa her body curving sinuously as she sought to balance. Upright and holding on, equilibrium was gradually restored and she could see again, a wispy reality of marginal utility, but serviceable, her breathing eased and a sense of smell returned. For a delirious moment she felt whole before the physical dissipiation of their existence impinged and overpowered her.

The moment slipped and Bernadette slid with it, gliding in and out of consciousness. She had no idea why she was standing in the middle of the room, her leg pressed against the sofa was numb, the only sound the tick-tack of the hot water pipes, her sisters were absent and she seemed to be alone. Rubbing feeling back into the forgiving flesh of her calf Bernadette thought she remembered why she was there, the reason she was who she was, the actor. She grasped Nanny under the arms, sensing a vestigial warmth, and hauled. Her aunt was not heavy but there was resistance in the curled body, already a stiffening of the joints, a pooling of the blood. How long had they been adrift in this end of life epilogue? Minutes, hours, days? Time was an elusive, unreliable servant, absent when you most needed it, missing from the plotline Bernadette had running through her mind. She had no idea where her attendant had gone. Rigour, both mental and physical, was now what was required and she was the only one of her sisters able to provide it. Nanny had to be moved for the simple reason they couldn't live with her anymore. The years together were over, the camaraderie, the intimacy, the deeper companionship of the devoted relation, so different from that of mere friends, was now just part of their history. The future promised much more, an eternity of harmony and joy, an infinite age of spiritual affinity. All they had to do was follow her and pass over. But before that she had to move Nanny out of sight, but not out of mind.

"What are you doing?"

The voice was commanding in tone, but groggy in execution. Mary, perturbed and dishevelled, her breathing staccato, was focusing hard from a half-raised position on the floor. Her weary mind labouring to tease meaning from the stippled pattern of facts in front of her – the overbearing juxtaposition of a towering Bernadette grasping a limp Nanny in her arms; the physical exertion being expended; the overwhelming sense of a lack of spirit – and failing to make out any arrangement that made sense.

"Mary let me deal with this. Nanny will be more comfortable in the dining room."

"Why? What's so uncomfortable about the sofa?"

"She can't be with us now in the same room."

"Don't be silly Bernie she should be with us now more than ever. We've got to stick together."

"Oh God!"

"We mustn't leave her alone."

"She's left us Mary."

"How can you say that?"

"Because it's true."

"Noooo."

The extended exclamation dissolved into fractured bars of liquid sobbing. The effect comically musical.

"Mary for Christ's sake. What does it matter?"

"It matters."

Anne's voice unexpectedly hard-edged.

"You can't always get your own way."

"I don't."

"You do Bernadette, you do. You always do, you always have."

"Oh, not this again, please."

"I hate you."

"You've no idea what I think of you, you silly little bitch."

Irritated Bernadette lowered Nanny's body to the floor and pushed her partially beneath the sofa, closed each vacant eye with the palm of her hand, brushed the hair from her brow, noticing that the deep furrows of consternation that had marred her homely appearance of late seemed to have disappeared, placed a cushion under her head, another between her knees, pulled a quilt down from the sofa, kissed her lightly on the cheek, then tucked her in securely. She wanted her to be comfortable.

"I'll leave you to it then, you ungrateful … I'm moving into the dining room."

"Good."

The sliding glass doors dividing the two rooms were an effective barrier in keeping out the incapacitated living – Bernadette was relieved to be shut off from her sisters – but the dead were irrepressible passing back and forth at will. And it was not just the recently deceased for Nanny's death had summoned a cavalcade of long dormant spirits to parade along the ancient intersecting pathways that formed the real physical geography of the place. Bernadette sensed them all and saw certain of the travellers in the gathering gloom. She was not surprised at their presence. Nanny had talked of the pilgrim spirits often to those who would listen. Many had thought of her as simply joking or of playing a blasphemous tongue-in-cheek game gulling the devout to rise, as they so often did, to take issue. But Bernadette knew differently. Nanny's spiritual compass had always pointed firmly heavenward, but she was not averse to straying off the path once in a while to commune with the spirits of place, cavorting with the true believers of earlier more holy times. The chosen of any age always had something to pass on if you would just listen and Nanny believed that it was only a fool who was not receptive to such wisdom, who turned their minds away. A place never forgot its history and neither did she. There were always slights to be righted, wrongs to be avenged and the local familiars were always striving to do that. They never ceased through aeons of time to seek out the sympathetic living to help them heal their spiritual injuries. It was rare to find a spot on the earth without such weeping wounds, ages-old, scarring the landscape. When you did – and Nanny believed Eden Avenue was one such place, even though it had to her chagrin been forsaken by modern developers – you could exploit the immaterial calm to promote your own wellbeing, resolving the slights and wrongs of your own life unheeded by vexatious spirits.

They were there now in their grotesque chattering brilliance but Bernadette was not scared, proximity to the dead was a comforting reminder of her, of their, ultimate fate. She did fear however that with Nanny gone the conduit would close and in the process be lost, communication would end, that without their guidance she would not be up to the task she felt her aunt had entrusted her with.

To be of such company was an honour, but she was uncertain, sensing she might simply be in their presence but not of them. Confined as they were, as she was, in limbo on the outer edges, she felt loneliness descending, seeping round like a bank of fog. Raw and alone – a precursor she knew of what was to come – Bernadette experienced a revelatory insight in which she understood that despite her faith, the passing of Nanny marked the end of an era, a generational change. She was meant to follow, as were her sisters, they had sworn to do so and knew it was the right thing to do. They were already travelling on the devout pathway, purging themselves of all that was impure in mind and body. On their knees, flaying their souls mercilessly as they climbed the rocky pilgrimage road to salvation. The clichés flowed – the murmurings of nuns, the mutterings of priests – insulting her intelligence, softening her logic, turning thoughts to mush. They couldn't save her now. But amongst the softness and fuzz there was a hard irritant core of belief that she stubbornly refused to abandon. She was not destined to die in this way, she was certain, but her sisters were. They were to be sacrificed to look after Nanny. She though was being kept back – Nanny hadn't said so explicitly but she had hinted at it. Bernadette was the one who was to speak to and for the ages. There was no one else who could do it, she was clear on that point. The irony was that she was too weak to do anything about it. There was nothing and nobody left, just the emptiness and the redemptive pain. The path travelled was pre-ordained. It would be God's will.

"I think Miss Walsh that we are very nearly done for today, but at this stage in your testimony I have to ask the question which I think everyone in this courtroom is burning to know the answer to. You have in what you said earlier hinted at some of the reasons, but I would like you now, if you can, to succinctly tell us why you and your family members decided to fast to the death and not say nurse Mrs Fanning through her inevitable decline and then continue with your lives?"

Bernadette had expected this question and had prepared an answer, which she would deliver with conviction. She thought she believed it and that belief gave her a great deal of comfort, particularly when the chill realization insinuated itself into a consciousness still somewhat befuddled by its own survival, that she was utterly alone.

"I am a deeply religious person, my family are as well ..."

"Not true, you can't say that. Suicide and murder are sins. You can't pull that one."

John was standing and staring at his sister, he was speaking at normal volume, but the pitch of his voice was monotonic.

"Mr Walsh please remain silent and sit down or I will have you removed from this courtroom."

John flicked his eyes in the direction of the Coroner, then sank down onto his seat.

"We believe in the life hereafter. In eternity. Nanny, my sisters and I lived together in this life and we planned to continue to do the same in the next. We believed deeply that that was possible, and to achieve it together was not a sin. Nanny was ill with a terrible wasting disease, her life on this earth was not going to be worth living, it was kinder for her to go at a time and place of her own choosing. We made that possible. It was an act of faith, an act of devotion."

The court was silent. Bernadette stepped back letting go of the rail bordering the front of the witness stand. Her skin adhered momentarily to the smooth metal surface – she realized she had been grasping it tightly. Each hand tingled with numbness. The Coroner cleared his throat before speaking.

"Thank you, Miss Walsh, we will continue tomorrow. The court is adjourned."

The sun was shining for the first time that Bernadette could remember since she had left the house on Eden Avenue semi-conscious on a stretcher. She could feel the wan heat radiating through the grimy skylight and rippling in soothing waves across the top of her head – where a thinning crown of brittle hair offered little protection for her scalp – then caressing the dry skin of her slightly upward tilted face. It was the filtered shining she recalled from the balmy summer of their death descent, each rising and setting marking a downward twist of the spiral. Every slippage brightly illuminated, the extreme perversity of her fast intimidating senses into accumulating false memories and seeking renewal from a natural order overwhelmed by her religious fervour and mental and physical decline. All intimations of impending darkness were challenged by the brightness of the light, whether caused by souls burning in the conflagration awaiting at the end or being purified by fire, Bernadette had never been certain in her own unravelling mind. Nonplussed by the unexpectedly bright nature of the season they had by chance ended up with as a backdrop to their exit, she had struggled to overcome the inherent optimism of the time of year. Days passed and the perpetual sun blazed, its presence filtering through the heavy drapes into the house where their diminished bodies reached out to grasp at the fingers of restorative light.

Nanny admonished her, whispering in her ear, "to face her tormentors" and she was prepared, but in her now weakened condition she needed precious moments of respite from the sights and sounds of the impending ordeal. Smarting eyes closed against the glare, shutting out images of the curious filing along the rows of seats in the courtroom, taking their places before sizing her up, as well as blanking out the accusatory stare of her surviving sibling, harsh and unforgiving. People were always difficult, often irritating and sometimes chastening in their unpredictability. Bernadette could live without them. She had arrived at the court early, seeking solitude but hadn't found it – the nudges, whispers and glances of onlookers following her every move – the concerned interventions of the Clerk nigglingly intrusive. Now hiding in plain view on the witness stand, if just for a few precious seconds, was the only time she had to be herself in those moments before the charade began all over again.

The courtroom pulsed in the buttery light, its rays smearing the worn furnishings and scuffed paintwork a greasy yellow, while everywhere sallow complexions flushed. It was going to be hot, jurors were removing their jumpers and coats, loosening ties while the security guard at the door had taken off his jacket and was rolling up his shirtsleeves. He was paying no attention to those passing in and out of the courtroom. Bernadette surveyed the scene and felt all-powerful. The feeling passed as the shuffling hubbub settled into an intimidating silence. The Coroner crashed into this expectant atmosphere, his presence resounding noisily as he crossed creaking wooden floorboards in his approach to the bench.

"All rise."

He sat down breathing heavily, each exhalation catching in the back of his throat – a ticking manifestation of physical frailty that made Bernadette grimace. Jurors noticed her expression as they settled back into their seats and felt uneasy at what it suggested about her true feelings towards the proceedings.

"Miss Walsh, will you, excuse me," the Coroner took out a handkerchief and coughed loudly, "Will you please continue your testimony, picking up with the events that followed the death of Mrs Fanning."

Bernadette closed her eyes. She could feel again the damp warmth of fetid air on her face, the swirling decay in the air that made her retch, the agitation of the hairs in her nostrils, the sneezing, the bile foaming in her mouth then spluttering in a fine mist onto her chest. She could taste the vivid pain of a burning throat, specific and localized, searing across the familiar landscape of hunger cramps and muscular contractions like a lightning flash. The fast was more real than real life and she understood why when she opened her eyes. The dumb need of these people in the courtroom was enervating, their yearning for an explanation, for understanding, was a tedious imposition. They would never grasp the truth, however hard she tried to spell it out to them. But try she must.

"It was cooler in the other room. The double doors into the garden were sealed and the curtains drawn but somehow fresh air seemed to find its way in. It was a relief after the crowded living room with all of us in there. I made a bed up near the window, got myself some bottles of water from the kitchen and settled down to listen to the radio. It took my mind off things. I could shut out the rest of the world and escape into myself. I left it on constantly with the sound turned right down. I was getting very tired at this point, nodding off during the day, having lurid dreams. I wouldn't call them nightmares exactly but they were disturbing, even upsetting at times. There was an evil spectre abroad and I had to keep him at bay. His plan was unclear but my faith sustained me. I, we, had a plan – and it was God's plan – and I was going to stick to it. Frightening me with images of my past, a distorted one at that, and people and places I had known and left behind didn't work for me. I had made up my mind and I was resolute, decisions taken long ago were exactly that, decisions made, and I regretted none of them. I was not afraid or ashamed of meeting anyone from my past again whether in heaven or on earth. I was on a righteous path and I would not be diverted, by nothing or no-one. The good Lord ..."

"Miss Walsh, I don't think any of us in this room question the sincerity of your beliefs and the intensity of your faith. You have left us in no doubt that you are a devout individual and genuine in pursuing the path you chose to follow. This court needs no further reassurance from you on this matter. What interests me is the events that took place in Eden Avenue that led to the deaths of your aunt and siblings and of which you are the sole surviving witness. I appreciate this is very difficult for you, but please redirect your testimony to these issues, thank you."

Unwelcome as the interruption was, wrenching her thoughts from a place of insight and calm introspection, it steeled Bernadette's resolve. If it was the prosaic detail he wanted then he would get it, story-telling was a thing of the past, no more embellishment, now it would be simple narration.

"I wasn't on my own long. A day or too later, it's difficult to judge exactly, both my sisters crawled in dragging their bedcovers after them. They couldn't bear to be in the same room as Nanny any longer. In the heat it had become impossible and the presence of a dead person, even one you love, is a difficult thing to get used to, we were all finding out, particularly in the dark at night. The adjustment is hard to make and they had discovered they couldn't make it.

Things settled down for a while. We had a routine of sorts. We talked a bit at the beginning, mainly about Nanny, but that soon became too much effort. We had said all we had to say a long time ago so we relied on the radio to fill the silence. The TV was out of the question as it was in the living room. Without having to clean the house or shop and prepare food you have a lot of hours on your hands. And meal times still dominated your life even though you knew they no longer had any meaning. The body is an amazing thing as for ages in the early morning, at midday and at five thirty in the afternoon the pains got worse in anticipation of food that was never forthcoming. It was very strange. You do imagine your favourite things to eat – you see them, taste them and smell them. But soon a few sips of water were all that was needed to banish these feelings.

I was the strongest of all of us then and still able to get around. I used to fetch water and empty the pots you know, that sort of thing. But I soon got too weak to do even that. We had to ration the water – I'd filled the washing up bowl and a couple of our big saucepans when I had the strength and we drank from those. The other containers just filled up – slowly as it turned out – but the smell got very bad.

My sister Anne was failing fast. She had always been the more sickly of the two of us, catching cold or going down with the flu before me. She was the one who fell ill with the measles or the mumps first, and suffered the most. She was always a demanding patient, needing attention and reassurance, seeking out company even when she was at her sickest. Not for her the calm and isolation of the sick room which so appealed to me. She wanted nursing full time, the calming word, the cool hand, the pain relieving medicine. And that was how it turned out to be during her last days. Passing in and out of consciousness she wanted me constantly, even though I wasn't able to offer much as I was barely keeping myself together. She started to hallucinate, raving in her sleep, about nonsense mainly, complaining, expressing anger at the pain."

Bernadette paused and looked directly at the jury.

"It was strange to watch someone you love and know well weaken and not be able to do anything about it. I know many of you will think me heartless…"

"Miss Walsh it is not for you to speculate about what the jury might or might not be thinking. Please continue with your testimony without any further comment."

"I was at peace with what was happening. We were all agreed on our chosen path as I have explained before. We had sworn to act together, pledged our commitment to each other, there could be no backing down. She was lucky in my opinion going before the rest of us, at least she had the company of her family during her final hours. Her last words were not heard by God alone, which is a blessing.

She died in the early morning. I could clearly hear the dawn chorus as she struggled for life, tangled up in her sheets and blankets. She called out my name as she passed over. Mary started to cry. I crawled across and kissed her. I was relieved as she had followed Nanny and wouldn't suffer any more. I was also a little jealous if I'm honest. Her struggle was over, she'd been true to her word, carrying out God's will. We had been left behind. I switched on the radio I remember to try and fill the emptiness – as it happens it was playing Elvis Presley singing some love song. We had always liked him.

I was now alone with my elder sister, which was strange for both of us, as it had never really happened before. Family life has a way of settling into a pattern and we both had never been that important or significant to each other. Which made it a surprise when the first thing Mary said after she had stopped crying was that, "this is how it should always have been, you and me."

"What do you think she meant by that Miss Walsh?"

"I think she was always jealous of Anne and our close relationship, the fact that we were twins, how we always did everything together, finished each other's sentences, that sort of thing. She was the oldest by several years, effectively an only child, as there was us – the twins – and a brother who had little to do with any of his sisters. She was the quiet one, keeping herself to herself, never really joining in. Being younger we probably didn't understand and weren't always that kind to her. She had a bossy side and we didn't like that. She also had quite a temper so we tended to keep out of her way. That's children for you, I suppose. When we got older Mary was the one who got married and moved away so we didn't see that much of her until she left that pig of a husband and came to live with us. It's strange now I come to think of it but the relationships quickly settled back into how they had been when we were younger, with Mary the loner. Nanny tried to include her in everything and she seemed happy enough, but it's true that she was always having a go at Anne for this and that, trivial things really, but she obviously got on her nerves. Whereas she left me alone, never scolding me about anything. I sense Mary had always liked me – I'd go as far as to say she preferred me over Anne – and now she had me to herself at last. She probably hadn't expected that given our ages."

"So, what happened when you and Mary were alone, Miss Walsh?"

"Mary got very emotional, crying all the time, although tears wouldn't come more often than not. She was gushing feelings, words, thoughts, sayings, noises. It was hard to keep up and difficult to understand what she was talking about. I tried telling her to calm down, consider her words, not get so upset but it only made her worse. In the end I gave up and just listened. Much of what she said seemed to be about her love for her family, how she'd never really shown it and other heartfelt stuff. She held my hand constantly. Then she got on to her husband. She was still married to the b… even though she hadn't lived with him for years. As a good Catholic she would never have divorced him, even after what he did to her. He's been hanging around lately I've seen him, probably hoping they'll be some money coming to him, that's what he's like – greedy."

"Miss Walsh, I've warned you before about commenting on things outside the remit of your testimony. I hope I won't have to mention it again."

"Their marriage was not a happy one, he was violent towards her both verbally and physically."

The Coroner raised a hand.

"That's a matter of record your honour. The police were called a number of times to their house when it got out of hand. She told me things I didn't know, about how cruel he had been locking her in the bedroom, starving her that sort of thing. He was always drunk, but he was a clever drunk, he never got completely out of control. He hit her in the stomach and nowhere else, so it wouldn't show. This abuse went on for years. She believed he permanently damaged her innards. Mary was always in pain when she ate and felt sick more often than not. She lost weight, got so thin people said things. Her waterworks were messed up too. So, it was a horrible time for her. It isn't really funny but she said over and over that fasting like we were doing was easier than living with him. She cheered up a bit when she said this. That was the last laugh I had with her. Mary never had much of a sense of humour so it surprised and pleased me that she at last saw something funny in our situation."

Bernadette smiled wistfully and shrugged, momentarily losing herself in a reverie of benign thoughts. She had liked Mary but in a distant way, never with any intimacy or respect. Their relationship had been useful to her in the constant games she played with her twin over the years, using Mary as an ally when needed then discarding her until the next time her help was required. Trickery lay at the heart of it, there was never any meaning in its own right.

To Bernadette this had been only too apparent as she lay enmeshed in her own private memories listening to Mary's ravings without any sentiment or compassion, companionable only because she now had no choice.

"Miss Walsh?"

"Sorry, Mary eventually left him, moved out of their home and came to live with us. She was nursing many wounds and we helped to put her back together in her mind at least, physically she remained a bit of a wreck. She told me several times over those final days together how important we had been to her. I was glad we spent that time together, even though she was a bit confused, I could tell she meant what she was saying and intended it to be understood. This may sound odd but it was the best time we had ever spent together."

The creased handkerchief smelled of lavender, pungent and sharp. Bernadette dabbed her moist eyes with it then blew her nose. The astringent vapours cleared her head, inducing a giddiness that taken with her physical frailty planted doubts in the court about her ability to continue. Inadvertently, the toll her testimony was taking was becoming a factor in the jury's determination of her truthfulness. Noticing the softening of expression among the Jurors and sensing a change of attitude Bernadette's posture hardened and she focused her thoughts, crumpling the damp handkerchief and tucking it into the sleeve of her blouse. A habit of her maternal grandmother that she remembered dimly from her youth. A recollection that was reassuring to Bernadette reminding her of the strength of female character running through the generations in her family.

"We soon found we couldn't stay where we were with Anne lying there so we decided to move into the kitchen, again it seemed to be cooler in there and we'd be closer to water. It was a good idea in theory, but we were already too weak to stand up and reach the taps so we had to crawl, pulling our quilts and stuff after us. Mary wasn't really fully aware of what was going on by this stage. I did my best to make her comfortable. She didn't want to lie flat on her back as she was having difficulty breathing and the shortness of breath would panic her, which was terrible to see and hear. So, I helped prop her up against the fridge, which we had earlier pushed against the back door. There was a cat flap there, which allowed some fresh air to get in. You could hear it rattling whenever the wind blew outside, particularly at night when it was quiet. Mary didn't seem to notice and she liked the breeze, but it started to get on my nerves. Clatter, clatter, clatter. There was nothing I could do about it as the flap was behind the heavy fridge. It became part of the trial I had to endure, part of the cross God asked me to bear. There was no escape, no shutting out the noise, as I was lying near Mary on the floor to keep her company. She would have been distraught if I had left and I couldn't do that.

She became more and more delirious. I kept giving her water, but she often brushed it aside, unaware I think of what she was doing. Her temperature was all over the place, first she was hot then freezing cold. Pushing off covers and pulling at her clothes one moment, then shivering and calling out to be tucked in again the next. She was very demanding and this made it hard for me. I was feeling weak myself by this time and unsure about what was happening. I think I blacked out on occasions. As a result, time seemed to be a variable thing. It would be daytime, the sun a bright orb silhouetted against the white sheet we had stretched across the window, then suddenly a pale silver glow of moonlight would have replaced it. Hours disappeared without me knowing it. The shining and the glow are what I remember most. The light."

She took a sip of water, then another.

"Mary was noisy but more docile physically if you understand me. Her strength was fading surprisingly fast. As was mine, but I still had a purpose of mind that she was missing. She was child-like in her demands, crying out for something to eat, for an end to the hurt, things I could do nothing about. I wanted these things too but I could still remember why we couldn't have them. If I'm honest I was glad to be able to sleep or pass out whatever it was.

Mary didn't seem able to do that, muttering constantly mostly nonsense, moving about, twitching her hands and legs, unable to settle and find any rest. I wished she had been able to if only for a few moments."

Wiping the tears from her eyes struck Bernadette as an overly sentimental thing to be doing and was aware that cynical jurors, of which she was sure there were a number judging by their stony faces and rigid bearing, would see it as just that, an attempt to wring every last drop of sympathy out of their more gullible colleagues. Bernadette supposed there was some truth in that as thinking these thoughts in the middle of an upsetting retelling of Mary's final ordeal suggested a degree of emotional detachment and scheming that any intelligent member of the jury was right to be sceptical about. But playing the grieving sister flooded with guilt was the part she was committed to and it required an element of grandstanding to be believable to the wider world, after all it wasn't just the jury she had to convince. The local press was following the proceedings keenly and there had already been requests for interviews. Her public would be expecting tears and she would have no difficulty delivering them particularly as she felt the sadness too, even if the pain had eased months ago lying alone in that sweltering kitchen, contemplating eternity.

"I have one regret that I wasn't there when she died. I don't mean I'd actually gone anywhere, I could barely move, but I had passed out. I came round to the click-clacking of the cat flap, otherwise silence. I knew. It was unnerving."

The tears flowed unimpeded. Her cheeks were wet and glistening in the filtered sunlight. Individual droplets trickled down the runnels of her neck – a ticklish distraction – dampening the collar of her blouse.

"Mary was leaning there against the fridge peaceful at last. She was looking directly at me with her eyes wide open. I wanted to reach up and close them but I couldn't, my body was drained and I remember craving sleep. I was alone now and wanted it to be over. All the people I cared about were dead and my own death felt very close, very real. I started to pray for the end to come but was overcome with shame at the vanity of my beseeching. I was making it about me and it wasn't meant to be. This was a family affair and I was asking God for special favours. I felt ashamed. I began to shiver even though it was hot inside. I felt cold and sweat chilled my skin. The shaking became so violent I thought I would die. It felt like I was being pulled apart. My body was out of control. I tried to get a hold on myself, pulling a duvet over me and curling up into a ball, but if any of you suffer from arthritis in your hands you'll know the terrible sensation of not being able to grip anything firmly, so I failed and lay there exposed shaking, quivering … it was awful."

"I think we should take a recess at this time. Please return in half an hour. Thank you, Miss Walsh."

Tea had never tasted as it should since the events, which she had taken to calling them, at Eden Avenue. The elixir of her former life was now a great disappointment to her – it failed to revive, refresh and satisfy like it used to. Even adding spoonfuls of sugar, which she had never done in the past, offered up no antidote to the loss of flavour. The taste remained bitter, the sensation warm, but little else registered. She sipped tentatively, holding the mug in both hands, the heat easing the ache in her fingers. It was a regret the loss of taste, the levelling out of sensation, that she was experiencing. Life was undoubtedly diminished. Her doctor said feelings might return if she was lucky but it would be a slow process. Her body had been placed under enormous stress, it was not uncommon in such circumstances for parts of the nervous system to shut down to protect the core being. But it was not without a cost and damage had undoubtedly been done. Only time would tell. This phrase amused Bernadette. Such preoccupations seemed trite to her. When you had measured out the time left to you in hours as she had then anything longer than that seemed like forever. She knew she had time in her hands. What she did with it was for her and her alone to decide. She set down the mug on the scuffed table, damp with spilled tea and sighed, "how long would this go on?" There was an interminable aspect to all she did these days and she was not sure how long she could tolerate it.

"The mice, or they may have been rats, appeared first at night. It was soon after Mary died and they were just there. It was as if they knew. I could hear them scampering around, rustling, gnawing at things. It was the sounds they made that were so frightening. You know how everything is amplified in the dark – it's your imagination I suppose given free reign – and I saw the most awful things in my mind that first night. My throat was so swollen I couldn't call out to scare them away and they just ignored any movements I made. They seemed to sense my helplessness and understand I was no threat and soon they got more daring, scampering over me, squeaking at each other. It was as if they were communicating, discussing me, sizing me up, it was frightful. I don't think I slept a wink. I was shattered. Daylight brought no relief, it was horrible. I tried to scream, I desperately wanted to but nothing came out. I was dried up and useless. I could see them moving under Mary's clothes, bulges zig-zagging here and there. It was like they were playing hide and seek or games of tag. Every so often they would stop and I imagined what they were doing. It was unbearable. Mary did not deserve this. In our wildest imaginings we had never contemplated such an end. This was God playing tricks with me, after all Mary was oblivious, she had ascended already, thus it had to be his final test for a doubting daughter. I would fail if I wasn't careful, I was aware.

In the bright sunlight the rats seemed wary of me staying in the shadows and keeping their distance, but I knew I was next. You could see it in their eyes and the way their noses twitched as they sniffed the air. It was an obscenity. I had to get away.

It was only strength of will that got me out of that kitchen. Mind over matter – there is much wisdom in that old saying. I was too weak to walk so I crawled across the floor. My palms were damp from my fearful sweats and they stuck to the shiny surface of the kitchen tiles and I was able to pull myself along. I have no idea how long it took me but I finally made it into the hall. I imagined the rats following me like the Pied Piper and my horrors would begin all over again, but they stayed in the kitchen with Mary and I escaped. I managed to pull the door closed after me, and felt safer even though I knew rats could squeeze through very small spaces and would do eventually. Looking back I could see Mary hazily through the scalloped glass of the door, a dark slumped figure silhouetted against the bright white door of the fridge. I felt sad for the first time, it was as if I was finally saying goodbye to someone I loved. I must have passed out then because I remember nothing else."

There is life and there is death and Bernadette existed somewhere in between. It was a narrow and rarefied place, ablaze with shining light and brimming with sound, bereft of substance and replete with desires. Shadows, a steady stream of them, drifted by. Many she knew or thought she did, others she recognized from their faces or voices or bearing. There were friends, enemies, neighbours, relatives, acquaintances, work colleagues, parents, priests and lovers. A human flock moving through lush landscapes, spreading across the face of the earth. Bernadette had cut out from the herd and was ranging wild. She could see clearly what the others were doing, understand their needs and motivations, anticipate their actions, read their minds. She was all-powerful. She would influence them for the better. Expiation had always been her destiny.

She had attendants, Nanny for one who had been helpful, but the whole escapade was mainly of her doing. Shepherding those she cared about along the path to beatitude, dispatching them from this place of suffering with maximum efficacy into the arms of a greater being. And she was soon to follow and then what celebrations there would be. A party of sublime resolution would be held, prayers would be answered, wishes would be met, frustrations washed clean away, a life expunged of slights and hurt, thwarted desires met, all raw thoughts of revenge salved. From such a heady night comes a hangover of eternal redemption.

The bass thudded below – the party was wild, as debauched as she, with her sparse experience, felt able to cope with – she could sense it through the floor, tripping the hard edge of her spine, and tingling splayed flesh. The back of her head throbbed against the bare polished boards, her mind full of high blown passions liberated from any feelings of guilt by smoky games and shots of bourbon. The distorted guitar line scorched the space in front of her closed eyes. An incendiary brass section fueling the fire. Spontaneity lay at the music's heart, sweeping away inhibition. Bernadette was recast, her identity and form taking new and ebullient shapes as she stretched out and soared.

Her fingers raked the tangled hair of her lover, his head wedged between her clamped thighs, his tongue tip divining, hands grasping her bare breasts. She watched his curls bobbing and shaking, his face hidden behind the wadded band of her skirt rucked up round her waist.

Yells echoed from below filling the space between tracks, a door slammed and there was laughter. Then the explosive bass rumble pulsed again through the bones of the building, re-exerting its grip on her senses, cheers surfed the rising cadence of the guitars, and the air surged with the latent energy of the dancers. Bernadette could feel it and was lost.

She didn't dare move any part of her body except for her grounding hands, out of fear of spoiling the pleasure she was experiencing. An ardent explorer of the charismatic boundaries of her faith she had never had to contend with ecstasy so all-encompassing. Her imagination had ranged over the otherworldly transport of the women she had seen in pictures of Bernini's statues of the "Ecstasy of Saint Teresa" and the death of the "Blessed Ludovica Albertoni", and had been attuned to their feelings but uncomprehending of the flights of passion sculpted into the exquisite white marble. She now understood after having spent so long staring through a closed window on to the world of these pleasures of the flesh. Her guide an illustrated travelogue to Rome proffered in innocence by a guileless priest after his pilgrimage to the Vatican as an introduction to her of all that was uplifting in the Holy City. This window had now been flung wide open and she had clambered adeptly through it.

Minutes later when Rick entered her she had been unable to pinpoint the exact centre of her enjoyment, her whole body resonating to the vibration. It was incessant yet wonderful, a mutual physical endeavour that was exquisitely wholesome. She wrapped her legs around his heaving body, entwining her ankles, and held on.

His juddering climax, following closely on her own, her first, invoked a stillness, a sensation of calm well-being that she had never known before. It was a moment of heightened sensitivity, an overload of sensory riches. The creeping return of feeling – the dampness between her breasts, the brush of his stubble on her cheek, the delicious chill of her cooling body – made her shudder.

He had rolled off her and they had lain side by side listening to the sounds from downstairs as their breathing calmed. He had reached for a joint and lit it. Smoke billowing in clouds above his glowing face, refracted the light from the streetlamp outside into whorls of orange and yellow.

"The fun has only just begun", he spluttered as he passed it over to Bernadette. She inhaled deeply and floated away.

They had made love again later that night, Bernadette still flying barely aware of the physical mechanism of the act yet emotionally engaged. She now loved Rick with unabashed fervour. It had not been her original intention to get so involved, that had been a purely mercenary motive prompted by self-justifying good intentions – deprive Anne of an unsuitable boyfriend, scupper her plans for staying in the US and gets things back to normal between her and her twin sister. But events had overtaken her plans and his physical beauty and undoubted prowess in bed had astonished her. She now felt spiritually wedded to Rick – it was her present and future, her petty machinations a thing of the past. It was hard to believe but he had said he loved her. The words expressed through gritted teeth, their faces close, his dopey breath warm on her cheek, the whites of his eyes startlingly bright.

There was emptiness there now, deeper and more enduring than any post-coital malaise, for as usual her original plans, which had not included any consideration of her own emotional attachment, just Anne's, had worked. Rick left days after the party and disappeared without trace. She, they, had been unable to track him down since.

Pondering her miscalculation over the years and the silence that had descended over their time in America, Bernadette came to understand that this act of betrayal had formed the bedrock of the sisters' relationships ever since their return to Northern Ireland – and that had been nearly thirty years ago.

There had been two brides jilted at that particular altar, but only one could publicly bemoan the fact, the other one, mired in her own duplicity and stricken by guilt, had to hide her feelings away forever. Mary had finally sensed something was wrong but was too emotionally barren herself to be able to articulate anything meaningful and had lapsed into a welcome silence. The sisters had never spoken about it until their dying breaths blew it out into the open.

Bernadette would be a bride, come what may, not on this earth probably but in heaven. A bride of Christ.

A longing for a change tinged the music with melancholy. The sounds of happiness were touched with a prevailing darkness. The guitars, drums and thudding bass never left her, she could hear them clearly filling her mind with sound. The swirl of an organ, an infusion of storming brass peppering the soundscape with brutal scattershot, the strident vocals urging, commanding, the echoing chimes of a bell resonant and loud …

The doorbell was ringing. A persistent onslaught, interspersed with a rapping on the glass of the front door, which rattled in its frame. There was a voice calling, a man, peremptory and stern.

His words indistinct and muffled, as if being broadcast from a great distance. In her ears a shrill whistle, running in counterpoint, muddied comprehension. Huddled on the floor in the hall, her cramped body squirmed, blankets fell away, freeing her face, which turned seeking the location of the intruder. Unseeing eyes stabbed by needles of light, just made out the darkened outline of a figure at the door. A refracted face loomed close to the glass, breath fogging the uneven surface. A hand raised to shield the eyes touched, the contact a finger of black in the glare.

There were voices in her head gabbling a multitude of words with the syntax of the insane, garbling meaning.

"This is purgatory. Is there anyone in there? I know you are."

Bernadette could only nod in agreement as she lapsed back into unconsciousness. Her head sinking down, settling, her breathing muted. The bell pealed again and again.

There was a relief to be close to the end of narrating her ordeal. She found her words slowing, drawing out the final moments, allowing time to take a look about her – the spectators arrayed to the front attentive as always, the jury off to the right a mix of attitudes, which in her fatigued state was becoming increasingly unreadable and the Coroner to her left, a solid block of imperturbability that she had come to actively dislike.

"... The next thing I knew was when I came round in hospital."

She looked directly at the bench and nodded. The words had been spoken and she was finished. Feeling returned and for brief seconds she was conscious of each breath that she took and of the rapid beating of her heart. Lacking any understanding of how she now really felt or about the impact of her testimony on her tormentors, she remained standing, challenging them to release her.

"Thank you for your deposition, Miss Walsh. I have a number of further questions I'd like to put to you before I dismiss you from the stand."

It was an irritation, his persistence, but she smiled in assent.

"They are questions I am confident the jury will benefit from hearing your answers to."

The man was a pompous ass, but Bernadette knew she must contain her feelings, particularly at this late stage in the legal game. Her brother was po-faced, she noticed, seated in the back row. He would be hoping for more, he wasn't difficult to read, never had been. Inextricably linked in her mind to their domineering father, she felt disdainful. Assailed by men at every turn, she would defeat them with strength of will. Fortitude and faith were her crutches and little damaged Bernadette would resolutely use them to hobble her way to salvation, ahead of them all.

"Miss Walsh, apologies for being so blunt but I feel we need a direct answer to this question: did you, your sisters and aunt mean to commit suicide?"

Bernadette stared at him, uncertain how to respond. Directly and succinctly would be honest but might appear brutal and unfeeling, however to offer further explanation at this stage could reveal more than she intended.

"Did you fully intend when you entered the house and sealed yourselves in to take your own lives?"

Her silence took on a form greater than her physical frame, burgeoning outwards with the passing seconds to press against the far walls of the courtroom. Everyone present could feel the stillness on their faces and hear nothing but the fluttering unsound of a distant, indistinct whisper.

"Miss Walsh, did you intend to kill yourselves? Please give us a direct answer."

"Yes, we did. It was something we had discussed beforehand and all made our choice. We were agreed."

"None of you had any doubts about such a momentous decision?"

"No, we were certain it was the right thing to do. We had looked at it from all sides and we always came back to the same conclusion. It was not something we decided in a hurry, we thought about it

166

over a long period of time. Any of us could have pulled out at any point, nobody was forced to do anything they didn't want to, if that is what you are saying."

"No, I'm not suggesting that, but it is a question many people will have, given the extreme nature of your actions."

"None of us had any doubts and no one was forced into it. We were family and got on well. There is no way we would have let any one of us do such a thing if we knew they were scared or frightened about what lay ahead. We were staunch believers. We loved God and as I've already said we loved each other. We were fasting to repent our sins, a lifelong tally of them. We had a lot to make amends for. By taking the ultimate step we were going to wipe the slate clean and appear before God as empty vessels. Free of sin. Love would be what filled our hearts, there would be no hiding place for evil. We would be there together, the four of us, holding hands, cleansed. We believed this strongly, none of us had any qualms about what we were doing. It was the only way forward for us. Repentance of your sins is fundamental to our faith and it was through fasting that we felt we would achieve this. We had no choice. I believe that with all my heart, we all did."

"I don't think anyone in this courtroom has any doubt about your beliefs and the strength of your faith, but I think many of us would not have been surprised to hear that you had growing doubts as your aunt and then your sisters passed on. Are you telling us that as time progressed you did not begin to question the need to continue with your er ... fast to the death? After all you could have stopped at any time."

The last sentence spoken as an afterthought was a clear indication that she had to be steadfast, show no weakness and not admit to harbouring any doubts. She could not let him think she was in any way the author of this drama, that she knew how the script would play out. She had survived but that had been pure serendipity, she could not have known that was going to happen. She was an actor improvising on the stage not the director in the wings. That much had to be made clear.

"I couldn't have stopped anything. I'm amazed you should suggest that. Nanny and the others had made the ultimate sacrifice, one we'd all signed up to. I couldn't be the one left behind. I had to honour them and continue my fast to the end. What sort of sister, what sort of niece would I have been if I hadn't?"

"But you didn't, did you Miss Walsh?"

A disturbance in the atmosphere of the chamber. A pivot point had been reached. Everybody sensed it. The Coroner's steely rejoinder was a challenge to the narrative direction of the witness's testimony. A renewed attentiveness gripped the courtroom as Bernadette struggled to hide her fear.

"What do you mean?"

"You survived Miss Walsh, while the others died. You didn't follow through with your fast."

"That was nothing to do with me. How was I to know that the rent collector was going to turn up when he did? I couldn't have known. I was barely conscious, the doctors said I had hours to live when I was discovered in the house. I was going through with our plan, but was overridden by events outside my control. It was God's will that I lived, nothing else."

"What would you say to those who might suggest that that was too convenient an explanation. That you survived because you changed your mind and decided not to go through with the pact you'd made with your aunt and sisters?"

"That, that is an awful thing to say about me…"

Bernadette's voice cracked with an emotion that she was far from sure was genuine. It was effective because it's genesis lay in indignation, in an outraged disbelief that they could dare to suggest that she was capable of such a disgraceful act. Her survival had surprised Bernadette, had she willed it, made it happen she didn't really know the answer herself.

"… I always intended to go through with it. The fact that I had the misfortune to be the last one left alive, although I was very weak, and to be discovered before I died is exactly that, a misfortune. Not something I wanted to happen or planned. I'd never do something like that."

"Liar!"

Her brother, John, was on his feet, red faced and shaking.

"Liar, liar. You've not told us the truth ever. You're, you're ..."

"Sit down this instant and be quiet or I'll have you escorted from this courtroom. I have warned you before and I'll not warn you again."

John was furious, unbowed.

"You knew the rent collector was going to come at some time, didn't you? You had it worked out so you'd be found. You planned it. You had no intention of killing yourself, did you? Tell us, go on."

The Coroner beckoned to the security guard seated at the court entrance. He got to his feet. Even as an adult it had never ceased to give Bernadette pleasure baiting her brother and she couldn't resist a smile. John slouched back into his seat. The guard sat down.

"Sorry about that Miss Walsh. Now normally I wouldn't countenance such an interruption, but I would like to put to you the point that has been raised as it follows on from my earlier line of questioning. And that is that you must have been aware that the rent collector would be turning up at Eden Avenue eventually once you fell into arrears. Did this knowledge influence your actions in any way?"

"No, not at all. We had discussed what would happen if he turned up and we agreed that we wouldn't answer the door. We thought we had plenty of time, several months at least, as it always took a while for the landlord to chase up this sort of thing and we expected our fast would be over before that. As I said earlier it was pure chance that he turned up when he did and that I was still alive, nothing to do with me. I view it as bad luck. I was in a dreadful way and prepared to die, God help me."

"I have commented before on the sincerity of your beliefs and I'm not casting doubt on them here. I know you have alluded to the answer to this question earlier in your testimony but I would be grateful if you could tell us again why you do not consider what you set out to do as a sin, given the very clear teachings of the Church on this matter?"

Sin was an endlessly fluid concept, Bernadette found, its seriousness very much in the eye of the believer. She was definitely a devotee of her faith, but an intelligent one, who found that the constructs of the Church, male dominated as it was, didn't always suit her or fit in with her vision of the way the world should be. She and Nanny had been of like mind on this and they had adopted a hybrid approach to living their lives. They broadly followed the teachings of their priest on most things, but when it came to sin they were more accommodating of deviance. They asserted the predominance of love and its unerring ability to mandate and mediate appropriate behaviour that was unassailable by sanction, other than by yourself and your own compact with God.

"I assume you are referring to the idea that it is seen as sinful to take your own life?"

"I am and I think you'll find it's a little stronger than just an idea. I think it is a very clear instruction."

"Sin didn't really come into it as far as we were concerned. No one ever mentioned it. Fasting has a long tradition in the church and in our family. In the past we often fasted as a way of ridding ourselves of all earthbound vanity, selfishness and sin. I hadn't really thought about it until now but I suppose if as a good Catholic you believe both in the redemptive powers of the fast and that killing yourself is a sin, then one cancels out the other and you come out even. A win-win situation. I know some people will say that they are not equal in the eyes of God, that suicide is a mortal sin that can't be erased by the mere actions of men and that my aunt and sisters sinned as a result, but that is not how we saw it then and it's not what I believe now. Cleansing ourselves of sin was how we saw it. We did it every year. What happened this summer was no different really we just followed it through to its logical conclusion."

"Miss Walsh, I think there may be a number of people in this room, myself among them, who would question the logical element in that decision."

"It was logical. Nanny was terminally ill and didn't have long to go. She had been our rock."

Bernadette paused for a moment, her hand went briefly to her mouth,

"No, that doesn't quite describe the relationship. She was more than that, she was our sun and we revolved around her. To all of us living without her was impossible, about that we agreed."

"Did your aunt, Mrs Fanning, agree with you? Was she happy that you were to die with her?"

"Happy isn't a word I'd use to describe what any of us felt about what was happening, joyful maybe, inspired, over brimming with confidence that we were right, but not exactly happy. To answer your question though, yes Nanny was very supportive of our plan – deep down she was obviously pleased – she thought it was the correct thing to do. She definitely approved. Dying alone and disregarded was not a pleasant idea for her."

"It isn't for anyone. I think everyone here would agree with that. But you could have been with her when she died and then gone on to live full and productive lives. You didn't have to die with her?"

"We wanted to. We were all of one mind. We had had enough of this world."

"One more question Miss Walsh. Given what you have just said about this being a joint enterprise, how do you feel about having survived?"

"As I've said I did not choose to live. It was pure chance that I was discovered when I was. It was not my time to die that much is obvious. It was God's will to keep me alive. He has other plans for me, I strongly feel that."

Secretly she had been thinking maybe she had been saved because she was the only one in her family who was not a sinner, the only one who was pure in thought and deed. But she couldn't say that, they wouldn't understand, not a single one of them.

"Do you feel guilty about being the only survivor?"

The syndrome was familiar to Bernadette and she had pondered its ramifications often in the months of her convalescence. Guilt was a powerful constraint on behaviour and was an emotion over which the individual had total control and responsibility. If Bernadette had not been responsible for her survival, she could not feel guilty about it, it was impossible, a contradiction. She had experienced a mix of feelings about what had happened: grief, sadness, anger – and was not prepared to own up to any of them here – but not guilt.

"Yes, I do feel guilty. We should all have died and I feel bad that I didn't. It will haunt me for the rest of my life."

Guilt was a simple emotion, easily understood by everyone. By admitting to being wracked by it, even though she was lying, Bernadette hoped to soften her edges and appear more human. Using such a tactic was not something she was going to have any qualms about, not in this world.

"Thank you, Miss Walsh. You may step down. Tomorrow we will resume with testimony from the police officer in charge of the investigation into the deaths at Eden Avenue, Inspector Michael O'Brien."

Part 4

Dead To The World

In those letters she wrote: "Proclaim a day of fasting and seat Naboth in a prominent place among the people.
1 Kings 21:8-10

Writing had passed the time. It had been reassuring, therapeutic, companionable, a cure for loneliness of both the physical and spiritual kind. It became a substitute for talking or not talking; it was cathartic as well as a disguise; a release and a camouflage for real feelings. It was a record of their ordeal and achievement; a palimpsest for their dysfunction; a means of communication when words failed; a salvation; a testament. They had written incessantly, at every opportunity, on all the pieces of paper they could find – writing pads, envelopes, a diary, notebooks, old shopping lists, toilet paper, the margins of newspapers and moldering paperbacks, the torn blank reverses of cardboard boxes and packets – cereal, soap powder, tea-bags – advertising flyers, scraps of crumpled waste. Every available unfilled surface was covered in their eager scrawls – precise, neat, block lettering, legible and not so, open, wild, carefree, rounded, swirling, scratched, smudged, rubbed out, pencil grey, multifarious inks black, blue, red and green – marking the passage of time, the physical deterioration and the steady descent into mental breakdown, with a progression into incomprehensibility and illegibility. The end always a scribble, an attempt to make their mark, to write their name for the final time, to lay claim to all that went before.

Some of these documents were meant to be read and these were left lying around on tables, chairs, the floor, in the pockets of jackets and cardigans, and some were even addressed to particular people and they were left propped up on the mantelpiece. Some of them were private and these were hidden in locked drawers, under piles of clothes, behind cabinets, down the back of sofas, under rugs, in a slipper. In truth nothing was secret, it would all be read and pored over, scrutinized for meaning and explanation, digested and regurgitated to the world. Bernadette had known this is what would happen and had not written anything down, keeping her thoughts and feelings to herself as she had always done. She had tried to make the others understand but to no avail, they had been driven to communicate. Their actions, their deaths, not being enough of a legacy for them, they had felt the urge to explain. Bernadette, however, knew only too well, that who writes history is the victor, the last woman standing, the one with the means to manage the record and have the final say.

There were always dangers. She had been physically very weak at the end, passing in and out of consciousness, and not able to keep a close eye on what the others were up to, so things could have slipped by her. The police had been very thorough in their investigation – it had been a high-profile case – and her brother had kept up the pressure on the authorities with his quest for understanding. Was she worried about what the police might have found? Was she concerned by anything her sisters and aunt could have written down? The answer was not really. She just had to point out that the writings were the rambling work of crazed women, all now dead, driven to extreme action by ill health and mental derangement brought on by hunger. Who could believe anything they had written?

It was another hot day as Inspector Michael O'Brien solemnly took the oath, sweltering as the sun beat down from the overhead skylight. He was an imposing man, tall, broad-shouldered, his uniform immaculately pressed, the glinting silver buttons burnished, with short cropped hair and a neatly-trimmed beard flecked with grey. Bernadette found this facial hair off-putting, but she knew others would be reassured by his smart avuncular style, business-like yet open and friendly, his voice a deep expressive burr. People would believe him.

Bernadette was relieved to be no longer the focus of attention. She was sitting in the body of the court next to her brother and his wife, Mairin, who was here in the courtroom today under instruction from the family lawyer to keep her husband in check, rather than out of any solidarity with her sister-in-law. It was an awkward situation, yet unavoidable as the family had to appear to be sticking together, even if the rancour between the siblings was growing. The relationship between Bernadette and Mairin had anyway never amounted to more than lukewarm pleasantries, which masked a deep-rooted antipathy based on mutually incompatible world-views. One was a devout convent school drop-out and the other a university educated scientist and non-believer. Periods of reconciliation rarely lasted and they spent most of their time sniping at each other, avoiding face-to-face battles. The main casualty was John who as a result hardly ever saw his sisters and was constantly poisoned against them by an often insulted and unforgiving wife.

She was here now at the end of the hearing, Bernadette knew, hoping to witness the shaming of an enemy. It made her seethe, as her sister-in-law's motives were so transparent. But she felt she had done well with her testimony and was sure she had nothing to worry about on that score. Let them puzzle over the meaning of human actions if they wanted to, it was of no interest to her, she knew all she needed to know on the subject. She'd be amazed if the Inspector could throw any more light on events, but wonders never ceased. It was with satisfaction she noticed that John and Mairin were holding hands. At heart they were simple creatures, so full of hope.

"Inspector O'Brien you have been in charge of the police investigation into the unexplained deaths at Eden Avenue in spring last year?"

"That is correct."

"I understand that somewhat atypically you are going to submit a number of documents into the record as part of your evidence to the court?"

"That is correct."

"Will you please explain to the jury the reason for this and then kindly proceed with your testimony."

"Thank you. Sir, it is very warm in here today, would it be permissible for me to remove my jacket before continuing?"

The Coroner nodded. The expectant mood in the room eased as the policeman stepped back and unbuttoned his jacket, looking around for somewhere to hang it, before the Clerk stepped forward and took it from him. Jury members shuffled in their seats, fanning themselves with their court papers, one scratching the back of his head, another sucking on a pencil, a woman in the front row reached for the handbag at her feet and took out a tissue, then dabbed her nose.

"This has been a very unusual case to work on. In my twenty odd years' experience I have never before come across a situation involving so many unexplained deaths. We had one witness – Miss Bernadette Walsh – who was helpful in providing information on what took place inside the house on Eden Avenue and you have heard her testimony."

Bernadette felt some satisfaction that this man, who had interviewed her over a number of days after she had recovered from her ordeal, should describe what she had told him as useful. She had been far from certain at the time that he was convinced by her and believed what she was saying. Her police interview or interrogation, as she persisted in describing it, had not gone well in her eyes. The line of his questioning had suggested a high degree of scepticism about what she was telling him and at points he had suggested she was lying and covering up what really happened. Her tears and eventual physical relapse, which had delayed her interview for almost a week while she recovered in hospital, had diverted and diminished the direction and force of police inquiries and it now appeared she had emerged from it all as 'useful'. She had though been remorseful for days afterwards fretting over her inadequacy in dealing with such people and in losing control of the story, but in the end it appeared she hadn't and all was well. There had been no need to worry.

"We have not been able to find anyone else who was privy to what was about to happen in the house or indeed privy to what did happen. We have therefore ruled out the possibility of there being a wider conspiracy behind the three deaths. We were helped in reaching this conclusion by the vast amount of written material that we found in the house, all of it apparently written by the women themselves and so contemporaneous with the fast and relevant to the events that unfolded. I should say at this point that we didn't find anything authored by Bernadette Walsh, and she assures us she didn't write anything for the entire period they were shut inside the building. Her reasoning being that she saw no need to communicate in this fashion while she was perfectly capable of speaking to her relatives. Once she was unable to talk there would have been nothing she wanted to pass on to them. But the three other women, Mrs Daphne Charlotte Fanning, Mrs Mary Elizabeth Reivers and Miss Anne Walsh left extensive written records. These took many different forms. We were able to identify who had written what by the handwriting. Miss Bernadette Walsh was useful in this regard. Mrs Reivers kept a diary, a hardback book that she appeared to make entries in on a regular basis until very close to the time she died and she also authored a number of letters. These were apparently intended as a means of communication with other members in the house – they were addressed and sealed in envelopes. Miss Walsh confirms that this was in fact the case and the technique was particularly used when there had been arguments between one or more people and they didn't want others in the house to know their thoughts or feelings. Mrs Fanning and Miss Anne Walsh also wrote a number of letters as well as extensive notes on a wide variety of types of paper and cardboard. These were left lying throughout the downstairs area of the house and were particularly concentrated in the living and dining rooms. Some of the documents had been put away in drawers and cupboards, often secreted under clothing, tablemats, cutlery that type of thing. Others appeared to have been more deliberately hidden – behind sideboards, under rugs, stuffed into pillow-cases, pushed down the side of sofas. Others were retrieved from a number of waste paper bins. They were often crumpled and unfinished, but useful none the less."

That word again, Bernadette was beginning to wonder when useful would cease to be helpful to her and would start to become a threat. She had only just grown used to living without doubt as a constant companion, now it was insinuating itself again into her life. Her silly sisters, and even sensible Nanny, had succumbed to this obsession to record everything, to write it down as if that gave it any credence. The three of them, under duress, had become prone to verbose prattling, mostly nonsense but occasionally they stumbled on a version of the truth that had the potential to disturb the direction of proceedings in ways that a juror, or a Coroner even, might misconstrue. They had bequeathed her a poisoned legacy, fraught with danger. In the closed stuffy atmosphere of the courtroom she began to sweat. Would her brother, John or his wife, squeezed into the seats beside her, notice her discomfort?

"The subject matter of these documents varied widely from the mundane, detailing the minutiae of their daily existence, to more weighty speculation on the meaning of life and the existence of God. My fellow officers and I spent several weeks reading the written evidence recovered from Eden Avenue. It was a challenge as some of the individual handwriting was difficult to read and make sense of and as the fast continued the script and style deteriorated, often becoming illegible in certain cases. However, we were able to read the vast bulk of the material. There is far too much of it to present fully to this court and a lot of it is not strictly relevant to the purpose of this hearing so we have taken the decision with the agreement of the Coroner to place a number of edited documents into the record along with documents from other sources that we deem relevant. I will read the contents of these papers into the court record and hard copies are available to the jury in the dossiers being handed out now."

The Inspector looked across at the jury as thick buff folders were passed out to each individual member by the clerk of the court. There was an initial tentativeness to each juror's handling of the file, uncertain what to expect, they all placed it carefully on the bench in front of them unopened.

"Each exhibit is numbered sequentially and identified by author, approximate date of authorship, if known, and will be referred to in future proceedings by its unique code."

Bernadette watched closely, itching to get her hands on the papers. By rights they belonged to her as the sole survivor of the fast, yet she had not seen many of them, had no clear idea what they contained and was as a result apprehensive. These silent posthumous declarations of the departed were always bound to be more evocative than anything the living could conjure up, the unending possibilities for misunderstanding and misinterpretation opening avenues of inquiry that could lead to troubling insights and half-truths, which taken together might ultimately be built into a legally sanctioned edifice of lurid lies. With no one alive to explain, contextualize and refine their words Bernadette would be trapped in this prison of untruths, powerless to escape and clarify.

Condemned, as she was certain she would be, to a lifetime of shame and anger that would corrode any residual joy she felt about her survival, Bernadette wished she was dead. After all, things could have been very different. It was a matter of timing.

Discomfited by her train of thought and concerned she may have been muttering out loud, she turned slowly to look at her brother. His face, strained in profile, was unmoved, his attention intently fixed on the Inspector who was arranging his papers on the witness stand. An escape of sorts she sighed. His obsessive fraternal attentiveness was draining and perversely disconcerting. She drifted back into the present, her disposition for the first time tinged with apathy. There was nothing that could happen to her that was worse than what she had already been through. With such an outlook bent out of alignment with any beliefs she still held dear Bernadette floated above the proceedings mentally immunizing herself against the expected findings.

"EXHIBIT 1/DF/10/04/03: This is a Bank of Ireland statement for the current account of Mrs Daphne Charlotte Fanning. On the 10th April, which was the last day the women were seen alive and is the day, confirmed by Miss Bernadette Walsh, when they shut themselves inside the house on Eden Avenue, the account was overdrawn by almost three thousand pounds – two thousand, nine hundred and eighty-nine pounds to be precise. Taken together with the rent arrears this means that Mrs Fanning was in debt for the sum of over four and a half thousand pounds. In the week prior to April 10th Mrs Mary Elizabeth Reivers and Miss Anne Walsh both closed their bank accounts with the same institution, withdrawing in total thirty-three pounds. Miss Bernadette Walsh, however, kept her current account open with First Trust Bank. It contained the sum of one hundred and eighty-two pounds. Asked to explain this discrepancy between her actions and those of her sisters, Miss Walsh said it was an oversight. Quote: "It was a very stressful time, we had so much to arrange. I just forgot to close it, after all we had no use for the money where we were going."

"EXHIBIT 2/DF/XX/04/03: Daphne Charlotte Fanning's partial medical records have been released into the public domain because they are deemed pertinent in addressing the issue of whether her physical and/or mental condition was instrumental in driving her desire to take her own life and in encouraging her relations to do likewise. We have heard testimony to that effect in this courtroom."

The jury turned their heads to look at Bernadette, it was involuntary, a collective stage instruction in the unfolding drama, obeyed then dismissed as the central character, oblivious, resumed his soliloquy. She sat there immobile and self-conscious, embarrassment burning her skin.

"Doctor Michael Leary, Mrs Fanning's GP, who she was a patient with for a number of years, was unfortunately unable to attend this inquest. So I will summarize the contents of Mrs Fanning's records for the benefit of the jury. I have consulted with Doctor Leary to ensure that I do not in any way misrepresent her state of health at the time she began her fast. Mrs Fanning was eighty-four at the time of her death. Her doctor says that for her age she was remarkably fit. There was nothing actually seriously physically wrong with her, as to her mental ..."

There was commotion among members of the jury, quizzical looks exchanged, gestures of surprise marking faces as this simple fact sunk in. Their understanding of what had motivated the women in the run-up to the events in the house on Eden Avenue was now open to question. Acknowledging the significance of this information the Inspector repeated himself.

"Nothing was seriously wrong with Mrs Fanning, and never had been according to her medical records, apart, of course, from the usual minor ailments of old age. She had high cholesterol levels for which she had been prescribed statins and aspirin, she had arthritis in the hands and neck, slightly high blood pressure and Type 2 Diabetes, for which she was also taking medication. She had a prescription for reading glasses. None of these were life-threatening or a serious handicap to leading a full and normal life. As to her mental well-being that appeared to be fine. There was no suggestion of the onset of any form of dementia. As Doctor Leary told me she was alert and in good spirits when he last saw her, which was in early April, just over a week before she shut herself away. In his opinion there was absolutely no medical reason why Mrs Fanning could conceivably have wanted to take her own life. She was not in any serious pain and was mentally and physically well. He pointed out to me that she was deeply religious and that this was a vital element in her life and as he saw it an important component in her general well-being. Consultations with her priest, Father Petrie, who in fact took her confession on April 10th the day she began her fast, confirmed her devotion to the Church and the stable balance of her mind at the time. He saw and heard nothing to suggest she was about to take the course of action that she subsequently did."

Bernadette was aghast. This was simply not what she believed to be the case. She had lived with Nanny and seen the physical and mental deterioration, gradual at first then accelerating, grappled with the swings in mood, the failures of recall and recognition, the bodily malfunctions. The Inspector and the doctor were lying. They were conspiring against her, painting a portrait of Nanny that was unrecognizable. Suggesting guilt by hinting at her fabrication of information was a cheap trick. The truth was she didn't believe any of this concocted medical history and in fact knew something quite different. She had told the court this in great detail. She should say something, object, but what was the point? Her fury at their scheming was righteous, the heat of her indignation flooding her body. She could feel the gaze of the court upon her and hear the hiss of their disapproval.

EXHIBIT 3/AW/21/04/03: "I would now like to move on to the documents that were found in the house on Eden Avenue. Starting first with those authored by Miss Anne Walsh. She wrote a number of letters during the fast to her sisters and to a Mr Richard Otis Kendrick, commonly known as Rick, an American citizen currently residing in Berkeley, California. I believe he had a short relationship with Miss Walsh during the time she spent in the USA in the mid-Seventies. I will detail some of this correspondence later but first here is a letter written from Anne to her sister Mrs Mary Reivers, which was found crumpled in a wastepaper bin in the dining room."

Dear Mary,

Please don't show this letter to Bernie I hate her at the moment. I don't think I can ever forgive her. What she said about Rick is terrible. How could she have done it? I'm her twin sister for God's sake. I didn't believe it at first. I just thought she was teasing me as she has always done, but then you confirmed it. I couldn't believe it, you as well. Please tell me if you are both lying as I can't bear it. I know it wasn't really you, that it was Bernie's idea, she can be such a bitch sometimes. But this takes the biscuit. This is the worst she has ever been. You saw how I was crying. I can't stand it. He was my boyfriend, my first one, I loved him I really did Mary. I was saving myself for him, you know that don't you? He was the one. It broke my heart, I never got over him going, now I know why. But I have a new boyfriend Mary, it's a secret Bernie doesn't know, I want to be with him, he's lovely. He's called Peter.

Please Mary can we stop this fast, please. I'm in pain, my whole body hurts. I don't want to do it anymore. My head hurts and my eyes are all fuzzy and I'm frightened Mary. I don't want to go on. I don't want to die. I'm so weak now I can't move very easily. My legs are numb. I'm trapped in here with Bernie and she scares me. I think she has secret food hidden away I've been watching her. She's not getting sick like us. I don't trust her. I love Nanny

183

but I don't believe she'd want us to suffer like this. It doesn't make any sense. We should stop this before it goes too far. I need to be in hospital, I need some painkillers. I need some food. We all do. Please Mary help me.

Your loving sister,

Anne.

The betrayal, the stab of non-recognition, was what Bernadette remembered about that letter. A boyfriend, how could Anne have had a boyfriend? Peter, my arse. She thought her twin told her everything. They never had any secrets. She must have been lying as no one had come forward with that name. They surely would have done with all the publicity. If they'd been that much in love he would have done. Anne was and always had been a fantasist. Making things up and then telling her stories to Bernadette, who else did she have to talk to? Over the years she had heard so much nonsense it was unbelievable. But at the time, when Mary had furtively shown her the letter as Anne dozed, she had not been so sure, taken, as she was, by surprise and in a weakened state herself. She was also annoyed her twin had gone behind her back to Mary, telling tales. Why Mary? The two of them had never got on and Anne knew Mary was weak and ineffectual and would never do anything to challenge or cross Bernadette. And she didn't of course, true to form, at the first opportunity she had showed the letter to her. Bernadette was so angry, snatching it from Mary, screwing it up and flinging it at a bin on the far side of the room. The crumpled ball of paper had bounced on the metal rim before dropping from sight. The flicker of success edged her fury and the sense of triumph at her accuracy still resonated. The letter had been forgotten as it disappeared from view, she now wished it hadn't and she had sought it out and destroyed it like many of the others.

Anne had been sleeping, wrapped up tightly, breathing deeply, the memory was clear amid the hazy recollections of that time and the hatred she felt then, immutable and pure, coursed through her body now, in this seat, in this courtroom her frame shook. A resurgence of passion was invigorating. She was restored, she was transcendent. The sentiments of this court, of any court, human or divine, couldn't touch her. Bernadette was certain her brother could feel it too. He was sitting upright, alert, a capricious expression fixed on his face, the look, she remembered from years ago, that he wore as he got ready for his night-time excursions with their father.

The Inspector continued: "We found a significant number of documents written by Anne Walsh and addressed to Rick Kendrick. They were scattered over the ground floor area of the house in Eden Avenue and there did not appear to have been any attempt to hide them. We gathered them together and placed them in chronological order as far as was possible. Not all were dated, but a handwriting analyst we consulted was able to place them in time order based on the deterioration in the writing style. What became apparent when they were collated in this fashion was that the documents were written in the style of a conversation with Mr Kendrick. One sided, of course, but Miss Walsh was engaged in telling her ex-boyfriend what was going on, giving an insight into her thoughts, assuring him of her continued feelings for him and ultimately appealing to him for help, obviously without any reasonable chance of success. We would like to place on the record an edited version of this conversation, which gives an insight into Miss Walsh's thinking and state of mind."

EXHIBIT 4/AW/11/04/03: Darling Rick, we are finally doing it. We have shut ourselves in the house and cut ourselves off from the rest of the world. Last night we had our last meal. Nanny was very happy. She is pleased we are with her and she said a prayer thanking God for bringing us together. We are fasting to wash us clean of sin. We are all sinners. I'm glad to be here, I really am. I know you'll probably not understand but it is the right thing to do. Family is everything after all. Isn't it?

I know now I'll never see you again in this world but if you ever read this, I want you to know I still love you. I always have, despite what you did. Rick, I don't understand why you left me, we seemed so happy and so in love. I wish you would tell me how you felt at the time, it's been on my mind for so long. I would like to know how you feel now.

EXHIBIT 4/AW/19/04/03: You were so handsome, Rick. You were the only person I've met who understood me. You got inside my head in a good way not like my sister Bernadette who rummages around breaking things and hurting me. I often think of you: where you are now? Who you are with? Are you married? Do you have children? I like to think you are happy, with a pretty wife and a lovely son and daughter. I want things to have gone well for you. Do you ever think of me?

EXHIBIT 4/AW/28/04/03: (I think. I'm losing track. It's so difficult as it is painful all the time). I wasn't going to say anything as I didn't want to hurt you but now that I feel myself getting weaker I'm going to. I don't want there to be any secrets between us. I have a boyfriend. His name is Peter. I really like him and he is very nice to me, but he's not like you. I still haven't done it with anyone. I wanted you to know that. All my life I've been saving myself for you. You were my ideal, I found out Peter couldn't match up. It's sad but what can you do but pray. It's so hot in here I can hardly breath.

EXHIBIT 4/AW/06/05/03 (Undated – estimated to be early to mid-May): HOW COULD YOU RICK? HOW COULD YOU? It must be a lie? Tell me it's a lie. Bernie says she slept with you. It makes me feel sick to think of it. You and that fat cow together like that. She says it was for my own good, she says you agreed to go away if you did it, she says Mary was in on it, thought it was a good idea. This is nothing to do with anyone else. This is my sister, she is evil, she had a smile on her face when she was telling me. I hate her.

I have to get back at her. I have to kill her. I'm crying all the time. My tears are dry. My eyes are raw. My life is slipping away.

EXHIBIT 4/AW/21/05/03: I forgive you Rick for everything. I now understand. It was my sister I know. She kills everything she touches, like she is killing us now. She is so ugly inside. I'm the only one who can see it. Everyone likes her better than me, except you Rick. I know deep down that is true, you can't have seen anything in her. It is not possible. She always gets her way. I can't bear to write her name. She isn't getting ill like us and I don't know why, I think she's a witch. I'm not speaking to her, just Mary and Nanny, although she is very weak now and quiet. Poor woman.

EXHIBIT 4/AW/16/06/03 (Undated – estimated to be June 16th): I feel dead all over. My guts are outside my body. Nanny has died. I'm alone now. Mary is OK but can't stand up to B. She wants to move Nanny, which is horrible. She is heartless. I wish you were here Rick.

EXHIBIT 4/AW/18/06/03 (Undated – estimated to be around June 18th): It's gone on long enough. I want to stop. I have to eat something soon. It hurts. My chest is tight. Have written so many times to Mary asking her to help. I need a doctor. Nothing. Help me.

EXHIBIT 4/AW/19/06/03 (Saturday – no certainty this is accurate – estimated to be around June 19/20th): Rick what did you think of me? I'm not too bad to look at, am I? I don't trust them, I trust only you.

EXHIBIT 4/AW/20/06/03 (Undated – estimated to be around June 20th/21st): Where are you Rick? Do you believe in God? Not sure I do anymore.
EXHIBIT 4/AW/11/04/03 (Undated – estimated to be around June 20th/21st): I'm very weak it hurts.

Rick had been easy to fall in love with, that much Bernadette knew, so it was no surprise that Anne had held him in her heart for so long. But to be honest it was much easier to recall the physical grappling and erotic charge of their lovemaking than to bring to mind his handsome face, the beguiling Carolina drawl and his slim, hard, athletic body. For a fleeting moment Bernadette felt sorry for Anne.

EXHIBIT 5/RK/12/10/02: "I mentioned when introducing the last set of documents that they represented one side of a conversation. Although not directly correlated the next set of documents could be seen as constituting the other side. They are a set of letters from Rick Kendrick sent from his home in California, addressed to Anne Walsh ..."

The drawer in her bedroom, another thing she had forgotten, Bernadette's attention was piqued. How would this play out? Anne's romance with Rick never had a future. When his letters addressed to Anne started coming to the house in Eden Avenue less than a year ago – she discovered them because as an early riser she always got to the post first – she read them without compunction and consumed by jealousy – there was never any mention of her – hid them away. The sisters had plans and Rick's re-emergence would be a distraction.

"...dated over a number of months prior to the commencement of the fast. We have no way of knowing whether Miss Walsh ever saw these letters but she makes no reference to them in any of her writings. The contents of the letters from Mr Kendrick would suggest she hadn't as they answer a number of the questions posed in exhibit 4. They are included here because they provide an outsider's perspective on the relationships between the sisters. We discovered them when searching the house. They were in a drawer in a dressing table in the bedroom, we believe, was used by Bernadette Walsh prior to the fast. They were hidden beneath clothes and held together in a bundle by an elastic band. The letters, four in all, were similar in content. The intention of the author was straightforward and clearly stated. To avoid repetition we include here the first and the last letters in the series.

12 October 2002
Shattuck Avenue,
Berkeley,
CA 94707
USA

Hi Anne,

How are you? Bet I am the last person you expected to hear from. I've been thinking of you recently (longer than that if I'm honest) and wanting to write you. I've missed you!!

You must be wondering how I got your address. Remember Kirsty Paine, who was a counsellor with you at the camp? I've kept in touch with her over the years and she thought that Roberta English was still living in Beaufort in her daddy's big old house. And she was and of course, as you know, she kept in touch with most of the old gang from back then. So here we are.

Anne, I wish we were back there now I would do things very differently. I'm sorry for what I did and for disappearing like that without saying anything. I'm soooo ashamed. Can you ever forgive me? I pray you can. I've changed. I'm a better guy now than I was as a kid. We were kids weren't we? Just starting out. I can't believe where all the time has gone.

I should tell you a bit about me. I didn't become that journalist I planned to or the great writer, but got into finance and made a pile of dough. Still at it now but planning to slow down soon. I'm a recovering divorcee. Married for 17 years to the same woman but it just didn't work out. The split was messy, but it's finished now. Got out with enough to start over and here I am.

Had two pretty daughters – Karen 17 and Anne (yes I know) 12. I see them as often as I can, but they live with their mom now in Kentucky, so it's hard. But I'm good Anne, my head's in a really cool place.

Write and tell me all about yourself Anne, please. I'm dying to know more about you. Are you married? Do you have kids? Looking forward to hearing from you.

All my love,

Rick

XXXXXXX

Ps. The pics are of me and the girls – Karen on the left, Anne on the right – can you believe the weight I've put on and the hair I've lost – huh! The other one is my house on Shattuck – a real peach?

Pps. I come over to Europe often for business. Never been to Ireland!!!!!

EXHIBIT 5/RK/02/03/03:

2nd March 2003
Shattuck Avenue,
Berkeley,
CA 94707
USA

Hi Anne,

I'm guessing given that you haven't replied to any of my letters that you are not interested in getting in touch. I'm sad about that I really am. I know it was me that blew it first time round and I was hoping to make amends, but so be it. I've told you many times that I'm sorry more than I can say about how things turned out. Won't you change your mind, please??

Maybe it's because you're happily married and this is an

embarrassment for you. I don't mean it to be sincerely. If you could just let me know that's the case and then I could be happy for you and leave things be.

I hope it's not because of something your sisters have said about me? I'm sure I can explain. They were not your friends back in the day. I don't know what you think of them now? You know it was their idea, it was. They were more brazen than you and I fell for it but I know that's no excuse. I was weak I see it now. You were the simplest soul I have ever met and the prettiest too. Please write, I want to be friends.

Yours hoping,

Rick
XXXXXX

Ps. I know this may seem pushy but I am flying over to Ireland in July. I hope we can meet up? I promise I won't come calling unless I hear from you.

Had he come? Had he visited Eden Avenue? July, it had been all over by then. Bernadette felt a twinge of regret, she would have been in hospital. Who would he have talked to? What would they have said? What would he have thought? Things could have been very different if she could have talked to him, could still be. Failed suicides once they had decided to carry on with life were, in her experience, eternal optimists. The thought of Rick and the challenge he posed thrilled her. There was so much that was possible. People were undoubtedly seeing her as a bitch after this travesty of an inquest, the police were biased against her, seeing things in black and white, needing a villain as they always did, but how different things would look if she got together with Rick and they moved to America. Anne would look like the silly deluded little miss she really was and Bernadette would be seen as having been her ally, shielding her from the ravenous predators out there in the big wide malevolent world and the disastrous consequences that inevitably followed on from meeting them. It was a satisfying fantasy to be wrapped up in, protecting her from the harsh winds of public sentiment blowing through the courtroom. Sex was a strange thing to be thinking about in these austere surroundings but Bernadette found it warmly alluring.

EXHIBIT 6/MR/10/04/03: "Mrs Mary Reivers kept a diary for the duration of her fast. It was a black A2 business diary for the year 2003, showing an individual week on each double page. This made it easier for my team to establish the time-line for her entries, in theory. I say that because in practice Mrs Reivers on a number of occasions states that she is confused about exactly what day and date it actually is. So we cannot be entirely sure that the dates quoted are the actual dates when the entry was made, but we are fairly confident that the entries were made in chronological order. Here is a sample of relevant entries that throw light on Mrs Reivers thoughts and feelings.

April 10th – It's such a big step we have taken. Everybody is very happy and in high spirits. Was sick again after our meal. Silly really as it will be my last one ever. Not feeling well. Bed early. It all seems strange – normal yet very different. The others stayed up talking. Nanny in full flood. Being reassuring as always. Anne needs her hand holding sometimes. I can't be there for her all the time.

April 17th – Been thinking a lot about Ian (could never see him as a Clive, hard as I tried) (**Captain Clive Arthur Stephens – British Army intelligence officer working undercover as Ian Peters. Former boyfriend of Mary Reivers. Disappeared while on active duty. His body has never been discovered.**). It frightens me to do it really. He was so important to me and yet he wasn't honest about who he was. It tears me apart. He was in the army, so I DO know what happened to him. It still gives me the chills! How did it happen though? How did he get found out? I don't think I suspected anything at the time. Even looking back after it all came out, about who he was, there was nothing I could think of that would have given him away to me. Nothing. Da didn't believe me I know. He was so suspicious, asking me questions over and over – but that is how he is. I hate him. And why has no body turned up? (there I've written it) It would be easier if it had just to be sure. What would have happened if we'd got married? Can't help feeling my life would have been very different. Stomach hurting as usual. I don't know why Brian (**Brian Alan Reivers, husband**) had to hit me so hard? My penance. Should have divorced him a long time ago. One more sin to be washing away.

April 23rd – Heating is on full but I feel cold. It's inside. Strange thing as I get weaker my stomach hurts less. I feel healthier. Slept all this morning. We are all downstairs together, sleeping in a row. It is better. Are we mad? Nanny is feeling it the worst. She is very quiet now. Nobody talks much. Watching TV all day.

April 30th – Trying to be sick but can't. Strained the muscles in my side. I can't bear to watch Bernadette pee in front of everybody – it's disgusting. I try and hide away but it's hard. No choice now, we are stuck with each other. Feel dirty.

May 12th – water tastes bad suddenly, can barely swallow but must. Can't focus on TV – will have to stop watching. Eyes hurt.

May 24th – Bernie told Anne about Rick. Why???? Said I helped set it up. Thought it was a good idea. Did I? Hard to remember, such a long time ago. Did nothing probably – as usual. feel terrible. Rick was not good for her but bad of Bernie to do that. no shame. I think she fancied him he was good looking. Feel sorry for Anne why did she have to find out. Anne v upset. We should be friends. Thank God Nanny didn't hear.

May 30th – letter from Anne wanting to stop, get help. Gave it to me when everyone asleep. Hard to read – long and whiny. It's too late can hardly move. Scared for first time.

June 4th – Oh no another letter (from Anne). getting a pain. Don't know what to do. Showed Bernie – mistake. She V angry threw it away.

June 15th – God save us Nanny died.

June 16th – Bernie gone next door, leaving us alone. In kitchen. Dream of Mammy. V pretty Wish she was here.

June 23rd – Ohhh Anne is gone. Must get to Bernie Can't stay here.

June 24th – ask Bernie to stop. No musn't.

June 26th – Bernie is a bitch says Anne told Da that Ian was a brit. Christ. The truth she says. Anne no way. How?? The twins … Ruined my life

June 27th – right. All bad.

Words from beyond the grave were chilling, lifting the hairs on the arms and evoking chance memories and emotions. Mary's voice, always so mild and inoffensive in real life, spat and clawed off the page, raking Bernadette's finer sensibilities with the hard truth of a death chosen. She had seemed too far gone, her mind in another place, when Bernadette, lying by her side in the kitchen, had told her only half the story about Ian, laying the blame, as she had done so often in the past, on her twin sister. It felt slightly disloyal now not to have come clean about his disappearance, to have told of how two young girls had taken a pathological interest in everything to do with their elder sister and this had given one of them the freedom to use with malicious delight a snippet of information to tell on Mary, with the intention of embarrassing her and getting her into trouble with their father, and how this teenagers' naïve misjudgment of the essence of that man and the blinding realization that followed of the evil at the core of their family had driven a wedge into her heart. At the time Mary had groaned at the news of her betrayal, but said nothing, her bloodshot eyes had opened wide and she had stared incredulous and unblinking at Bernadette. Waiting, the moment for honesty passed and Bernadette felt an intense regret that she had not been challenged, as always with her family, not been taken to task. Mary had made an entry in her diary, something Bernadette had no recollection of her doing, and it was affirming to know her words had not been ignored or misunderstood. Her sister had been listening and Bernadette felt humbled to be in her presence again. At last an edge that had been missing from her character had revealed itself, whether it would cut deep and wound was a question yet to be answered. She knew though that it wouldn't be fatal for her, she could live with it. But could her father? It was intriguing that Mary's diary entry was the first evidence the police had linking him to the case of the missing British soldier. Nobody had spoken to Bernadette about it yet, but that was not to say they wouldn't in the future.

EXHIBIT 7/DF/25/03/03: "Mrs Daphne Fanning left in the house a significant number of written documents or tracts, as we conducting the investigation have chosen to call them. We have done this because the vast majority of them related to religious themes and Bible stories and were not directly concerned with events taking place in the house or Mrs Fanning's thoughts and feelings about what was happening there. For this reason we have chosen not to include them in the court record. There is however one document authored by her that is of vital importance to this investigation. As far as we have been able to establish it was the only formal letter that Mrs Fanning wrote. It appears to have been written in the days before she started her fast. It was sealed in an envelope, which was an unusual occurrence among the documents we found in the house, and was addressed to her brother Mr Patrick Walsh, who is currently residing in a care home in Belfast. It had been hidden at the bottom of a clothes drawer in the wardrobe in what was Mrs Fanning's bedroom. Mr Walsh has been shown a copy of the letter and we are presenting it here because of its direct bearing on the case."

57 Eden Avenue,

Belfast

March 25th 2003

Pat,

I hesitate to use the word "dear" when writing to you, Pat, even when it's for the last time. It just isn't me and this isn't the time to be making amends.

I know I must have loved you once, but now after all these years it's not even a distant memory, and it doesn't seem right anyway. When we were young I was a big sister looking up to, and often looking after, their little brother, they are fond memories so I do believe love must have come in to it. You were strong and even kind at that time, I can remember that very clearly, but then you grew into something different. Mammy always said you had another family, a higher loyalty. I didn't believe it, not deep down, that is until a few years ago, but I'll come to that. Family is family in my book, you want them around you. You finally realized it with your own lot, but too late for me. I know you loved your girls in your own way, but even they saw the edge to you more often than not. You became a hard man, cruel and vindictive, petty in the exercise of your power. A local dictator, hiding behind the Church and the cause – you were too strong for your own good in my opinion. I do not believe Jesus will forgive you for what you've done, whereas I think he will me, what with the wrongs you've done to me and the ultimate sacrifice I've made in his name. I'll surely know and pray I'll be laughing on the right side of my face, as I'll already have passed on when you're reading this. My reckoning will have come and I'll have made my peace.

I'm writing this before me and your girls start out on our particular journey. You're reading it when we've arrived at where we were heading.

If I know you Paddy-Boy, you'll have been asking yourself why? Why did they do it? But not coming up with the right answer, not even close. The reason is it's YOU. You shake your mutton head. But yes it's YOU. You're to blame we are all dead. Not the first blood on your hands by a long way, I know that, but I hope the most galling. Children dying before their parents is never a blessing, killing them is a sin you can never make amends for, never confess away. At your age you've run out of time, you evil bastard!

You don't know what I'm talking about do you? No bloody idea. You always were a stupid gobshite. Our Mammy used to say "the man never outgrows the boy" and I'm sure she was thinking of you. You never had that much imagination. No subtlety. Always the direct approach with you. A fighter as a boy, I'm told, always in scrapes – why play games when you could lash out with your fists and win? As a man why talk when a bullet to the back of the knees does the job, eh Pat? I never could understand why they all thought you were so great. It all comes down to the size of the dog's bollocks as they rightly say around here. Girls just never get a look in, not in your family or anywhere in this God-forsaken land.

There is no reason for me to tell lies anymore. It is time for the truth. You need to know and I want to tell you.

Patrick, your name is hard to write, and it pains me to show any sign of civility to you. Patr, Pat, Pa, P ... I want to rub you out, wipe you off the face of this island, erase your memory..., but I want you to do it yourself. I want your mind to boil with the knowledge of yourself as an abomination. Big man what waits for you? Your lackey priests won't forgive you this one – in fact you won't be able to speak of it. Just you and I will know. I'm laughing now, believe me, even though the deed is not done. I have the power and there is nothing you can do to stop me.

Here it is my gift to you, my "old friend", my brother!

Boy I fell out of love with you many years ago, but I've only hated you for the last decade or so. I don't think you knew even though we lived in the same house for over 20 years and saw each other every day, you were never really there. To the extent you paid any attention to me at all you never gave any sign that you registered my hatred. Yours is the indifference of the brute, ordering the world around you to suit your own ends, your understanding of how things should be. I detested you with a passion (this you might understand) that has driven me to do what I'm about to do.

Since you've been in that care home I've had your girls all to myself. Eating out of my hand. Believed everything their ailing "Nanny" told them. We had always been together and always would be … for eternity. I've been a good Catholic and so have they and they loved me, even more than their poor dear Ma, who they can barely remember. Maureen, God rest her soul, could never accept what you were either, the brutal indifference and hard manliness, and gave up the ghost early, releasing her angels to my care. You just saw it as one more woman making your life easier, never another thought. Your weak spot right where you would never dream of looking for it.

What do women do in the company of bullies? You have no idea? Build a community of self-interest, protection and, yes, love. We spoke the same language, thought the same way, saw the world as one, there was no way we could ever be apart. Why? What else was there?

Well, that's how your daughters see things. I have a different view.

My little flock I call them. Sheep are simple beasts and that's what your children are. Rarely an original thought among them, and certainly nothing I couldn't deal with. They'll have done exactly as I say as you'll have found out. I am nothing if not persuasive.

I didn't dislike them when I moved in with you all, but it is as they say, "familiarity breeds contempt." You took for granted I would look after them "like a mother", but they were yours not mine. Try as I might not to, I could always see you in them, particularly Bernadette. The colour of their hair, a turn of the head, the hardness of their faces in the glare of the sun, a phrase they would use. You imbued them with an attitude, a set of the mind, a way of thinking. Poor Maureen barely got a look in.

Your actions, your wicked deeds filled their existence, seeping into their very cores. Poor things they were oblivious to the creeping corruption that was eating away at them and hollowing them out. They were empty when I picked them up and realized I could fill them with anything I wanted.

It didn't take long before living in your house began to repulse me. I began to understand that a family could be evil. The sins of the father and all that...

I don't exclude myself of course I am family after all. We are all sinners. I believe that with all my heart.

Brother, remember this you made it very easy for me to do what I've done. It was not difficult.

Now, you'll be wanting the meat, won't you, boy that you are?

You remember Sean, don't you? Of course you do, my husband was the love of my life and your best friend. Killed fighting alongside you in Iraq, blown to smithereens by an enemy grenade on the 20th May 1941. You must remember that, you were there. You told me all about it when you got back from the war, describing everything that happened in such detail I knew you must have really cared too. I respected you for not holding back, for suppressing your own feelings to help your friend's broken widow and your dear distraught sister. I knew it was difficult and painful for you. Such sacrifice. You helped me believe he died a hero, you helped me grieve.

You know for me there's never been anyone serious since him, don't you? How could there have been, a man such as that.

I know he was more than a friend to you, he was also a comrade in the good fight, he told me so. What you never understood – or come to think of it maybe you did – was that he confided in me, told me everything. I know he was up to something with you in London in 1939. You both disappeared for three weeks early in the year, but it didn't happen did it, Boy? And therein lies the rub. Sean said you changed after that, were never as friendly. Oh yes on the surface who would ever have known, but he felt it. It cut him deep as he didn't understand you. You were his best friend.

How could you?

You blamed him, didn't you?

The police were on to you and your comrades and you had to scrap your plans to bomb the place and run back home to Belfast with your tails between your legs.

It wasn't Sean who ratted you out, believe me. I knew him, he was as loyal as anyone, he would have followed you anywhere and done anything you asked. I suspect he did as he rarely talked about that sort of thing. As I say he was a loyal foot soldier.

Then you joined up, the Kings Own Royal Regiment no less – perfect cover he said – off the two of you went, thick as thieves, or so he thought, off to fight a "greater evil". Little did Sean know. Little did I know. My own people?

You'd hardly been out there in Iraq five minutes and he was dead. Blown up you said in a roadside ambush. "You gave them hell", you said, "paid them back." It was bad luck as nothing was going on fighting-wise out there at the time. It should have been safe, well away from the main action. He could have served out his time and survived. Should have done, like you. But he didn't!

It killed me, you know, when I heard the news. Never

recovered. The grief was too much. I didn't know how I would cope and I never really did. Spent my whole life looking for Sean and never found him. Nobody came close. It helped a bit to know he died in action. The pain did fall away, but the yearning never did. Got worse if anything over the years. I thought of him every day of my life. I loved him deeply, you must have known that. You did know that. I know you knew that.

So how could you have taken me in to live with you after what you had done? What's the old saying "keep your friends close, your enemies closer." Is that it?

There's no point in arguing, as I know you will, I'm dead and I know the truth. God is now my witness.

I don't have to prove anything to you, but I will.

You were different when you came back from the War – a harder man, driven, your Republicanism more deeply felt than ever and you used it as an outlet for your loathing of the Brits. I respected you for that, such a change rang true given what had happened to you and it took me in. I believed your story, why wouldn't I? My own brother, Sean's best friend, you were there, a witness to what happened, you'd have no reason to lie. What a fool I was and for so long. Do you think a lie gets worse the longer the truth is withheld? Do you Boy?

I DO.

Having lived with it for over sixty years, I DO.

The flames of my hatred had a far bigger bonfire to burn once I learnt the truth. All those years as kindling. I burned white hot.

A hatred that sucked all the oxygen out of my body – dried me up inside and left only a single ember glowing in the ashes of my life – revenge. It is more sustaining than you would ever imagine and I was good at feeding off it secretly, without anyone knowing.

Your surprise – I hope your dread – is proof of that. I wish I could see your face, now at this very moment. Maybe I will, yes God willing. You're starting to understand aren't you? Starting to get my drift.

But you need more information. How did I find out? How did I uncover your sordid monumental secret, so well hidden, you thought, by thousands of miles and the passing of the decades? Little Daphne was never going to go to Iraq, never even went to the mainland, she was losing her mind, slowly but surely. You sought safety in my relentless slide into old age. But you were wrong. I was paying attention.

Here you are then – here are the facts: it was early 1992 and out of the blue I got a letter from the Commonwealth War Graves Commission. Official looking letter – it had me worried I can tell you – and as it turned out with good reason. It said that the cemetery at Kut, where as you know only too well, poor Sean is buried, was flooding. The pumps that used to keep it dry had fallen into disrepair after the first Gulf War and the water from the River Tigris was seeping in, washing out the graves. They didn't say so in so many words but I could imagine what was happening. They said because of the "current situation" in Iraq the Commission could do nothing at the moment to rectify the situation, but when conditions improved it would be their top priority to get in there and sort out the problems. In the meantime as the listed next of kin they were sending me all the documentation they had on record about Private Sean Fanning, the Kings Own Royal Regiment, killed on 20th May 1941. They had a grid reference for his grave – Plot 3 Row D Grave 7 – and even a photograph of the headstone and inscription. Do you know what it said, Boy, do you know what that inscription told me? Do you?

It said: In memory of Pte S. Fanning, the Kings Own Royal Regiment, who died in a shooting accident on 20th May 1941. Remembered with honour. Kut War Cemetery, Iraq.

What is wrong with that? It all seems perfectly clear, tragic for me to have it all brought up in such an unexpected and blunt way, but clear. I was horrified at the thought of the dead being disturbed, of Sean no longer resting in peace. It was all such a long way away. There seemed to be nothing I could do – it took me a while to realize that that was not the case. I had nightmares, but not just about that. You can probably imagine about what. You know where this is going, don't you boy?

Excuse me but a shooting accident is not being blown up in an ambush is it? And both you and I know what "a shooting accident" means in your world. Why did you do it, you bastard, why?

I can hear you now from beyond my grave still objecting, always arguing. Let me stop you dead. Suspicious, but still not certain even you would have done something as evil as that, I (or I should say our good friend Liam Blake, the solicitor did) wrote to the Commission formally requesting more information. It took forever and several letters before they sent me the official report into Sean's death. It was short, hand-written and damned you to hell.

Here it is – I know you'll be interested to know how you got away with it.

25th May 1941. Kut al Amara General Hospital. Office of the Military Coroner, Hashemite Kingdom of Iraq South. Report into the death of Pte Sean Fanning, 7215/176, the Kings Own Royal Regiment.

Fanning's body was found the morning of 21st May in a drainage ditch running alongside the Baghdad Road, 3 miles north of Kut. His body was obscured by reeds and in the early stages of decomposition. There was evidence of animal interference post mortem. Cause of death was a single gunshot wound to the front of the head. His hands had been bound at some point prior to his death. Estimated time of death – within the preceding 24 hours. Pte Fanning had been reported missing from his unit on 20th May – last seen alive at 6.15 pm by Pte Patrick Walsh, 7214/193. Believed victim of an abduction. Reason unclear. No ransom demands were received. Kidnapping of military personnel uncommon, but not unknown. Murders so far rare. Inquiries continuing.

That's it nothing else was discovered. I wonder why? Funny how you were the last one to see him alive.

Why did you lie to me if you had nothing to do with his death?

You're a killer and you murdered my Sean for informing or so you thought – took the first opportunity you could and got away with it, you bastard. Hiding behind the perfect cover – the chaos of war. You got away with it until now. Now I've got my revenge – I've taken from you something as precious as that you took from me – your daughters. My only regret is that they never knew you for what you really were. But we all have to make sacrifices, don't we?

Rot in hell, Pat. I'll be looking down on you, forever.

Mrs. Daphne Fanning

Images of Nanny floated in front of her eyes, whispers filled the air – seductive, beguiling, wholesome, loving, trustworthy – Bernadette had absorbed them all. Now as the memory of how it began hit her, her body was rejecting them, their deadly toxicity destroying her history and understanding, her very being becoming anathema to her.

Comprehension stunned John Walsh. Bereft of all that he had thrived on, his compulsion and feelings of hatred and revenge, he could do nothing but stare palely at this sister.

The siblings, together for the first time ever, sat in the hushed courtroom. The inspector gathered his papers and stepped down from the witness stand. It was almost over.

The air was frigid, a mantle of off-white clouds drifted low through the trees, embracing the bare branches and swirling around the dark twisted trunks. Tattered shreds of mist kissed the frozen lake, the aching monochrome offset by the dark silhouette of a solitary mallard standing one-legged on the ice, its green head reversed and tucked neatly under its ruffled feathers. Shattered reeds and fractured bulrushes, their stems bent and bulbous heads hanging, ice blasted, spiked the far-flung fringes. A hoary willow bent low over an incongruous stain of darkening melt-water, an angled stump protruding, the tree's frieze of straggling branches dangling, trapped in the ice. A veneer of surface fractures extended web-like across the surface snagging jagged blocks scattered haphazardly – a field of miniature bergs each summit flecked with white. Fleeting relics of yesterday's thaw and childish enthusiasm, now solidified and holding back time. The lawns, paths, grassy verges, and planted borders of the park were rime-encrusted, the vivid desolation beautiful in the pristine morning light. It was a deserted bipolar world, infused with a smoky rigidity that was breathtaking. Imperfect – the myriad footprints of birds and animals crossing the path marring the perfect crystal dusting – but entrancing. Nanny and Bernadette were content to be alone, the lack of people chiming with their mood of introspection. They were walking slowly arm in arm in companionable silence – bundled up in overcoats, woollen hats, knitted scarves and gloves – only the sound of their footsteps on the frosty ground reverberant in the winter quiet. Billowing breath clouded their vision and the chill razored their exposed skin, yet the searching cold was exhilarating.

Bernadette was biding her time – nothing could ever be hurried with Nanny – waiting to hear about her aunt's consultation that morning with Doctor Leary. She was concerned, as her aunt had emerged subdued from the surgery, hunched and diminished. Not her usual self. The waiting room had been packed, the cold weather exacting its toll, and Nanny had said nothing, just nodding her head in the direction of the door. On the pavement outside she had hesitated and looked appealingly at Bernadette as if she had made up her mind about something, then changed it, pulled up her collar, adjusted her gloves and prepared to cross the road to the park on the opposite side. Her niece hurried to catch up with her, linking arms as they stepped onto the far pavement. Nanny briefly rested her head on Bernadette's shoulder – she had never done that before – and the inner warmth Bernadette felt was as flimsy as a memory from childhood, and as important. The formal intimacy of their relationship was a blessing – by Bernadette's reckoning her sisters did not spend as much time as she did with Nanny, nor were their interactions as physical or friendly. Nonetheless, they hardly ever laughed together and their relationship was still slowly evolving, even after so many years, and she found this reassuring. It was the closest Bernadette would ever get to understanding disinterested love.

They were now heading for the café near the park gates, where they often stopped for a cup of tea before catching the bus home. As they rounded the closed off bandstand two joggers burst past them, their breathless chattering brash and intrusive, their words swirling in the buffeting slipstream. And lingering for seconds in their wake lapping ripples of sweet-scented perspiration.

The café shimmered in the jewelled landscape, aflame, the glow from its clouded windows casting an ochre shadow across the glinting tarmac, smoke streamed vertically upwards in the still air from its soot streaked chimney and a fan in the side wall forced out a rolling torrent of pungent steam. As they drew nearer they could smell bacon and fried bread, toast and fresh coffee and over the last few yards they stepped up their pace.

Inside, the warm humid air was heavy with fragrance, almost tactile, condensation streamed down the walls and windows and the woman behind the counter was red-faced and sweating. The fluorescent lights were brilliantly harsh, obliterating contrast and throwing objects at the periphery into stark block relief. There was one other customer, a young man wearing a T-shirt, seated in the window with a laptop open on the table in front of him, and a mug of coffee. He looked up when they entered, smiled then returned to his work. Bernadette immediately shrugged off her coat and removed her hat and gloves.

"It's hot in here, nice though."

She rubbed her hands together.

"Are you OK?"

Nanny nodded and sat down at a table in the middle of the room. She pushed the ketchup and brown sauce bottles to the edge of the table furthest from her and straightened the napkin dispenser. She kept her coat buttoned up and her hat on.

"Beautiful morning, cold though. What will you be having?"

The waitress turned her head away and sneezed.

"Sorry."

"Two teas please. Anything to eat Nanny?"

She shook her head.

"And a bacon sandwich for me. I didn't have much for breakfast. You sure you won't have anything? You need to keep up your strength."

They waited for their order in silence. Enclosed and sealed off. Nanny appeared pale, smiling feebly at Bernadette, the chill chapped blue tint of her cheeks and lips already fading away in the moist clinging atmosphere. A translucent bead of moisture hung unnoticed at the end of her nose – a sign of distraction or old age Bernadette wasn't sure – but she hadn't the heart to point it out. She was determined not to be the one to pierce the bubble of their intimacy. That was a job for Nanny alone.

"Here you go, two teas. Your bacon buttie won't be a mo. Sugar's on the table."

"Thanks. You're not very busy, I expected there'd be more people around."

"The cold always keeps people away, although we usually get a rush around lunchtime in all weathers."

Nanny was grasping her steaming mug with both hands. The warmth was infusing through icy fingers and Bernadette imagined it spreading outwards through her body, reviving and reanimating. The change was sudden. Her aunt blew on the surface of her tea then took a tentative sip.

"Bernie, I'm glad it's you with me today. Thank you dear."

It was the first thing she had said since leaving the surgery.

"You know it's nothing. It's a pleasure. I enjoy being with you."

She nodded, taking another sip and breathing in deeply the aromatic steam.

"This tea is good. It's warming me up."

"You can't beat it can you? A good cuppa."

"No, you can't. I've always said that. I like talking to you Bernie, you're the most sensible somehow."

"What do you mean, Nanny?"

Bernadette blushed slightly. Compliments were rare in their family and she was pleased at this belated recognition from a woman she admired.

"You seem to understand me. If I tell you something you get it, that's not always so true of the others. They can be heavy going sometimes ..."

She fell silent as if reflecting on what she was going to say next, the mug tilted in her hand. Reluctant to interrupt, Bernadette was about to reach across and take the mug from her when Nanny noticed and righted it herself.

"Silly me."

She shook her head.

"Now where was I? Ah yes. I don't have to explain things to you ... and most importantly you can make the others understand. You have a way with them. They look up to you. They'll always do what you want them to. That's your talent Bernie."

She smiled affectionately. Bernadette was surprised at how emotional she felt and could not say a word. She was so grateful. The arrival of the bacon sandwich provided cover for her embarrassment and she smeared it with brown sauce and cut it in two, avoiding Nanny's gaze.

"Sure you wouldn't like half?"

"No dear, it's all yours."

They ate and drank in silence. Steam hissed from the espresso machine on the counter. The young man stirred at his table, looked at his watch then packed up the computer, put on his jacket and walked up to pay the bill. The till chimed and the cash drawer slammed shut. The door opened then swung shut. A gust of cold air swept over them. They shivered.

"That was delicious."

Bernadette wiped her lips and crumpled the napkin onto her plate. Nanny placed her empty mug on the table and coughed, covering her mouth.

"I hope I'm not catching something."

Her expression was off-key, disturbing. Emboldened Bernadette looked directly at her aunt.

'What did the doctor say Nanny?"

A fleeting smile, then another cough.

"It's not very good I'm afraid."

The words were delivered quietly, deliberately enunciated.

"What?"

Bernadette felt the impact of the news physically in the pit of her stomach, she bent forward, in her confusion banging her mug on the table and slopping tea onto the Formica surface.

"I wasn't going to say anything just now. I didn't want to worry you."

"Oh Nanny."

Bernadette could feel her reserve slipping, the tears welling behind her eyes, the ache of regret for a time past. Nanny glanced over at the counter, where their waitress was drying plates, ignoring them. She nodded resolutely to herself.

"Doctor Leary says that I'm exhibiting the first signs of dementia."

"Dementia?"

"Yes, I know. He said it was early days but the tests have confirmed it."

"You've had tests?"

"Yes, several weeks ago."

"Who came with you?"

"No one Bernie. I went on my own. I needed to know before telling you. As I said I didn't want to worry you unnecessarily."

"Oh my God. You should have said. What happens now?"

"They can't do much. It's the aggressive kind. I just get steadily worse until …"

"No."

"They can give me medicine that will help ease things but there is nothing they can do to stop it happening."

Bernadette had started to cry. She felt adrift.

"I can't believe it."

"No one lives forever, Bernie. There's a dear."

She reached across and touched Bernadette on the hand.

"There must be something they can do?"

Her words were strained and loud. The waitress looked across at them with concern.

"There isn't really. He's very nice Doctor Leary and he spelt it out for me. It's unclear exactly how long it will take but I haven't got much time and I will become less and less capable of looking after myself and as to knowing what is going on, and recognizing people …"

She gulped.

"… well that will just get worse and worse …"

Shortness of breath clipped the end of her sentence and tears began to run down her cheeks. Bernadette scraped her chair closer to Nanny and embraced her.

"You'll have us, we'll always be there for you. You don't need to worry about that."

"I know, I know."

"Here you go loves. It sounds like you need this."

The waitress placed two fresh mugs of tea on the table in front of them. They pulled apart, nodding in gratitude. The warm tea steadied Bernadette's racing mind, and she began to feel capable of sensible thought. Nanny had retreated, slumping back in her seat clutching her mug close to her body.

"We can get a second opinion."

"No Bernie. Doctor Leary has been very thorough. He has asked around. I don't think there is any doubt. I trust him."

"We can't just accept this. I can't accept this."

"You must, Bernie, for your sake and mine. We'll go mad if we don't and that will make things much worse. I need you Bernie, I need you to be strong."

"I will be Nanny. You can rely on me."

"For your sisters too, they'll need you. You must all stick together."

"There must be something that can be done. Doctor Leary may have got it wrong."

"I don't think so. Now that it's sunk in, I'm wondering how much of a surprise it really is. You know I have been noticing things recently."

"What do you mean? What sort of things?"

"You know forgetting what I'm doing halfway through something, not knowing where I am, not recognizing people, forgetting names, shopping, all those sorts of things. It's been worrying me for a while. I put it down to being tired and a bit out of sorts, but now I know …"

"Oh, Nanny you mustn't worry anymore. We can help you get through this."

"You must have seen it too? You must have noticed? Deep down you must have been wondering about it? What was going on?"

It was an awakening for Bernadette as all the incidents, minor in themselves, came together and began to make sense – the stumbles, the blank looks, the bewilderment, the puzzling answers, the memory loss – a joining of the dots that was drawing in her mind an unpleasant and unwelcome image of a woman failing.

"No nothing Nanny."

"Oh, come on Bernie."

She had never felt more awkward about giving her truthful opinion.

"I just thought it was old age, nothing to worry about."

"There you go. You can be wrong."

She smiled and leaned in towards Bernadette.

"I have something I want to tell you Bernie and I know I can trust you."

Bernadette nodded assiduously. Nanny's conspiratorial words were barely audible.

"I don't want to hang around to the bitter end, to be in the state when I'm incapable of doing anything, can't remember what I did five minutes ago let alone yesterday, forgetting to eat and drink, not recognizing anyone. What about when I won't know who you are Bernie? That would kill me and you I think."

"You shouldn't be saying this Nanny, let alone thinking it."

"But I am. I want to end it before then. I am certain about that. I don't want to lose myself and not know who I am. I don't want to lose control of my body. I particularly don't want to lose you. I don't want you watching me fade away, existing only as a shell."

They stared at each other

"But it would be a sin?"

"Oh Bernie," she laughed, "I think a benevolent God, which I believe him to be, would forgive us on this one. The ending of suffering for one of his creatures has to be a good thing. No one is meant to endure the humiliation of dementia I really believe that. I know it's all part of his great creation, his scheme of things, but so is free will and I choose not to suffer. I will end my life when I'm still me, while I still have my dignity."

They hugged each other again.

"I can't believe I'm asking you this but how will you do it?"

"I'll fast like our Lord did, but I won't stop. It's the simplest and purest path, just fading away. Everything else seems so violent and I can't bear the thought of that. And taking an overdose of pills is unreliable, particularly if you are losing your mind."

Again the same laugh mixing with regret.

"If you look there are so many examples in the Bible of fasting, in both the New and Old Testaments – in Kings, the Psalms, Luke, Corinthians, you name it."

Bernadette was surprised that she understood the logic of this argument, was not appalled at the prospect, more intrigued. It would be easy to achieve she acknowledged that, all it needed to succeed was a reliable support network and Nanny had that.

"You've obviously thought about this."

"Rest assured I have. I've always been a devout person as you well know. This seems the right way to go to me. I hope you'll help?"

There was no hesitation on Bernadette's part.

"Of course I will, you can rely on me."

Nanny's voice was a plaintive appeal.

"I don't want to die amongst strangers. I don't want to die alone."

"You won't be alone," Bernadette reached across and patted Nanny on the hand, "you'll have the three of us."

After two days of deliberation the jury returned their findings of death by suicide in the cases of Mrs Daphne Fanning, Mrs Mary Reivers and Miss Anne Walsh. They had asked two questions of the Coroner: first whether they could find that the women had conspired together to kill themselves? and second could they state on the record that they believed one of the women (they were prepared to name her) had exerted undue influence on the others? In response the Coroner had told them that the finding of death by suicide pact was not available to them and that it was not their role to apportion responsibility to an individual or individuals for what had happened to the women. It was for the police service to decide if they wished to pursue such a line of inquiry and that decision depended on there being sufficient evidence of wrongdoing. At the current moment, the Coroner understood that the police did not think there was and that the case of the deaths on Eden Avenue was closed.

Epilogue

The Osborne Arms, High Holborn, London, 1939

The vanilla tan foam glided slowly down the outside of his glass, lumpily ponding at its base, before bleeding a damp stain over the polished surface of the bar. The jet-black pint, crowned by a dense head imprinted with the fading outline of a shamrock, stood forlorn and untouched.

"None of these bastards know how to pour a Guinness over here. What are you supposed to do with that?"

Inspector Harry Grimes laughed.

"Drink it you old Fenian. If you don't like it Pat, you should stay your side of the water."

"You could be right. I never learn."

Patrick Walsh shrugged and lit a roll-up. The match flared in the dim, smoky air of the crowded public bar. He exhaled and turned to stare at the policeman, sitting beside him. The man was whistling quietly to himself and keeping time with the rolling tempo of the piano in the far corner of the bar. People were singing along. The two of them had known each other for over two years and had engaged in mutually beneficial business on a number of occasions. Their relationship had grown into one of grudging respect, teetering on the brink of actual friendship. Their meetings always brief enough for their beliefs never to interfere with their common cause – an amicable pint and the commercial exchange of information.

"You should be going, I can't afford to be seen with you."

"Anything more I need to know about this campaign you fellows have planned for over here, Pat?"

"No, I've told you everything."

"And you've got your money, so I should be off. As always…"

"Just give me time to get on the boat back to Belfast. Nothing too hasty now."

"You know me Pat."

The inspector drained his glass of beer, wiped his mouth with the back of his hand, then cleared his moustache of foam with index finger and thumb. Standing he buttoned up his overcoat and lifted his stained fedora from the bar.

"It's been a pleasure as always. Until the next time."

"Pat."

The sound of his name was distant but distinct, carrying over the hubbub. Pat, who had been relaxing against the bar, straightened up and turned. His world spun. His brother-in-law was waving at them, a puzzled look on his face.

"Sean! You're early."